A Kiss in the Dark

Also by GINA CIOCCA

Last Year's Mistake

A Kiss in the Dark

GINA CIOCCA

SIMON PULSE

NEW YORK   LONDON   TORONTO   SYDNEY   NEW DELHI

SIMON PULSE
An imprint of Simon & Schuster Children's Publishing Division
1230 Avenue of the Americas, New York, New York 10020
First Simon Pulse hardcover edition March 2018
Text copyright © 2018 by Gina Ciocca
Jacket photographs copyright © 2018 by Michael Frost (couple)
and Thinkstock (car and ground)
Photo-illustration by Steve Gardner/PixelWorks Studios
All rights reserved, including the right of reproduction in whole or in part in any form.
SIMON PULSE and colophon are registered trademarks of Simon & Schuster, Inc.
For information about special discounts for bulk purchases, please contact
Simon & Schuster Special Sales at 1-866-506-1949 or business@simonandschuster.com.
The Simon & Schuster Speakers Bureau can bring authors to your live event.
For more information or to book an event contact the Simon & Schuster Speakers Bureau
at 1-866-248-3049 or visit our website at www.simonspeakers.com.
Jacket designed by Jessica Handelman
Interior designed by Heather Palisi
The text of this book was set in Janson.
Manufactured in the United States of America
2 4 6 8 10 9 7 5 3 1
Library of Congress Cataloging-in-Publication Data
Names: Ciocca, Gina, author.
Title: A kiss in the dark / by Gina Ciocca.
Description: First Simon Pulse hardcover edition. | New York : Simon Pulse,
2018. | Summary: "By revisiting the horrible events of junior year that
found Macy Atwood heartbroken and at odds with her best friend, she hopes
to discover the boy who kissed her the night the lights when out at the
high school football game"—Provided by publisher.
Identifiers: LCCN 2017021937 |
ISBN 9781481432269 (hardcover) | ISBN 9781481432283 (eBook)
Subjects: | CYAC: Kissing—Fiction. | Friendship—Fiction. |
High schools—Fiction. | Schools—Fiction.
Classification: LCC PZ7.1.C56 Kis 2018 | DDC [Fic]—dc23
LC record available at https://lccn.loc.gov/2017021937

For Andrew, the best part of sunrise, sunset, and everything in between

A Kiss in the Dark

One

It's funny how they say a picture is worth a thousand words, because the one I'm looking at has me pretty speechless.

There's nothing special about it. Not to anyone else, anyway. It's a snapshot of me, Joel Hargrove, and Ben Collins after an impromptu game of basketball in Ben's driveway on a sunny Saturday junior year.

The beginning of what was supposed to be something amazing.

But being that our friendships went up in literal smoke since the photo was taken almost a year ago, I have no idea why it's currently staring back at me from the smudged surface of Jadie Donovan's cell, posted to the school's share site for everyone to see.

1

"So who put it there if it wasn't you?" Jadie yells over the bustle around us on the football field, blinking lashes coated in electric-blue mascara. Her lips are painted silver, and spiral ribbons of silver and teal spring out from her glossy black ponytail. "I thought you were finally talking to both of them again."

I sneak a peek at Meredith, who's jumping up and down, waving her pom-poms a few feet to my left. She's looking anywhere but at me, which I should be used to by now.

"I mean, we are. Sort of. But it's not like this." I hold up the phone, indicating the photo. Not even close.

Jadie shrugs and slips her cell into the back pocket of her jeans. "Guess you won't be spotlighting that one on the blog this week. Not that a crap ton of people would notice if you did." She shakes her head and returns her attention to the fancy black camera tattooed with RIDGEDALE YEARBOOK labels, flipping through her last shots of the game.

She's talking about our newest endeavor—the one that rose from the ashes of our defunct cheerleading careers—as yearbook photographers and keepers of the Ridgedale's Finest page, the site where students and administrators upload their snapshots of the school year. She's also exaggerating its obscurity, just a little bit.

But I'm still hung up on the picture itself, and my eyes automatically dart to the metal platform in the center of the field, which is usually reserved for homecoming and graduation ceremonies. Because during tonight's halftime, in addition to the usual performances by the dance team, cheerleaders, and marching band, we're welcoming Mr. Hargrove—one of the algebra teachers and Joel's father—back to Ridgedale after a yearlong tour in Afghanistan. Wearing his army fatigues, he's an exception to the sea of silver, white, and teal. He waves at the crowd from behind a podium wrapped in a giant yellow ribbon. Joel, looking a little overwhelmed, stands next to his father with hands in his jeans pockets as he surveys the crowd.

As if he senses me staring, Joel looks over and catches my eye. His hand lifts in a hesitant wave.

"He's got some nerve kissing ass to you and Ben all of a sudden," Jadie says in my ear. She gasps and grabs my arm. "Do you think *he* posted it?"

"How would I know?"

I'm trying to act like it hasn't occurred to me. But the minute Ben began *sort of* speaking to me again, instead of closing up like a sun-deprived flower every time I get within five feet of him, is when I sensed Joel circling cautiously, trying to close some of the distance between us. Searching for weak spots in my armor.

And now a picture of the three of us mysteriously appears where he knows I'll see it. It's a little too coincidental.

Before I can say anything else, Jadie brightens. "Let's have someone take a picture of us. Now that we're always behind the camera, we're never *in* pictures anymore."

When the "someone" she grabs is none other than Meredith, I stiffen. I know Jadie's intentions are good. But her efforts to orchestrate a truce between Meredith and me have started to feel like theatrical demonstrations of, *Look! I'm living proof that fights with Meredith Kopala aren't a death sentence!*

In Jadie's case, it's true. In mine, not so much.

I stand there, trying not to look uncomfortable as Jadie gives Meredith a quick tutorial on operating the camera. Then Jadie bounds over to me and puts her arm around my waist. We press our faces together, and I do my best to smile. In the few seconds it takes for Meredith to snap the picture and hand off the camera to Jadie, she doesn't look at me once.

Probably because all she'd see is the traitor responsible for the blackened, ash-coated remains of what had been our junior-year homecoming float. And that wasn't even the biggest thing I ruined.

As she rejoins the rest of the cheerleaders, I think about how strange it is to be standing in the middle of the football field when so much has changed. Not the hot-dog-and-popcorn-scented air crackling with competitive energy and celebratory yells and school pride—that's exactly the way I remember it. But now that I've traded my teal-and-white pleated skirt and shell top for street clothes and a black camera a lot like Jadie's strapped around my neck, the only indicator that I used to be part of the group of clapping, kicking girls to my left is the injuries. Hence the flesh-colored brace clamped around my left wrist and hand like a robotic glove.

Not to mention the damage that no one else can see.

A scuffling sound scratches through the speakers as Mr.

Fielding, our principal, steps up to the podium. I ready my camera as Jadie jogs away to work a different angle. Mr. Hargrove waves at the crowd, then salutes the football players, who are lined up on the opposite side of the stage next to the marching band. The football players have removed their helmets, per Coach Simmons's orders. Fielding lays his arm around Mr. Hargrove's shoulders.

"Good evening, ladies and gentlemen!" The crowd erupts into cheers as if he'd announced that everyone had won a million dollars. "Tonight is a very special night. Not only are our Ravens playing their very first game on home turf"—he pauses, waiting for the roar from the stands to quiet—"but we're also here to welcome back our friend, algebra teacher extraordinaire and father to our very own Joel. Please give a hero's welcome to Mr. Cedric Hargrove!"

The crowd explodes into a fresh frenzy, and my camera captures frame after frame of Principal Fielding proudly squeezing Mr. Hargrove's shoulder while Joel maintains his uneasy posture in the background. On my other side, Meredith jumps and kicks so vigorously that my ponytail sways in the breeze her limbs create.

"Thank you, all. It's so good to be home!" Mr. Hargrove says into the mic. He pulls Joel into a side hug while the stands roar. "I want to thank everyone who kept us in their prayers and who took care of my family while I was gone. Especially everyone who kept my boys in line." He ruffles Joel's blond hair, then waves to a spot in the stands, where I assume Joel's mom and younger brothers are seated, before leaning back into the mic. "One of the things I get asked a lot before I leave for duty is 'Are you scared?' It's been a long time since I've had to answer that question with 'yes,' and I'll tell you why.

"During my first deployment, I was injured pretty badly. I woke up in the hospital with a collapsed lung, a broken leg, and a host of other nasty injuries, including a broken jaw. With all that time stuck inside my own head, unable to walk and barely able to talk, I did a lot of agonizing over what would happen if my family had to live without me."

He stops and looks at Joel, who's hunched into his jeans pockets like this is something he'd rather not remember.

"Now, you might think this is crazy," Mr. Hargrove continues. "But what made me the most determined to get out of that hospital was the fact that I'd promised this kid"—he reaches for Joel's shoulder—"that I'd teach him to ride a bike."

Joel stares at his feet, looking like he's wondering how this speech became about him and what he can do to stop it. And I'm wishing this story weren't so endearing, because empathy is the last thing I want to feel for Joel.

"Summer came and went," Mr. Hargrove says, "and I never got to make good on my promise. But somehow, when I finally did get home, what do I see but my boy, zooming around the driveway on a shiny blue bicycle that he'd taught himself to ride."

He's holding on to Joel like he's afraid he'll disappear, and Joel looks like he's wishing he could do exactly that.

"I knew then that if I had to lay down my life defending my country, my family would find their way. Because they had a strong foundation of faith and courage and they were more than capable of forging their own path." He hugs Joel to his side again. "So if there's one thing that I want to instill in all of you, aside from 'a squared plus b squared equals c squared,' it's that you have the power to do anything you put your mind to." He turns to Joel, whose face is downright gray. "Anything at all."

The crowd roars. I could've sworn Joel and his father didn't get along, but Mr. Hargrove's speech told a different story.

The words "I hate him" emerge from my memory as clearly as if Joel had come up and whispered them into my ear. When did he say that before?

Mr. Hargrove motions for Joel to take the mic, but he shies away. Someone in the crowd shouts Joel's name, igniting more whoops and whistles to egg him on. When it becomes obvious that he's not getting out of there until he says something, Joel steps tentatively behind the podium and swallows hard before leaning into the microphone.

"Thanks, everyone. Uh, it's been a tough year without my dad." With his voice magnified from every corner of the football field, the hitch of nerves is unmistakable. And I assume it has at least something to do with the other thing I hear: snickers from the token hecklers. My jaw tightens and my hands clench. Well, my right hand does. My left fingertips press into my brace. I'm not exactly the president of Joel's fan club, but I have no patience for people who get their jollies off public assholery.

I scan the sea of teal jerseys, glad to see that Tyrell Davis, the quarterback and Jadie's boyfriend, is scowling into the crowd. But it's Noah's eye that I'm hoping to catch. He's not hard to find, being that he has biceps bigger than some people's heads, long black hair that brushes his shoulders, and a jaw chiseled into a permanent state of *Don't mess with me*. And since an injury kept him from dressing for the game tonight, he's wearing his jersey with jeans and a black brace over the knee he reaggravated in practice earlier this week.

He might be new to Ridgedale, and he might've defected from the same rival territory as Joel, but I'm sure a stare down from Noah could end the sneering in two seconds flat.

Except that when I locate him, Noah is doing some sneering of his own—at Joel. Until he sees the disgusted look on my face, and then his eyes dart to the ground and he shifts on his feet.

Joel starts to speak again, but his words are lost in a loud screech of feedback. And then, as if the night had swallowed the field whole, everything goes black.

Cheers and chants morph into hollers of confusion. All around me, commotion swirls in the darkness.

"The power went out!" someone yells, as if that much weren't obvious. I blink furiously to adjust my sight. My night vision has always been terrible, and all I can see are bright dots dancing in front of me where the grid of stadium lights were glowing two seconds ago. When I extend a hand and come in contact with nothing, I decide my best bet is to stay put. The last thing I need is to trip over something and add another broken bone to my running tally.

Except that's when I hear Coach Tori shout, "All my girls, get over to the fence! Wait for my instruction!" I change my plan and shuffle toward the sound of her voice. That's when I slam into another body. I shriek as hands clasp my arms, steadying both of us. I'm pretty sure it's a boy— or maybe it's a tall girl—until his fingers bump my brace and a very male voice says, "Macy?"

I know that voice, but I can't tell who it is. Despite the chaos, he spoke as quietly as if we were the only two people on the field.

In the next second I'm aware of only two things: one, his hand has moved from my arm to the back of my neck. And two, his lips are pressed gently against mine.

There's an instant of horror, a fleeting moment when I realize I shouldn't let this happen. But there's something about the way his mouth finds mine, tender and sweet and urgent and desperate all at the same time. It's . . . *familiar.* It's not so much a thought in my head as a reaction in every synapse of my body: *I know you.*

My hand dislodges my camera from where it's squeezed between our bodies and then brushes the hem of a short-sleeve shirt as I ignore the minuscule part of my brain still capable of logic and make a clumsy attempt to pull him closer. I want to hold the back of his neck the same way he's holding mine. I want to make him tell me who he is.

Except that I think I already know.

Then, as if my own thoughts have burst the magic bubble of that moment, he pulls back.

"Joel?" I gasp.

The air shifts with his retreat. I'm still standing with my hand in the air, fingertips warm from his skin, when the lights come on a second later. The collective cheer that rises in the stands registers as static in my ringing ears as I shield my eyes from the sudden glare. I whip around, scanning the turf. My heart is beating like I'd sprinted the entire length of it.

I don't see anyone running away from me. I don't see anyone close to me, period.

My mind is a million miles away. I don't even notice that Jadie has jogged over until she grabs my arm.

"Oh my God," she says. "That was so freaky! What happened?"

I wish I knew. It takes me a second to notice that I'm staring dazedly instead of responding, and to realize that she's talking about the blackout.

Because no one saw the other thing that happened.

"It was really weird," I finally say.

Inwardly I'm still freaking out, and Jadie is looking at me like I've spontaneously changed species.

But there's no way that I imagined it. Someone kissed me in the dark. But why?

And more important—who?

I take out my phone and fumble to pull up the Ridgedale's Finest page. "Who did you say posted that picture? The one of me and Ben and Joel?"

"Uh, I didn't. It was anonymous, remember?"

Somehow, hidden identity has become the theme of the night. As I stare at our smiling faces and touch my still-tingling lips, I'm suddenly convinced that the timing of this photo's resurfacing wasn't an accident.

Because there's a story behind it, or at least the beginning of one.

Two

JUNIOR YEAR

Football is no joke in the South, and homecoming is no joke at Ridgedale High.

That's why the varsity cheerleaders are gathered around a trailer in Meredith Kopala's garage, trying to figure out the best way to morph an old hay truck bed into a nightclub on wheels for this year's homecoming parade. Our float's theme is the Ravin' Ravens, and so far the oversized cardboard boxes we scored from the grocery store don't even come close to resembling the giant stereo and speakers in our concept sketch.

I'm helping Jadie measure paper circles for the face of the speakers when Meredith gripes, "This stupid thing is sagging in the middle." She rips a piece of duct tape off the roll with her teeth, curling her lips so as not to smudge her lip gloss. There are two things Meredith is almost never without: the color baby blue and lip gloss. Not baby-blue lip gloss, though. She scowls when the box wilts despite her careful surgery over the seam. "Tape isn't gonna cut it. We need something to prop it up."

"Daddy will be home in half an hour," Mrs. Kopala says from her post at the door that leads into the house. She and my mother are both leaning against the frame, sipping mugs of tea. "Spray-paint the boxes in the yard, and once they're dry, he can build something to support them from the inside."

"But Ben Collins is outside playing basketball," Jadie says.

The floats are considered a school project, so parents technically aren't supposed to help. It's a rule that no one enforces and everyone breaks. Unlike the secrecy rule—nobody messes with that.

Every year the football players and the cheerleaders face off for the best float. It's 100 percent an unofficial contest, but we take it as seriously as if every victory of the season were riding on it—no pun intended. Even the location of the float building is top secret, and changes every year, because the football team is notorious for pranks. They once spied into someone's shed, saw the Best-Team-Under-the-Sun-themed float, and then replaced all the planets in the solar system with giant cutouts of their faces. Which makes no sense, since the floats are in *their* honor, but that's jock brain for you. So the first rule of building homecoming floats remains Don't Talk About Building Homecoming Floats. And definitely don't take your props outside in broad daylight where possible moles can spot them.

It's not surprising that we all scream when a basketball flies past the open garage door literally seconds after the words leave Jadie's mouth, followed by a flash of dirty-blond hair and Ben Collins's lanky limbs in pursuit.

"Sorry!" Ben calls, trotting back to the driveway with the ball against his hip. "Ball hit the backboard and bounced across the street." He stops to catch his breath, and shrieks of protest bounce off the walls, the loudest cry being Jadie's.

"You can't be here, Ben!" she yells.

"Hey, relax!" Meredith says, bolting to her feet. "Ben is cool. He won't say anything." She turns a sunny grin on Ben's shell-shocked face. "Right, Benny?"

"Hell, no. I'm man enough to admit that you guys scare the shit out of me."

A burst of laughter sounds from the door, and my mother says, "I'm with you, Ben. I can't believe how seriously they take this." She walks away, shaking her head into her mug.

Football culture in Georgia is something my mom still hasn't quite grasped, having gone to a small high school in upstate New York, where we lived until I was in fifth grade. There, it was no big deal—no parade, no fanfare. Not even a homecoming *dance*. I'll never forget the way Mom's eyes bugged out of her skull at the throngs of people the first time she came to watch me cheer. Or the perplexed, horrified look on her face when bare-chested, teal-and-white-painted boys charged through the oversized inflatable replica of a Ridgedale football helmet, each carrying a flag that spelled out RAVENS. They might as well have been wearing mammal-skin loincloths and waving clubs around.

Maybe it was silly, but football is a big deal. And I love it.

The tension in the garage breaks as we all chuckle at Ben's remark, and he tosses the basketball into the grass before strolling inside to take a better look.

"So you're in charge of smuggling the float this year?" he says, circling the trailer. "What's the theme?" He jostles it a little, runs his hand over the surface like he's testing it.

"Ravin' Ravens," I reply. "Does it pass inspection?"

Ben's eyes flick up to meet mine. "Wasn't that the theme last year?"

"No, that was Ravens *Rock*. We had a rock-climbing wall and a giant Indiana Jones boulder. This one is going to be a nightclub. Totally different."

"Ah, I see." Ben pats the trailer again, like he's pronouncing it worthy. Then he picks up the sketches near Meredith's leg. "This what you're planning?" His eyes dart from the papers to the sagging boxes. "Need some help?"

A few of the girls, including me, blurt out "no" at the same time Meredith says, "Yes!" She turns to us, undoubtedly sensing the daggers shooting from our eyes. Letting our parents pitch in is one thing, but a guy who's friends with half the football team? No.

"Guys," she says, "Ben is amazing with his hands."

Jadie snorts. "Oh *really?*"

Ben turns so red, he's practically glowing, but Meredith rolls her eyes. "He built our doghouse, perv. And a bunch of other stuff, and he's been my neighbor for five years. So I think I know when someone is trustworthy."

"Thanks, Mer." Ben runs a hand over his hair, which is thick and the color of beach sand. It stands straight up, then bounces right back into place like some kind of cartoon coif. "Trustworthy until Hargrove gets here, anyway."

There's a collective gasp. Joel Hargrove is new at Ridgedale. Not only is he a football player, but he's a former member of enemy camp. He transferred from Mortonville, Ridgedale's sworn rival. To some, that alone puts him only a step above the spawn of Satan. But add in the fact that Joel cost us the play-offs last year when he tackled Ken Davenport and broke his collarbone, and Joel pretty much *is* Satan.

And still, some of us can't help but be curious about him.

Ben chuckles. "He's coming over later to shoot some hoops. You've got plenty of time to blockade the door or rig booby traps or whatever you need to do." When he's met with nothing but aghast, anxious stares, he holds up his hands. "Seriously, I'm not going to say a word."

"Okay, let's do this fast, then," Meredith cuts in. She explains the situation to Ben, who grabs a measuring tape and assesses the boxes from every angle, jotting down notes on the back of the sketches while she talks.

"This should be easy." The tape snaps into place. "I can

make crates out of some scrap wood I have in my shed. I'll be right back."

"Wait," I call after him when he starts out of the garage, paper in hand. "You're doing it now? What if Joel gets here early?"

Ben shrugs. "It'll go a lot faster if you want to help me."

If I gave any impression that I knew the first thing about power tools or woodworking, I didn't mean to. But I kind of like the idea of learning, so I hop down from my stool and follow him up the driveway.

"So I haven't seen you at the soccer field in a while," he says as I fall into step next to him.

I almost forgot that my seven-year-old twin brothers, Aaron and Michael, are on a rec soccer team with Ben's little brother. Lately I've gotten into the habit of staying home during their games, to take advantage of the rare quiet and get my homework done.

"Michael says I'm bad luck, because they lost the last two games I went to." Still, I feel like a terrible sister. I make a mental note to watch them play next weekend. "Speaking of games, you were holding the giant cutout of Joel's head on a stick at the last football game, weren't you?"

I don't mention that it distracted me for all the wrong reasons.

"Hey, he's a nice kid," Ben says. "Someone needs to get the ball rolling for everyone to stop treating him like a curse."

We cross the street, heading toward the big white house with green shutters on the corner. "Why did Joel's family move out of Mortonville, anyway? Is it because his dad teaches here?"

All I know is that if I'd taken down Ridgedale's wide receiver during one of the most important games of the season, it would be the last place on earth I'd transfer to voluntarily.

"Mr. Hargrove taught over there for a while too. But he's getting deployed to Afghanistan. I guess Joel's parents wanted a house that was smaller and easier to maintain while he's gone. They ended up in Willowbrook, right around the corner."

In truth, we all kind of live "right around the corner." The homes in our town are mostly clustered into subdivisions, with restaurants and businesses and shops lining the main roads. The entrance to Meredith's and Ben's community—called Scarborough Farms, though there's nothing farmlike about the stately Colonials—sits directly across the street from the high school's driveway. My neighborhood is about a mile down the road to the right, and Joel's is less than half a mile on the left.

"Gosh, that's so scary. My mother would be lost without my father." Immediately I feel like an ass for being hesitant to get to know Joel. Everyone has been so focused on Joel-the-Mortonville-Pirate that no one, except Ben, has bothered to find out who he is off the field. And I'm glad it's still early in the year, because there's plenty of time to change that.

Ben leads me toward the back of his house. The yard is

small but neatly manicured, and in the far corner is a toolshed built to resemble a little cottage. Next to it is a white-and-black doghouse with a nameplate that reads SULLIVAN. It looks a lot like the one in Meredith's yard, the one I never realized Ben built, until five minutes ago.

"This shouldn't be too hard," Ben says as we head toward the shed. "You won't need anything fancy. Might not even have to break out the nail gun."

"Damn." I snap my fingers with mock disappointment. "Hammers are so inferior."

Ben stops so quickly, I almost trip over him. "Wait, have you really used a nail gun?"

"No," I admit.

He grins. "Man, then I'm definitely not letting you near it. If you nail your foot to the ground and can't cheer, Mer will rip my nuts off."

"I think she has other plans for them." I clamp my hand over my mouth and feel myself blush right to the roots of my hair. My natural color has always been strawberry blond, but if I looked in the mirror at this moment and saw it glowing a fiery magma red, I wouldn't be surprised in the least. "That came out *so* wrong."

Ben laughs, and there's a sudden shyness to the set of his shoulders as he opens the shed door. "Mer's a cool girl. Too cool for me."

"Why do you say that?"

"She's . . ." He motions at me, like whatever magic word he can't conjure up is hidden in the fibers of my clothes. "She's Meredith Kopala. And I'm not a jock."

I step closer to him and put my hand on his shoulder, biting back a giggle and making my face as somber as possible. "Ben, this might come as a shock to you." I lower my voice. "We're not living in an after-school special."

His eyes widen with feigned surprise. "No?"

"Nope. Cheerleaders date people who aren't jocks. Jocks date people who aren't cheerleaders. Those rules? It's a conspiracy. They don't exist."

He whistles like I've blown his mind and ushers me inside, looking thoughtful. The shed is small but neat and smells like wood and mulch. Ben heads to the far corner, where slats of plywood and a few two-by-fours lean against the wall. "So you think it's that easy, huh?"

I shrug. "There is a right and a wrong in the universe, and that distinction is not hard to make."

"You did *not* just quote Superman."

Ben gapes at me, and I try not to look too self-satisfied. I'm both surprised and impressed that he picked up the reference. "I have two brothers, remember? They're obsessed. My mom actually framed that quote and hung it in their room."

Though, I'm pretty sure she did it as an effort to keep them out of beast mode, a move of pure wishful thinking on her part.

"Come on," Ben teases. "Don't pin it on the testosterone in your house. I recognize a fan when I see one." He points to the locket hanging around my neck. "I'll bet that's where you hide your *S*, huh?"

I clutch the silver heart. "I'll never tell."

He gives me an approving once-over. "Wow, who would've thought?"

"I'd also never tell if, say, you were thinking about asking Meredith to homecoming?"

His eyes fix on me, and in the light filtering through the shed window, they look almost the same color as his hair. "For real?" The piece of wood fumbles through his hands and clatters to the floor.

"Are you nervous just thinking about it?" I snicker.

"I don't know. I guess I *haven't* really thought about it. Okay, that's a lie—I've thought about it. A lot," he corrects, testing the plywood between his hands. "But I suck at figuring out if she's flirting or just being Meredith. I mean, we joke around, and sometimes we walk to school together. But then she goes her way and I go mine. Separate circles, you know?"

Lately I've begun to suspect that Meredith's feelings for Ben might be more than neighborly, but I choose my response carefully, wanting to convince him without selling out my best friend. "All I know is that if anyone else had gone near that float, Meredith would've come at them like a spider monkey. I'd bet money that if you asked her to homecoming, she'd say yes."

He nearly loses the board again, then brandishes it when he regains his grip. "See, this is what happens. Everything's fine when you're friends with a girl, but throw in words like 'homecoming' and 'together,' and suddenly I can't walk and chew gum at the same time."

"Guess I'd better handle the nail gun after all."

He actually lets me too. Only a couple of times, since my job is mostly "hold this," but when I'm not keeping boards steady like a champ, I take great pleasure in pulling that trigger. We work pretty quickly, and soon we're carrying a rectangular crate for the body of the stereo back to Meredith's garage.

"The speakers will be a little trickier because they're taller, but I can throw something together tomorrow if you want," Ben says, smiling proudly when we're met with cheers and claps. He sets the crate on the trailer, and Meredith helps him slip the box over it.

"Perfect!" she exclaims, ruffling his hair. "Nice job, Benny."

Ben backs away with a shy smile, pushing his hair into place even though it didn't go anywhere.

"Glad I could help. I should jet, though. Joel'll be here soon, and I have to act natural."

He waves good-bye, and we wave after him until Meredith closes the garage door.

"I guess we're not getting much more done today," she says. "You guys can stay for lunch if you want, but I'm not bringing the boxes outside for spray-painting with a Mortonville Pirate right across the street."

"*Former* Pirate," I point out.

"Once a Pirate, always a Pirate," Anna Chen butts in. "He is a hot Pirate, though."

"Blasphemer," Meredith shoots back.

I start gathering stray shards of cardboard and paper from the trailer bed to take my mind off the fluttering in my stomach. My insides dance like this every time I think about Joel, and it's been happening for longer than I care to admit. Talking to Ben seems to have made it worse, which probably explains why the next words that tumble out of my mouth are in Joel's defense.

"I'm pretty sure a player's loyalty is to the game, not to the team. He didn't have to play here if he didn't want to. Besides," I add before anyone can argue, "Ben told me Joel's dad is being deployed to Afghanistan soon. I'm sure Joel has a lot more on his mind than football."

The murmur that goes up through the garage tells me I've won Joel a sympathy vote. Especially from Jadie, who was adopted from China as an infant. She's never spoken to her birth parents and has a huge soft spot for people who lose theirs.

"Still," Meredith says. "We need to be careful around all the guys. But him especially."

I fight the urge to point out that letting Ben help with the float despite his buddying up to Joel doesn't exactly qualify as "careful." But I've seen the way Meredith lights up around Ben, how she ruffles his hair the way she did moments ago. I'm convinced that she didn't grant him exemption so quickly on the off chance that her family might need to borrow a cup of sugar one day.

The rest of the girls head inside, where my mom and Mrs. Kopala are putting together egg salad and tuna sandwiches. I hesitate, staring through the small window in the garage door at the spot where Ben's basketball is still lying at the edge of the Kopalas' driveway.

"I'll go with you if you want to bring it back," Jadie says through a mouthful of mayonnaise and egg. I swear she appeared next to me out of nowhere.

I'm assuming Ben has a spare if he hasn't come to retrieve his ball, but part of me wonders if the new light I shed on Joel has Jadie thinking what I'm thinking.

I hop off the float and dump my paper scraps in the trash. "Let's go."

When we get outside, Ben and Joel are walking up the street together. My breath catches in my throat, and Jadie murmurs, "Geez, he really is hot."

It's unfair to other boys, really. Joel could easily be a movie star. Blond hair—much blonder than Ben's—blue-green eyes, a smile that can knock the wind out of you like a quarterback sack. No complaints here about the broad shoulders and flat stomach, either. Joel Hargrove really hit the jackpot in the genetic lottery.

"Hey," Ben calls when he sees us. He eyes the basketball I dribble as we approach them. "Are you challenging us to a game?"

"We thought it might be kind of hard to play without your ball," Jadie says. She swipes it from me in one swift move and passes it to Joel. He looks surprised, but recovers quickly and breaks out that Hollywood smile.

"Nice," he says. He offers his hand to Jadie first, then me. "I'm Joel. I know we met at the preseason banquet, but remind me what your names are again? They introduced me to ten thousand people that night."

Jadie chirps her name, and I follow it up with, "Macy." I'm surprised *I* remember my name, because all I can think about is how warm his hand felt in mine. "How do you like Ridgedale so far?"

He gives a lackluster, one-shoulder shrug. "I'm still getting used to it, but it could be worse." I get the feeling that's his stock answer, the thing he tells people instead of flat out, "It sucks." And it makes me feel terrible.

"It'll get better," I say. And the way he holds my gaze, like he has every intention of holding me to that promise, makes me want nothing more than to keep it.

"Starting now," Ben agrees, nodding toward the ball. "Are you guys up for some two-on-two?"

"I don't think—" I start to say, but I'm cut off by Jadie's bony elbow jabbing my ribs.

"Totally," she says, and I know she got the same vibe from Joel's response as I did. She turns to me. "You and Ben versus me and Joel?"

And before I know it, we're running up and down Ben's driveway, dribbling and passing over the asphalt, laughing and sweating in the bright end-of-August sunshine. It doesn't take me long to realize that Ben is some kind of basketball ninja, so when I'm not sure about a shot, I find a way to pass to him. But Joel has some sweet moves himself, and Jadie is a scrappy little thing, so when Ben and I score the final two points, it's by the skin of our teeth.

"Good game," Joel says, holding his hand up for a high five, which I oblige. "I'm impressed."

"Never underestimate a cheerleader."

"Wouldn't dream of it." He smiles at me, a real one without reservation this time. It's something I could definitely get used to. I'm so busy thinking as much that it takes me a second to register Jadie's hand next to my face.

"Hey, don't leave me hanging!" she shouts into my ear.

I laugh, slapping her five. "Come on. Meredith probably thinks we got kidnapped." I grab my cell phone off the retaining wall, but then decide that one more minute won't hurt. I hold my phone out to Jadie. "Wait. I want a picture of the winning team."

Jadie makes a face. "I don't know about *winners*, but I can take a picture of the cheaters who think they beat us."

Ben and I convene beneath the net. He slings an arm around my shoulder and says, "Take the picture, quick!" before balancing the ball on his pointer finger.

"Totally missed it," Jadie says, shaking her head. The ball clomps toward the garage door. "Do it again."

Ben runs to retrieve it and comes back to my side. "Okay. This time on three. One . . . two . . . THREE!"

Moving fast, I make a Rosie the Riveter–style muscle, and Ben flashes a huge grin as the ball is once again steadied on his fingertip like an orange-and-black leather globe. But then, as the camera clicks, another arm wraps around me.

A third person pops into the frame, and before we know what's going on, Joel's face is right between Ben's and mine.

When Jadie hands back my phone with the picture on the screen, I giggle. Joel and I are grinning, and the basketball hovers in space next to Ben, where Joel's photobomb knocked it from its orbit. Ben is looking at him as if to say, *What the hell happened?*

It's a question I'll ask myself many, many times in the months that follow.

Three

SENIOR YEAR

After the blackout, Principal Fielding reclaims the podium to apologize for the glitch, apparently caused by the power company doing some work down the road. Then the game goes on like nothing happened. But the more I think about it, the more I'm wigging out. Jadie's reaction when I tell her what happened doesn't help either.

"Someone kissed you?" Her face contorts like she caught a whiff of something foul. "That's *assault*! How gross."

She, of course, has a point. Who bumps into a girl in pitch-blackness, kisses her, and then walks away without another word? But I didn't have to kiss back. I chose to. Because it was so far from gross.

And honestly, the first thing that struck me was how

familiar it seemed. Like a reminder of something I'd lost. Or some*one*.

Maybe someone who'd dredge up an old photo from the depths of obscurity and put it where he knew I'd see it.

Even though Joel's name was the first word to leave my mouth following the kiss, I backpedaled on my hasty conclusion almost immediately. But there were only three people in that picture—Ben, Joel, and me. If my theory is that the picture and the kiss are somehow connected, then Ben is an automatic no, because he's not here. Jadie and the other girls will see him later, at Buck's Diner, where the football players will walk in yelling "COLLINSSS," and he'll reply "Suuuup!" before dishing up fries and floats for the post-game feeding frenzy we've dubbed Friday Night Eats.

And obviously I didn't kiss myself. Which leaves Joel. I have no idea where he's disappeared to, but he was onstage when the power went out. Which means he would've had to find his way off the platform and over to me in pitch-blackness. It doesn't seem likely, but it's not impossible.

It's very possible, though, that the picture and the kiss have nothing to do with each other. People share throwback pictures on the site all the time. And no one could've planned for a freak blackout, so it makes zero sense that someone posted the picture and then waited for their opportunity to sneak up on me.

It's strange, but every time I remember the likelihood of the kiss-and-the-photo-being-unrelated phenomena, I find myself alternately tracking Noah Granger's every move and avoiding his gaze like the plague. It's not like I'm wishing for it to be him. I've spent the past few weeks making it crystal clear that We Are Not a Thing. And yet if I superimpose his face onto the memory of that kiss, it's kind of difficult to remember why I've been fighting so hard to stay in the friend zone.

Maybe the world doesn't implode if a Mortonville Pirate kisses a Ridgedale Raven. Even if there are some serious sparks.

I shake off the thought, opting to study every boy on the field instead. I snap picture after picture in the hope that my lens will see something I don't—a wink, a secretive look, a flare of someone's freaking nostrils—any indication that those stolen seconds in the dark were *our* little secret and not just mine.

When the cheers die down after the final buzzer finds Ridgedale victorious over its visitor, Noah trots over to me. I can't help but hold my breath.

"Hey," he says. "Fielding's offering hot dogs on the school if we go to Fuddruckers instead of Buck's tonight. You're in, right?"

Oh.

Call me crazy, but if I wanted to craft the perfect follow-up to a secret, electric kiss, I probably wouldn't lead with hot dogs. Something deflates inside me. But before I can answer, Joel reappears and jogs up to Noah's side.

"Hey, Mace," he says like we're old pals and not ex-friends. Like he has no grasp on the depth of my contempt for him. "My dad convinced Fielding to spring for hot dogs. You need a ride?"

"She can ride with me," Noah says, his tone a dismissive block of ice.

"Relax, dude." Joel gives him a derisive once-over before turning his attention back to me. "Either way, you coming?"

I'm not very hungry, though my answer would be the same regardless. "Thanks, but I'm gonna pass tonight."

Arms wind around me before I even realize Jadie has bounced over to us. "You pass *every* Friday night," she says. "We're going to keep asking until we wear you down. I'm not a cheerleader anymore either, and I still go."

"That's different. Your boyfriend is on the team." Not to mention there's way more to it than that, and Jadie knows it.

Noah raises a hand. "Uh, hi. Boy who's your friend and also on the team, right over here."

I give him my best regretful smile. "No, thanks. My parents are here. I'll head out with them."

"Do you want me to skip out and make you s'mores instead?" Jadie asks.

Jadie is the only person I know who can microwave chocolate and marshmallows into stew. So I tell her I have a bag of S'mores Oreos to keep me company, which leads to her usual fake retching and staunch declaration that Double Stuf Oreos are the only Oreos worth eating. Normally I'd go to bat for my equal-opportunity Oreo eating, but in all honesty, the solitude of my bedroom is the only company I want right now. Nothing is making sense to me, and I need time to sit and process all the questions in my head. So I concede, say my good-byes, and start toward the stands.

"Mace?" Noah calls after me, and I turn around. "See you Monday?" He fixes those smoldering eyes on me as one side of his mouth quirks up into a smile, and my heart stops.

That's the kind of look I've been waiting for.

I'm tempted to backtrack, to stick around after all. But as I hesitate, I spot Joel watching me a few feet away. The way he's looking at me, like he wants to say something but isn't sure he should, sets off a flutter of warning in my belly. He turns and walks off as if he's thought better of whatever he almost said.

In a sudden burst of bravery, I open a text message and type: Did you want to tell me something?

It's not until I'm dropping into the backseat of my parents' car that Joel's response vibrates in my hand:

Lots of things.

Like? I type back.

I wait for an answer that never comes, my temple pressed against the window and my wrist throbbing dully beneath my brace. Joel's face is still flashing through my mind long after we get home. Meredith's, too.

I keep thinking about the way she would look at me only through the lens of Jadie's camera. Last year we talked about being roommates if we got accepted to UNC, and scheduling all our classes together. Now I think I've become invisible to her. I've thought the same thing about Joel, about Ben. I've asked myself a thousand times how we went from being friends to floating around one another like ghosts, acting like we no longer exist on the same plane. The picture on the Ridgedale's Finest page is proof that at one time our friendship was real. As I stare at it again on the screen of my phone, I have to wonder—hope?—if maybe that's the point someone was trying to make in posting it.

Four

JUNIOR YEAR

As a cheerleader, I'm used to being at the center of crowds. But when Jadie and I get back from our impromptu shoot-off with Joel and Ben, I'm more aware of the eyes on me in Meredith's living room than I've ever been in an entire stadium full of spectators.

The girls have gathered around the TV and are watching a video of last year's regional competition, analyzing what to emulate and what to improve. The second Jadie and I enter the room, sweaty and flushed, the routine is forgotten.

"Details," Anna Chen says. "Now."

"Relax, weirdos," Jadie says with a dismissive wave. "We were playing basketball. There's no law against it." She squeezes herself into the space between Anna and the arm of one of the two sofas in the room. "Where's Meredith?"

"I think she went up to her room."

Mrs. Kopala pokes her head in from the attached sunporch. "Why did Meredith go upstairs? Was she not feeling well?"

"I'll go check on her," I say, turning on my heel. I have a feeling that Meredith's escape has nothing to do with her health and everything to do with the vantage point that her bedroom offers: a perfect view of Ben's driveway.

When I get to the top of the stairs, her bedroom door is cracked open, so I knock and push it wider. Meredith is sitting at her desk in the far-left corner of the room, staring disinterestedly at the computer screen.

"Hey. Sorry. I didn't think we'd be gone that long. Are you mad?" I ask.

Meredith looks away from the screen long enough to shake her head. "Watching that video too many times gives me ADD. I'm trying to get some new ideas for the Halloween fund-raiser." Unsurprising. Not only is Meredith the co-captain of the squad, she's also the student council vice president. She has her hands in everything, and makes it look like child's play. The mouse clicks as she asks, "Did you have fun?"

Anyone else would think it an innocent enough question. But the gold *M* that hangs from her necklace is pressed between her thumb and forefinger as she drags it back and forth along the chain, the way she always does when she's worried or nervous, right before she pulls the necklace up over her bottom lip. And . . . yep, there it goes.

"Uh-huh. Proved once again that Pirates are no match for Ravens." I settle at the foot of her bed, where Ben and Joel are visible through the window next to her head. There's a red-haired little boy with them now, and they clap when he shoots the ball, even though he misses. When Meredith sees me staring, she leans back in her chair.

"Isn't he cute?"

"Ben's brother?" I say, raising an eyebrow. "Or Ben?"

She rocks forward again, closing out the page she had up. "Whatever do you mean, Macy Jean?"

"I put in a good word for you."

Meredith's lips tighten. I can almost see the tug-of-war inside her head, that split-second decision of whether to keep denying once you've been caught red-handed. She goes for the cop-out, coyly twisting the chain of her necklace around her finger.

"He's not my type."

I raise an eyebrow. "We both know that your 'type' could use a makeover."

She snorts. "Speaking of which, Ken asked me to homecoming."

"Tell me you didn't say yes."

Ken Davenport might've done a great job of playing the victim after Joel broke his collarbone, but it doesn't change the fact that he is a royal douche, something we both learned firsthand during his and Meredith's short-lived relationship last year.

"I told him to roll naked in dog shit infested with fire ants." We both crack up, and I relax into one of her cushy down pillows.

"So Ken gets an ass crack full of poisonous ants, but Ben gets to help with the homecoming float. What does that say?"

Meredith shrugs. "It doesn't say anything. Yeah, Ben is nice. And funny, and sweet, and he has beautiful eyes—"

"Sounds to me like he *is* your type."

She grabs a package of lip glosses off her desk and chucks it at my head. I block it with my hand, giggling as the transparent pouch of shimmery reds, pinks, and peaches bounces onto the bed next to me.

"He's also a goofball, and he's too short—" She cuts off when she sees me making a face. Meredith is five feet, seven-and-a-half inches tall. My guess is that Ben is somewhere in the ballpark of five nine. Being five feet, three inches myself, "short" would not be a word I'd use to describe him. "Short for me, I mean," she amends. Her fingers find the *M* on her necklace again. "Plus I'm a jerk magnet, so he's automatically disqualified."

"Meredith, come on! You're assuming the worst without even giving it a chance." I sit up, taking the package of lip glosses into my lap. "He thinks you're out of his league, you know."

"Of course he does." She mock tosses her hair. "I am."

I roll my eyes and pull a gloss from the pouch, tipping the tube as I spread the strawberry color over my bottom lip. "Love Spell," I read aloud. Then I notice the label on the front of the package. "The Seduction Collection?" When I turn it upside down, I have to stifle a snicker at the name stickered on the bottom of each tube. "Heartbreaker, Crush . . . Pillow Talk? Wow." I fix suspicious eyes on Meredith. "Didn't you buy these right after we gave Ben a ride to Smoothie King on our way to the mall?"

Meredith groans and throws her hands up. "You are *so* reaching, Macy Jean. Ben and I are friends, and that's how it's staying. Got it?"

She seems dead serious, almost annoyed, and I'm ready to drop it. Until she turns to grab a pile of papers off her printer, and I catch the way her eyes wander toward the window as Ben sinks a basket and lifts his brother over his head in victory.

A wistful smile tugs at her lips. A smug smirk pulls at mine. If I can help it, Meredith will be eating her words by homecoming.

Five

SENIOR YEAR

I usually wait until Sunday morning to go for a run. But by the time eight a.m. rolls around on Saturday, fifteen different tricks for lulling myself back to sleep have already failed, including counting the pink and white flowers on my bedroom curtains. So I roll over and face the parallel wall, the one that proudly displays uniform rows of framed eight-by-tens of my best sunset photos.

The first time I picked up my mother's camera and aimed it at daylight's swan song, I never imagined it would be the thing to eventually fill a huge gap in my life. I'd never slowed down long enough to appreciate that the same sun in the same sky could take on so many unique, spectacular appearances. Once I did, it boggled my mind that people weren't trampling me for a front-row seat at the lake each night. I wondered if they even noticed.

And then I think about last night at the football game, and remember that my own days of not seeing things that are right in front of me aren't over. Although, some pretty amazing things can happen in the dark.

I shudder and throw the covers off me, deciding to exhaust my racing mind into submission.

"Hey," Mom says from her spot in the laundry room when she spies me coming down the stairs. "Up before nine on a Saturday? Are you feeling okay?"

"Couldn't sleep. I'm going for a run."

"That was a nice welcome back for Joel's father last night." The fact that she totally ignored me and swooped in with a comment about Joel makes me wonder: Did she somehow see the picture on the Ridgedale's Finest page? I'm still trying to craft the perfect nonchalant answer when she adds, "Maybe now that he's back, he can teach his son how to act like a man."

The tension whooshes out of my body. No suspicion here, just good old-fashioned bitterness toward the boy who ditched her daughter the night of the junior homecoming dance. Sometimes I think she's more hung up on what he did than I am.

"Low blow, Mom."

"Maybe, but not uncalled for." She gives the shirt in her hand a quick, rough fluff. "Did he ever give you an explanation? Or an apology, for that matter?"

"Not exactly, but I think maybe it's been eating at him. He's been weirdly nice to me lately."

She stops mid-fold to give me a look. One that says *Watch your back* as clearly as if she spoke the words out loud. I grab my phone, earbuds, and key lanyard off the dining room table and reach for the front door before she can say more.

It's hard not to feel a *little* more peaceful in the early quiet of my neighborhood. The breeze is cool and the sun is mellow and warm, nothing like the unrelenting brute it'll be in a few hours. Neighbors are taking advantage of the reprieve by washing their cars in their driveways or walking dogs on leashes and babies in strollers.

I pick up my pace and adjust my earbuds, turning the volume up on my phone. Still, no matter how loud I blast my music, my thoughts are louder. I can't go more than sixty seconds without being ambushed by the memory of that kiss, and the flush of heat it sends rushing through my body every time it replays.

Like right now.

It isn't long before I find myself jogging down the wide wooden steps that lead to the lake at the center of our subdivision. According to the community website, it's actually two lakes, but to me it looks like one big lake, bisected by a damlike path lined with willowy shrubs and staggered wrought-iron benches.

Whatever it is, it's one of my favorite places to be alone with my thoughts. I love that the water is the sky's mirror, the only place where the clouds ever take the same formation twice. I love that I can come out here with my camera to capture the sunset, and every night it's new and different and breathtaking. And still, every time I watch the bright gold-and-pink light fade from the clouds, I wish it didn't have to be over so soon. As I plop down on one of benches, the events of last night replay in my mind, and I think about some of the other things I wish I could've held on to a little longer.

I shoot to my feet, shaking yet another rehash of that kiss out of my head. If I'm going to outrun my thoughts, I have a lot farther to go.

I'm not heading toward the school. I'm not going back to the football field to look for clues. I'm really not. To prove it to myself, I veer off the sidewalk and make a pit stop at Mugsy's Coffee Shop. There are a few dollar bills crammed into the license holder attached to my lanyard, and I dig them out as I order my usual, a salted caramel latte.

"Some things never change," a voice behind me says.

I whip around to see Ben sitting alone in a corner booth near the back entrance that opens to the parking lot. He's wearing a green hoodie, and his cell phone sits on the table in front of him like a weapon at the ready. He does not look happy.

"Hey," I say with a nervous titter. "I didn't see you there."

"I'm used to being invisible."

If he's trying to make me feel guilty, that comment is a direct hit to my feel-like-shit-o-meter. Ben Collins is not the kind of friend I imagined walking away from. But he turned his back on me, too. And every time I peered over my shoulder in hopes that he'd be looking my way, he kept right on walking.

I keep my discomfort at bay by chattering senselessly. "What's wrong with sticking to my usual?" I nod toward the cup next to his phone. "Next one's on me if that's not a hazelnut Irish cream."

His eyes flick over to the cup and then back to me. "Still hating on hazelnuts?"

"Hey, if you enjoy eating something that tastes the way the janitor's cleaning fluid smells, that's your business." A hint of a smile plays at the corner of his mouth, just enough that I don't quit while I'm ahead. "You missed a crazy game last night. The power went out at halftime while Mr. Hargrove was onstage and—"

The smile vanishes, and Ben looks disinterested to the point of angry. It occurs to me that I don't know where I'm going with this anyway. He's the last person I'd talk to about the real reason why the blackout was such a big deal to me.

"You should probably know I'm here to meet Meredith," he says.

"Oh." The barista hands me my cup, and I stand awkwardly in the space between the counter and Ben's booth, not sure what to do with myself. I'd planned to make a bold move and sit down with him, but the mention of Meredith is the opposite of an invitation. "Should I go?"

Ben pushes his cell phone to the edge of the table. "I'd rather we talk about this first."

I step closer and peer at the screen. It's lit with the image of him, Joel, and me. My eyes dart between it and Ben's face, trying to read the solemn line of his full lips before I open my own mouth.

"I'm guessing it wasn't you who posted it?"

His expression doesn't change. "You mean it wasn't *you*?"

"Of course not. It's an anonymous account, and that's the only picture they've shared." I slide into the booth, keeping one eye on the French doors that overlook the parking lot, in case I spot Meredith's car. "Besides, I haven't spoken to Joel since the night of the fire." Ben raises an eyebrow, and I hold up my hand before he can call me out. "I know. He's been coming around again lately. But I don't know why, and I'm not sure I want to find out."

Except that I do. Especially after the way he looked at me before I walked off the field last night. And even more so now that two out of three people in the photo that's currently fading to black on Ben's phone have been eliminated as its posters.

But if Joel posted the photo, it only makes sense that he's also the one who kissed me. The back of my neck goes hot, and my first sip of coffee is suddenly doing an impression of the Bellagio fountains inside my stomach.

Ben shifts in his seat and rests his elbows on the table. "Don't you think it's time we talked about what happened last year?"

I take a sip of my coffee, purposely avoiding his eyes. "What is there to talk about?"

"A lot, and I think you know it."

"That's funny, because there were a few things you could've said *before* that night that would've made everything pretty different."

For a second we lock eyes, both ready to draw our respective swords. But then a flash of red car pulling into the parking lot catches my attention, and I scoot from my seat.

Meredith never forgave me the last time she found Ben with me when he should've been with her.

"Time to go. You're right, though. We should. Talk, that is." I motion to his phone. "I would've had someone warn you about that last night if they'd gone to the diner. But I guess everyone went to Fuddruckers instead. Sorry if you were waiting."

Ben shrugs. "They let me off early when they saw how dead it was."

"Okay." I inch toward the front entrance. "Tell Meredith I said hi." Why would I say that? Meredith wouldn't care if I said hi. Meredith wouldn't care if I turned into a tap-dancing monkey. "Or, you know, don't."

I speed to close the distance to the paned doors at the front of the shop, but stop when Ben says, "Mace?" He turns over his shoulder, and I follow his stare to where Meredith is still sitting in her car, applying lip gloss in the rearview mirror. When he turns back, he doesn't look directly at me. His hands twist together on the tabletop. "I think we should talk about what didn't happen that night too."

My coffee turns to sludge in my throat. I swallow hard and manage a nod. But my mouth opens at the same time as Meredith's car door, and I slip outside without saying a word.

When I get to the gas station on the corner, I chuck my cup and make a left. Then I start to run at full speed.

I lied. I'm jogging on the track that surrounds Ridgedale's football field, still trying to tell myself that I'm not here because of that kiss. That stolen, cryptic kiss that's hiding in every corner of my mind. Only now I'm trying my hardest to push what Ben said into one of those corners too.

What didn't happen that night.

I spent so much time thinking about everything that did happen that night—the fire, the fight with Ben and Meredith—that I managed to convince myself that the other thing must've been my mind playing tricks on me. And maybe it was. Maybe Ben meant something totally unrelated to what I'm thinking.

An abandoned GO RAVENS sign curled against the bleachers catches my attention, prompting the memory of last night's kiss to barge in again. I come to a stop, kicking my legs to stretch them out, and breathing deeply to distract myself. It's bugging me like crazy that a moment that came and went in the blink of an eye has left its imprint on every minute since, and now it won't leave me alone. What's worse is that I'm not sure I want it to.

Screw it. I give up all pretense and jog out to the middle of the field. I can only hope that someone else somewhere is obsessing over last night the same way I am. Maybe they want to reveal themselves but they don't know how. Or maybe they're waiting for the perfect opportunity.

But since I have zero reason to believe either of those things, I'm resorting to blindly combing the scene of the crime, knowing full well that the only evidence is locked inside my head.

There are a few other random people using the track for their workouts this morning, so I try to appear casual as I trot the length of the field, hoping something other than gum wrappers and napkins will pop out at me. And right when it's looking like my little mission is as pointless as I thought it would be, I reach the spot where the metal platform stood last night.

Here, I think. *It happened right around here.*

A round of tingles floats down my neck, and I circle slowly, scanning the ground. I stop when, about three feet to my left, I spot the creased, jagged corner of something sticking up from the green turf.

I dart toward it. At first glance, it looks like a bent, trampled piece of paper, and I'm disappointed. But when I bend down, I realize it's a photograph. Not an actual four-by-six picture but a grainy printout on letter paper. It's creased like an accordion and bowed in the center where it was folded, but it's mostly intact. And it's definitely not anything I recognize from the Ridgedale's Finest page. Or anywhere, for that matter.

The image is a black-and-white close-up of a tattoo on the back of someone's neck. Based on the muscle tone and hairline, I'd guess the subject is a boy, and he's lying on his side. The tattoo is an intricately detailed snake, its body coiled and redoubled into the shape of a fern. It's beautiful, and it strikes me in a way that surprises me. I trace the design with my finger for a few seconds before remembering where I am, and stand up with it. On impulse I snap a picture of it with my phone before stuffing it into my sports bra.

I very much doubt that this picture is somehow connected to the kiss. But just as I was certain last night that someone had posted the photo of Ben and Joel and me as some kind of message, I have a feeling that this picture is telling a story. It's what pictures do.

An image that's very different from the one pressed against my chest conjures in my mind then, and I have to physically shake myself to force it out. A thousand words indeed. And depending on the words Ben wants to say to me, I might finally have to acknowledge something that I've been perfectly happy to believe I imagined.

Which means admitting to myself when things really started to go wrong.

Six

JUNIOR YEAR

"Hey!" Ben greets me as I walk away from my car toward the rickety bleachers at the edge of the soccer field alongside St. Mary's church. "You made it."

"I did. I probably won't stay long because I have a crap ton of homework, but I made it."

He shades his eyes with his hand and gives me an assessing once-over. "Not that it isn't good to see you, but you don't look any different. How did you break the bad-luck spell?"

"Swigged a bowl of Lucky Charms cereal this morning while the twins watched me like hawks. Michael dug every green clover marshmallow out of the box and made me eat extra."

He chuckles and motions toward my locket. "I thought

maybe your Superman *S* was your lucky charm, since you wear it all the time. But hey, whatever works."

I touch the surface of the rounded silver heart. "The boys gave me this when I turned sixteen." I press the tiny latch on the side of the pendant, and it swings open, revealing the picture inside. Not the picture I would've chosen, since Michael has his fingers hooked into either side of his mouth, stretching it wide, and Aaron's eyes are crossed. But coming from them, it's perfect. "They try to pretend they hate it when I take their picture, but they're full of it. Plus I used to be obsessed with the movie *Annie*— Have you seen it?"

"Orphan with a broken locket who gets a carnival of elephants and flame-eating dancers when a loaded bald guy adopts her?"

"Yup. They gave me this with a card that said, 'So you can remember us if Mom and Dad give you up for adoption or if you kill us when you start driving.'" I snap the pendant shut, adding an affectionate, "Little shits."

The game starts, and Ben and I take a seat on the bleachers behind our parents. Michael scores a goal within the first fifteen minutes, and for a while I'm fooled into thinking that the clover-shaped chunks of sugar I consumed might serve a higher purpose than merely decaying in my stomach. The Blue Dragons guard a slim, nail-biting lead throughout the game.

And then, with barely five minutes left, the other team scores twice.

Aaron goes rigid in the middle of the field. He finds me in the crowd and glares like he's hurling a knife at my head with his eyes. My mother and I exchange an anxious glance.

"So much for not staying long, huh?" Ben says, oblivious to the nervous way I'm fiddling with my necklace or how quickly my parents are gathering their things. "For a bunch of seven-year-olds, that was pretty intense."

Unfortunately, it's about to get even more so.

Aaron's fists ball at his sides, and his face turns cherry red. "This is *your fault!*" he screams in my direction. "I told you not to come!" He looks around wildly, and I'm pretty sure he's trying to find something to throw at me.

"Macy," my mother says hurriedly. "Why don't you head home? Daddy and I will take the boys out to brunch once we get him settled, okay?" She nods toward Ben. "See if your friend wants a ride in case his parents are staying."

In other words, *This is about to get ugly. Get out while you can.*

The confusion in Ben's eyes is clear as they dart from my mother to me. "Uh, sure. Thanks."

"Oh," my mother adds as she's scurrying away from the bleachers. "And pick up Aaron's prescription on your way, please."

"Prescription?" Ben asks as we head away from the field, where adults are distributing post-game snacks and discreetly discouraging their children from staring at the spectacle that is my crimson-faced, screaming brother. "Is he sick?"

I shake my head. "No. Aaron's been . . . going through some stuff. He has been for a while. He's always had a quick temper, but his meltdowns are getting out of control. My parents are sending him for a bunch of tests to try to figure out what's going on."

"Oh." Ben looks over his shoulder at my brother. "I didn't know he was having problems. He seems like a normal kid to me."

I shrug. "Having problems *is* normal, when you think about it. Nobody's perfect."

"Uh, speaking of which. I'll have you know that ever since you mentioned taking Meredith to homecoming, I have no idea what to say around her."

He pauses at the passenger door of my car and shoots me a loaded look over the hood.

"Well, 'Do you want to go to homecoming with me' usually works for asking a person to homecoming."

"No, I'm serious," he says with a laugh. "Ever since you said that she might—you know—want to, it's like I can't even speak to her anymore. And everything I do say is dumb."

"Aw, that's so cute that you're nervous."

"Yeah, freaking adorable," he grumbles, dropping onto the passenger seat and slamming the car door.

I join him, pausing before turning my key in the ignition. "If it makes you feel any better, I get the same way around—someone."

I could kick myself. Right in my big, stupid mouth.

Ben shoots me a quizzical look. "Are you talking about Hargrove?"

"Ugh. That obvious, huh?" I start the car and back out of my parking space, like the inevitable verbal diarrhea will somehow be less embarrassing if we're in motion. "I don't know why it's such a big deal. Am I really not supposed to like him just because I'm a cheerleader and he used to play for Mortonville? I think the whole rivalry thing is stupid. And it's not like he *meant* to hurt Ken, right?"

"Aha. So I guess there's some truth to the after-school special conspiracy after all?"

"Maybe." I reach absently for one of the individually wrapped Life Savers in my cup holder. "But you hang out with him. He's nice, right?"

"Hargrove's cool. Kind of quiet, though. Can't say I blame him— he was like a god at Mortonville, from what I've heard. It's gotta be tough having that held against him every day." Ben side-eyes me. "Do you want me to say something to him? Like, on your behalf?"

"No!" I almost choke on my candy. If Joel's going to notice me, I want him to do it on his own.

As if he read my mind, Ben says, "There's no way you're not on his radar after those sweet layups you made the other day." He holds up his hand. "But if you'd rather work solo, I'll keep my mouth shut." He unwraps a Life Saver for himself. "And if there's ever a Butter Rum apocalypse and I need"—his face puckers as he puts the candy into his mouth—"really *warm* Life Savers, I guess I know where to go." He shakes his head. "You use your cup holder as a candy dish. Meredith uses hers as a makeup bag. Girls are so weird."

"Says the boy who used to paint his chest and run screaming out of an oversized inflatable football helmet every Friday night."

"You remember that?" Ben looks incredulous. "My flag runner career lasted about five minutes."

"Why'd you stop?"

He makes a muscle, and for being so lean, a respectable bulge appears beneath the sleeve of his red T-shirt. "I got tired of the objectification of my body." He chuckles. "Kidding. I had an allergic reaction to the paint, so I quit. Hives don't really go with our school colors." When I laugh, Ben sighs. "Definitely not my coolest injury."

"I don't know about cool, but I've had my share of crazy injuries. We should compare notes sometime."

Not now, though, because I'm not ready to drop the subject of Joel.

"But back to what we were saying before . . . I mean, if Joel mentions me, I wouldn't be opposed to hearing about it. And I definitely wouldn't be opposed to you maybe fanning the flames a little. Assuming they're good flames."

Ben nods, his expression mock contemplative. "I suppose I wouldn't have a problem being human gasoline if, say, there was something in it for me."

I raise an eyebrow. "Like?"

Ben tugs at his seat belt. "Like maybe some help untying my tongue? I feel like I need—I don't know—practice,
or something, before I ask Meredith about homecoming. Is
that stupid?"

"Not stupid at all." I give him what I hope is a reassuring smile. "It's a deal."

He looks away, grinning to himself, and I can't help but
think it's adorable. "You know," he says, "not to use your
brother as a bargaining chip or anything, but Joel told me
that one of his brothers is on the spectrum. He sees a thera-
pist for that and ADHD."

"Really? Aaron is about to go through the testing process for spectrum disorders."

"Maybe you should ask Joel about it. I get the feeling he
could use more people to talk to, and it's always nice to have
someone who can relate to what you're going through."

"Thanks. I'll keep that in mind."

After I drop Ben off, I spend the rest of the afternoon
singing happily to myself, my mood buoyant. I've always
thought of Ben as Meredith's neighbor, but I like the idea
of just calling him my friend. And not only do we have the
chance to get to know each other better, but we'll do it while
helping each other out in the best possible way.

And I love a good win.

"I cannot believe she voted against me," Meredith says,
yanking the ribbon around her ponytail tighter. She's also
shooting stone-cold glares at Jadie, who's stretching on the

brick-colored surface of the track a few feet away. "And then she comes right out and admits it. What the hell?"

I try not to cringe. For the past few years, the cheerleaders-versus-football-players pennant hunt at Old Mill Park has been a tradition. But this year some of the girls felt like it was getting tired and predictable. Meredith was the hunt's most staunch supporter, while Jadie piped up more than once about wanting to try something new. So we ended up taking a vote, and by a super-slim margin, the hunt got scrapped.

I thought Meredith would be over it by now. Clearly I was wrong.

"Would you rather she lied about it?"

Meredith props a leg up onto the fence and bends into it, part of her pre-game warm-up. "I guess not, but what's up with her lately? Just because the hot black quarterback makes googly eyes at her all the time doesn't mean she gets to constantly one-up the co-captain of the squad. She pulled the same shit last week when we were practicing the new routine. In front of everybody just, 'Oh, hey, I think it would be better this way' and doesn't even run it by me first. And now she voted to ax the pennant hunt in favor of that stupid put-makeup-on-the-football-team idea?" She stretches her arms behind her head, scowling. "Like there's any team-building value in slapping guyliner on a bunch of jocks."

Maybe not, but it does sound like fun. I don't dare say as much.

Luckily, Meredith is distracted by something behind me. Her face breaks into a grin, and she switches from stretching her arm to waving it vigorously.

I turn around to see Ben approaching the track, wearing a button-down shirt that has his name sewn onto a patch beneath his left shoulder.

"Hey," Meredith says, leaning closer to me while Ben is still out of earshot. "Did I see you leaving his house the other day?"

"The other—? Oh, right. I drove him home after the boys' soccer game."

"Oh."

So she noticed. And she cared enough to bring it up almost a week later. And was that a trace of relief I detected in that oh-so-loaded single syllable?

Not my type, my ass.

"Look at you," I say to Ben as he nears the fence. "Are you here to watch the football game or change the oil in my car?"

Ben tugs at the name patch on his shirt. "I can change your tires if you want, but I'd rather make you a milk shake. You're looking at Buck's Diner's newest employee."

Meredith claps and laughs. "Every time I think that floats couldn't get any better, Benny shows up to make them for me."

"One scoop of chocolate ice cream, one scoop of vanilla," Ben says.

Meredith winks. "You know how I like it."

Okay, Meredith may be a born flirt, but dirty innuendo is definitely my cue to see my way out of this conversation. Before I can come up with an excuse, Ben asks, "How's your brother doing?"

I shrug. "He's all right. Mostly good days this week, with a few bad moments. Better than the other way around."

"I bet. But I was reading this really interesting article earlier about how music can be therapy for behavioral disorders."

"Oh?"

"It's supposed to reduce anxiety and boost all sorts of healing hormones in the body. Especially instrumental and classical music, stuff where the patterns repeat. And I know your brother's not gonna want to sit around listening to Mozart on loop, so I wanted to ask you—what if I taught him to play guitar?"

"You play guitar?" I don't know why this surprises me, but it does.

"He's a man of many talents," Meredith says. "And he never brags about it, so I will." She must realize how that sounds, coming from someone who claims Ben doesn't occupy extra space in her head, and she nudges me a little too hard. "Told you he's good with his hands."

I rub at my arm, and Ben looks embarrassed. "Aw, thanks, Mer. I quit taking lessons a while ago, but I remember the important stuff. Enough that I could maybe help out by giving Aaron something to focus on."

"I bet he'd love that!" My mother has been beside

herself, trying to dull the edges of Aaron's outbursts while dealing with Michael's accusations of being ignored. This could be a tiny ray of hope to alleviate some of the tension. "That's so, so sweet of you to offer." I turn to Meredith, taking full advantage of my shot. "You're right. He *is* great."

Meredith responds with a playful ruffle of Ben's hair, which he shyly pats back into place. "It's nothing I've been meaning to get back into playing for a while, anyway." He eyes the brace on my wrist. "And what's your story?"

I hold up my hand. "Sprained my wrist at practice. The same one I broke three months ago."

"Ouch." Ben winces. "You're on a roll."

Meredith hooks an arm around my neck, making my camera strap dig into my skin. "Macy's sitting out tonight, so she's playing team photographer instead." She turns to me and runs my ponytail through her hand. "I hate when my road dawg goes off-roading."

"Relax. You're not getting rid of me." I snap a picture of her pouting face. "And I'll still be at the diner later."

"Awesome." Ben grins. "What kind of pie do your brothers like?"

"Apple crumb. One of the few things all three of us agree on. Why?"

"They throw away whatever doesn't sell at the end of the night, so instead of trying to eat everything myself, like I did last time, I'll sneak some aside for you to take home. See you there."

"And blueberry for me!" Meredith calls after him, waving her arm in the air.

"Don't worry, Mer," Ben calls back. "I've got you covered."

I flash a grin at his retreating back, because that's a promise I intend to make sure he keeps.

Seven

SENIOR YEAR

My sleepless night and restless morning of running finally catch up to me, and after lunch I pass out on the couch in my dad's office while I'm waiting for him to install a program on my laptop.

It's not long before I wake up to the sound of the rain announcing its escape from the clouds with loud slaps against the roof. Dad jumps up from his chair, swearing softly. "Forgot to pull my car into the garage. Be right back." He starts off, but doubles back when he sees me rubbing my eyes.

"It's not like you to crash in the afternoon. Are you feeling all right?"

I flex my fingers around my wrist brace. "Still sore and

kind of swollen. I don't know why this keeps happening."

"Which is exactly why you should have it looked at."

I open my mouth to protest, but the beat of the rain intensifies and Dad starts off again. He does a little shuffle like he stepped on something, then bends and scoops my phone off the carpet. "Here," he says. "You dropped this."

The screen lights up, showing two new text messages. When I see that one is from Meredith and the other is from Joel, my heart does a funny extra beat.

Meredith's is a group text that says: FLAG HUNT @ OLD MILL CANCELED. STUPID RAIN.

I'm disappointed. I thought maybe she was trying to reach out to me. But it was just a formality, the only type of interaction we've had in a very long time.

Frowning, I click on the message from Joel.

CAN WE TALK BEFORE SCHOOL ON MONDAY? AT THE FIELD?

My heart does that weird skip again, and I stare at the screen. I start and erase a response three different times. Finally I hit send:

PROMISE TO TELL ME EVERYTHING?

A full minute goes by before my phone buzzes with a reply, and I wonder if Joel was similarly angsting over his answer. Until I see that all he's written is:

SEE YOU THEN.

I have every intention of getting to school half an hour early on Monday. But somehow a blueberry from one of Mom's homemade pancakes explodes on my shirt, and after I change, I reemerge from my room to find that Michael and Aaron have missed their bus—an almost impossible feat, considering the stop is our next-door neighbor's driveway. Still, they managed it, and by the time I'm finally dashing to my locker after dropping them off at school, I'll be lucky if I can make it down to the football field with five minutes to spare.

I can feel Noah watching me as I unload my bag. He's talking to Tyrell Davis at the opposite end of the hall, but each time I look up, I catch him averting his eyes one second too late. I get the feeling he has something to tell me, and it's making me irrationally nervous. Then again, so does everything lately. I silently will Tyrell to keep their conversation going until I can get my book bag loaded.

It's not that I don't want to talk to Noah; I just don't have time right now.

I honestly have no idea what I ever did to catch Noah's attention. After Joel became the thing that made me think *I will never be that stupid again*, I had no intention of going on another adopt-a-former-Pirate campaign when Noah transferred to Ridgedale. If anything, I'd planned to totally ignore him. Then we got paired up for a biology lab. When I told him my name, he said, "Like the department store?"

"No," I replied. "Like my great-aunt."

"Ah." He rubbed his chin. "Well, I'm Noah."

"Like the ark?"

And even though I realized my mistake immediately and wanted to crawl under the table, I swear the grin that lit his face might as well have been the sun breaking through the clouds after forty days and forty nights of rain. It was that beautiful.

"Noah *built* the ark," he said through guffaws. "That was cute."

His chuckling was so warm and without a trace of mockery that I couldn't help but crack up too.

That was really all it took to break the dam. He was so open and friendly that I couldn't not be nice to him. Before I knew it, he was sharing the story of how his parents were divorced and he'd been living with his mom in Mortonville, but after a knee injury that required surgery left him (and his grades) in a funk, he'd decided to move in with his dad in Ridgedale for a fresh start.

I revised my plan of action, telling myself we could be friends. As long as that was *all* we were and I stayed in control of my better judgment, it seemed totally doable. Until he started walking a little closer and his jokes became a little more suggestive and he started texting me for no real reason.

And, of course, until someone snuck up on me in the dark and kissed me senseless.

I slam my locker door shut and almost drown out the voice that says, "Hi."

I turn to see Meredith walking past me. I blink at the sight of her tall frame and her chestnut-colored ponytail pooling into the hood of her tight, baby-blue zip-up, and then I scan the hall to see who else could've spoken. There's no one. So unless my ears were playing tricks on me, Meredith just acknowledged my existence for the first time in ages.

"What do you mean, 'hi'?"

Meredith stops. One shoulder lifts slightly, like she'd been hoping I hadn't heard her. She turns. "It's a pretty standard greeting. Doesn't usually require an explanation."

"Right, but"—I hoist my bag onto my shoulder—"you haven't directed any kind of greeting at me in a while."

Meredith hooks her thumbs into the pockets of her hoodie and looks at the floor. "I know. But Ben told me you said hi. So . . . Hi."

She starts down the hall, and all I can do is watch her go. I've tried to open dialogues with her at least a dozen times since last year's homecoming, but Meredith Kopala runs the Hotel California of shit lists: Once you're on it, you never leave.

It doesn't make sense that a message relayed through Ben is what finally broke the seal, except that it kind of does.

"Wait, Meredith!" I bolt after her, hoping the window of opportunity isn't about to slam down on my fingertips as they catch her arm. "Do you—can we please talk?" I pull her toward a nearby exit to a courtyard without giving her a chance to respond. "Please come outside."

She resists but ultimately lets me lead her out the door.

I dump my bag onto the ground when we reach one of the stone benches at the center of the courtyard, and sit. Meredith doesn't. Before the tidal wave of words building in my throat can come crashing out, she says, "You knew how I felt about him."

"I—yes, of course I did. *You* were the one who kept denying it, remember?"

"Did it ever occur to you that there was a reason for that?" She tosses her bag onto the grass but still doesn't join me on the bench. "You knew the kinds of guys I dated. They were all goddamn mirages. The minute I got close—*poof*—all the good stuff disappeared. It was like a self-fulfilling prophecy that it wasn't going to work out."

"Meredith, you're not a jinx."

"Well, that's how it felt, okay?" She finally drops down next to me, her expression pained. "Ben . . . Ben is different. He's like a sacred cow or something."

I laugh before I can help it. "A sacred *cow*?"

She smiles, albeit fleetingly, before her lips turn down and her fingers find the *M* on her necklace. "You know what I mean. Once I realized I had . . . a crush"—she falters on the word, like she's never said it out loud before—"on him, I didn't want to do anything about it. Because he was so different from what I'm used to, and because I liked him so ridiculously much." She presses the *M* into the underside of her bottom lip. "I knew screwing it up would suck ass." She stands abruptly, like she's said too much. When she retrieves her bag from the grass, she turns to me and adds, "Only, I didn't have to worry about screwing it up, because you did that for me."

She might as well have taken a pen out of her backpack

and stabbed me with it, for how deeply her words cut me. And still, when she starts for the door, I shoot to my feet and call after her.

"Meredith, I swear to you, nothing happened. Not before homecoming, and not during. It was only a dance, and I know it was stupid for the two of us to be out there together, but it was all my fault for even showing up in the first place. Ben was trying to cheer me up, and I'm sorry he left you alone to do it, and I'm even sorrier that it looked like something it wasn't."

"There was a lot more to it than what it *looked* like, Macy."

"I know, and I'm sorry. Part of you must understand how bad I feel, or you wouldn't have said anything to me in the hall before. I don't know what else to say except that you were right. If I'd listened when you said Joel couldn't be trusted, none of this might ever have happened."

A shadow of something that looks a lot like confusion passes over her face. "You still think he set the fire?" She stiffens, steeling her expression like she said something she shouldn't have. The change in her demeanor is so quick and yet so unmistakable, I feel like I've missed a very important detail.

"Everyone thinks Joel set the fire. It's the only thing that makes sense . . . isn't it?"

Meredith grips the strap of her bag against her shoulder. "He says he didn't. And maybe it *doesn't* make sense, but I want to believe him. I guess it says a lot that I'm willing to trust Joel Hargrove over someone I used to call my best friend."

She disappears inside the building, and I sit down hard on the bench. My mind is reeling. What did Joel say to Meredith to turn the tables? And why did she forgive him and Ben so easily, but any steps I make toward progress are destroyed as quickly as footprints in sand?

I wasn't the only one who hurt Meredith last year. But somehow I'm the only one she still sees as a traitor.

Eight

I almost don't see Jadie coming toward me as I adjust my camera lens before the halftime show. The marching band is spilling over the football field in their bright white-and-teal uniforms, and I've been having so much fun capturing the energy and action of the game, freezing moments in time, that I decide to keep snapping.

"Meredith's really mad at me about voting down the pennant hunt, isn't she?" Jadie says.

I bite the inside of my lip. I don't want to get in the middle of this. "You know how Meredith is. She's used to being the leader, and she doesn't handle it well when people don't think that her way is the best way."

Jadie crosses her arms over her chest. "Well, it's not like I was the only one. I'm not going to apologize for remembering that there's no *I* in 'team.' I mean, don't you think she's a little ridiculous sometimes?"

"What's ridiculous?" another voice cuts in. Joel is suddenly on my other side, his football helmet dangling from his hand. He's sweaty and dirty and his hair is a mess, and somehow he still looks like he should be strutting in slow motion toward a movie camera while cheesy music swells in the background. I lift my camera and snap a picture of him.

"That catch you made in the second quarter," I say.

"That you never come to the diner for Friday Night Eats," Jadie adds without missing a beat.

Joel bumps her with his helmet as if to say *Good one.* "Thanks, but I won't be there tonight, either. My dad ships out tomorrow."

"I'm sorry," I say. "It must be so hard on you."

He shrugs. "It's not the first time, and it might not be the last. And I get that he has to go, that it's his duty or whatever, and I'm proud of him. But I still feel . . ." He trails off, scratching his eyebrow.

"Abandoned?" Jadie offers.

Joel points his finger at her. "That. Exactly that. I mean, he's got a wife who has to work, four kids, one of them is about to be admitted to the hospital—" He cuts off when my eyes go big and Jadie gasps. "It's nothing serious," he adds quickly. "Well, I mean it's not life-threatening. Peyton, our littlest guy, has cystic fibrosis, and every so often they bring him in for what they call a 'tune-up.' He stays about ten days while they pump him full of antibiotics and do breathing treatments. So it's not like we don't need my dad *here*, you know?" His features harden. "I think it's fucked up to put your country before your family."

"I get it," Jadie says. "My birth parents gave me up for adoption because I wasn't a boy. And even though I love my mom and dad, part of me is always, *always* aware that the people who created me thought I wasn't good enough for them." She spots Coach Tori waving her over, and squeezes Joel's wrist. "Let me know if you ever need to talk," she says before jogging back to the squad.

"Wow," Joel says, scratching the back of his neck. "I feel like an idiot for complaining."

"Don't. You have a right to your feelings. That saying about no one being able to make you feel inferior without your permission? Total bullshit."

There's an all-too-brief second where Joel's blue-green eyes are looking at me with a mix of appreciation and something else that I don't have time to decipher. Because someone slams into his back then, and he crashes into me with a grunt. Joel is able to catch himself, but I hit the Astroturf hard, seeing stars of pain as my bum wrist breaks my fall.

"Shit, are you okay?" Joel says, rushing to kneel next to me. "I'm so sorry."

I hug my wrist to my chest. "It wasn't your fault. Who the hell was that?"

"Davenport," Joel spits out. "Fucking douche bag." He

gently pulls my hand away from my body and inspects my brace. "Did you hurt it again?"

"Well, I definitely didn't help it."

Joel's features twist into a snarl of disgust. "Forget his collarbone. Next time I'm breaking his face."

He cringes, probably because that would've been the wrong thing to say in front of anyone else. But I can't help it—I laugh. And soon Joel is chuckling right along with me, and it's like there's no one else on the football field except the two of us.

Joel takes my good hand and helps me to my feet. But he doesn't let go once I'm standing.

"I'd better get back," he says. He gives my fingers a gentle squeeze. "Sorry I'm such a high-risk person to be around."

I squeeze back. *Some risks are worth taking.*

I cut out of the game a little early to avoid the post-game traffic jam, and arrive at Buck's before everyone else. It's not a huge place, but the atmosphere is great. It's like stepping into the 1950s, with red leather seats atop silver stools that line the counter, a black-and-white checkerboard floor, and even a jukebox beneath the window that overlooks the street outside. I love coming here after the games almost as much as I love the games themselves.

When I see Ben standing behind the polished silver counter wearing a soda jerk hat, I can't stop myself from giggling. He gives me a sheepish tip of the canoe-shaped

A KISS IN THE DARK

headpiece, and I pull myself onto one of the stools, marveling at how empty the place is.

"Where is everybody?" I ask.

"Haven't you ever noticed that the only people here on a Friday night are the same ones who just rolled up out of the football stadium? It's a morgue before the game gets out." He nods toward my camera. "How'd tonight go?"

"We were killing them when I left. Wanna see some pictures?"

I free the camera from my neck, and Ben leans on the counter as I scroll through my frames. I captured some pretty sweet action shots, and I'm super-pleased with myself when Ben looks impressed with what he sees. But when I scroll too far and accidentally show him a picture I snapped of the lake at sunset, he takes the camera right out of my hands.

"Wow. Did you take this one too?" He studies the screen, where the houses and treetops edging the water are silhouettes against a sky full of brushstroke clouds in gray and white and pink and yellow. The colors blur in the water below, a distorted mirror image.

"I did." My stomach does a little flip of embarrassment when he continues scrolling through more of my sunset shots. "I took all of those. It's a weird hobby of mine, I guess."

"It's not weird. It's awesome. These look like they belong in a magazine."

That makes me blush. Maybe it's because the only other

73

person I've shown those pictures to is my mother, and that's only because it's her camera. I'm used to being known as the bubbly cheerleader. The introspective part of me isn't something many people see, and giving someone a glimpse into my quiet time is weirdly personal. But Ben seems to appreciate it, and I kind of like the way that feels.

"That first one was from a few nights ago," I say. "Aaron was having a bad day, so I suggested we all drive down to the lake to watch the sunset. It seemed to help . . . for all of five minutes."

Two of Ben's co-workers burst in from the kitchen, and Ben jumps, like he just remembered that he's supposed to be working. So I order a banana milk shake, and Ben makes it before checking on the whole two tables that are occupied.

When he comes back, I'm fiddling with my brace. My last dose of ibuprofen is wearing off, and whether I make it tighter or looser, nothing seems to help.

"That had to hurt," Ben says, nodding toward my wrist.

"This is a walk in the park compared to some of the things I've done." I swivel on the stool and point to my right leg. "See this knee? When I was thirteen, I broke it in the middle of the Avalon ice rink while news reporters were filming a story about their Christmas village. My kneecap split in half, and the gap was so wide that I could fit two fingers between the pieces." I demonstrate by holding my index and middle finger over the spot that was once a canyon separating my bone. "And they got the whole thing on tape."

Ben laughs, even as he shudders like a thousand tiny

bugs are crawling over him. "You might as well send me the link, because I am so googling that tonight. Okay, my turn."

He tells me about the time his brother flung a stick at him while they were building a tree house and it hit him in the eye.

"My eyeball was huge," he says, shaping an example with his thumb and pointer finger. "I thought it was going to pop right out of my head."

I scrunch up my face. "That sounds gross."

"I had to have surgery, and I still ended up with a trauma cataract. It's small, but if you look close, you can see it."

He leans over the counter and angles his head toward me so that I have a direct view of his right eye. At first I don't notice anything unusual except for the sheer number of colors in his iris. When I followed him to his shed the first time he helped with the homecoming float, I thought his eyes were the same color as his hair. Up close I can see that there's nothing on the spectrum to describe them. They're not any one color; it's like a solar flare of gold and green and brown and blue, or an artist's interpretation of the sun reflecting in the ocean. I've never seen anything like it.

"Can you see it?" he prompts.

I blink when I realize I've been staring. I recover by squinting and taking a closer look. "I think so. Right there," I say, pointing at the tiny translucent spot to the right of his pupil.

Ben nods, looking proud of himself. "Hard-core."

His face is still only a few inches from mine when the

bell that signals the opening of the door sounds. I turn around to see Meredith and two of the other cheerleaders filing into the restaurant. She bounds up to the counter and takes the seat next to me. She's all bubbliness and energy, but the once-over she gives me out of the corner of her eye isn't lost on me. It's the same ice-cold look she gave Jadie on the football field earlier.

Nine

I never make it down to the football field to meet Joel. By the time Meredith and I end our mess of a conversation in the courtyard, there are only two minutes left until the first bell. I send him a text asking if we can reschedule, but when he still hasn't answered by the start of lunch, I check my message to make sure I wrote actual words, since I was so rattled that I can't be sure.

"Hey," Noah says, sidling up to me as everyone is filing back into the school.

We've finished up lunch outdoors, and the promise of fall is in the air—which really just means that stepping outside of an air-conditioned building no longer feels like venturing onto the surface of the sun. Real autumn weather is still at least a few weeks away, but for now I'm enjoying the warmth on the back of my neck that would've burned me to a lobster-red crisp up until a few days ago.

"Hey yourself." I catch sight of myself in his aviator sunglasses, and I hate that I look a little unnerved.

"So it sucks that the flag hunt was canceled," he says. "I was kind of looking forward to it."

"I'm sure Meredith will reschedule it. No way she'll let it get sacked two years in a row."

I look up at that second to see Jadie and Tyrell walking parallel to us a few feet away. Jadie's stare is fixed on me as if to say, *Are you seriously sharing your personal bubble with another Pirate right now?*

I pretend not to notice.

"What happened last year?" Noah asks.

I stifle a snort. "A few of the girls wanted to change things up and try new team-building exercises. So we voted the hunt down in favor of something else, and Meredith was *not* happy. But now that she's the senior captain, it's back."

Noah pushes his sunglasses to the top of his head. "It's weird to hear you say 'we' when you talk about the cheerleaders. I know you were on the squad for a long time, but it's hard to picture you waving pom-poms when I'm used to seeing you with that thing"—he motions to my camera—"hanging around your neck all the time. You carry it around like it's your kid."

I finger the edge of the lens. It might not share my DNA, but this camera has definitely become part of me.

I lift it to my face and snap a picture of Noah. "You never know when you'll need to capture a moment."

He smiles, but holds up his hand to mock shield his face. "Let's keep this off the record. Then you can tell me the real reason why I need a bathing suit for the flag hunt."

"What do you mean, 'the real reason'? Everyone goes swimming in the waterfall afterward."

He makes a face, and I can understand why he's confused. Old Mill is a park built around the ruins of a Civil War–era manufacturing mill that burned down in the 1800s. The creek alongside it was dammed in order to use the water for power, and the result was a gorgeous waterfall that looks like it should be tucked between picturesque mountains, not around the corner from a main drag in the suburbs of Atlanta.

When I tell Noah as much, he stops walking. "Wait, is this the park near that country club? The Mill Club, or whatever?"

"Yep. Have you been there?"

"Nah, but I've heard of it. At least now I know it's not some kind of prank. Like, tell the new kid to bring a bathing suit, and then hang it from a branch while he's bare-assed and covering his junk with a rock."

I really wish he hadn't said that. Because now I am definitely picturing him naked.

"Um, no," I say, shaking the image out of my head as we approach my locker. "No one ends up naked. Unless they want to." OH MY GOD. A flush of heat crawls up my neck, burning hotter and faster when a roguish smile spreads across Noah's face. "I mean—I meant—no one's ever stolen someone's bathing suit. At least not that I know of." My face is so hot that I'm convinced wisps of smoke must be rising from the top of my head.

My phone vibrates in my bag, and I fumble for it, grateful to have somewhere else to look. Until I see that Jadie has texted me a picture of herself with a mock stern look on her face. She's pointing two fingers at her eyes, and then a second photo pops up of her making the same motion toward the camera, as if to say, *I've got my eyes on you.* Beneath it is the caption: FRIENDS DON'T LET FRIENDS CHASE PIRATE BOOTY!

As I'm reading it, a second text pops up: TWICE.

I clear the screen before Noah can see, though I'm not sure he even has a chance, since a couple of football players walk by and nod at him at that moment. It's crazy to me how smooth Noah's transition from Mortonville Pirate to Ridgedale Raven has been, at least in comparison with Joel's. Maybe no one's willing to test Noah's take-no-shit vibe, or maybe the novelty of a Pirate on Raven turf has started to wear off. Either way, Noah's arrival hasn't brought a fraction of the drama that Joel's did.

So far. But I have a tendency to speak too soon, and that's the exact moment when Joel walks by.

"Mace," he says. "Can we regroup after school tomorrow? I have to work tonight."

I wonder why he'd phrase the question in such a dodgy, nonspecific way, until I see him eyeing Noah and realize

Joel must not want him to know what we're going to do. Even if it's only having a conversation. Which is weird, but I've noticed friction between them before, and I get the feeling it has some pretty deep roots.

"Do you purposely wait until you see us talking to come up and start bothering her?" Noah says, giving Joel an acidic once-over.

"Because what, you own her?" Joel shoots back. "You don't need to act like a caveman just because you have the hair, you know."

A muscle in Noah's jaw twitches. "Fuck off, Hargrove."

"Guys, stop," I cut in, holding up my hands like that would actually prevent them from pummeling each other. I look at Joel. "After school tomorrow is fine."

"Sounds good." His gaze cuts right back to Noah. "You're the one who needs to fuck off. Right back to where you came from."

Noah doesn't flinch under Joel's glare. He stretches an arm toward the hall, glowering right back at him. "After you."

I slam my locker and grab Noah's outstretched hand before the sparks in Joel's eyes can set something on fire. "No one's going anywhere, except to class," I say, tugging Noah away from my locker. "Let's walk. Joel, I'll see you later."

"Yeah," he says, still scowling at Noah. "Later."

"What was that about?" I ask as we head toward the science wing. I try to drop his hand, but he doesn't let go. So now I'm walking down the hall awkwardly holding hands with Noah Granger two minutes after seeing him naked in my head.

"Hargrove's a prick." He side-eyes me. "But I get the feeling you don't need me to tell you that."

"What was your first clue?" I'm asking how he knows about my history with Joel, given that he didn't go to school here last year, but he must think I'm referring to whatever beef the two of them obviously have, because he says, "I've known him a long time."

"And did you learn that lesson the hard way, or have you always hated him?"

"Mostly column A. Watch your step around him. He can be pretty heartless."

Don't I know it. But before I can harp on it, Noah stops walking and pulls me into an exit alcove. "Listen, back to what we were talking about before. Why don't you and I go over to Old Mill after school? I was going to say tomorrow, but—" He throws an annoyed look in the direction of where we left Joel.

I'm about to tell him I can't because I have cheerleading practice, until I remember it's a knee-jerk response that's no longer true. So instead I say, "Don't you have football practice?"

"We can go afterward," he says with a shrug. "My knee's not up to snuff yet, so I'll probably cut out early anyway. You can give me a tour of the park. That way if the hunt's rescheduled, I won't be wandering around like a blind dog."

He glances out into the hallway like he's half expecting Joel to reappear, then turns back to me with a conspiratorial gleam in his eyes. "And maybe you and I can finally have a conversation without being interrupted. There's something I want to talk to you about anyway."

My pulse picks up speed. My first thought is that he's going to confess to kissing me. But if that's the case, I want to know *now*.

"What is it?"

"Nothing that can't wait. So what do you say? Is it a date?"

Alarms start flashing in my head, telling me I need to find some way to say no. That saying yes is the first step down a road where I already crashed and burned last year. I hold up my brace-bound hand. "I can't really swim" is the best I can come up with.

Noah flashes a grin. "There are ways around that. Text me your address, and I'll pick you up at four?"

"I—okay." I'm still nodding dumbly as I watch his back retreat down the hall, knowing I might've just done something supremely stupid. But when he looks at me over his shoulder and smiles before disappearing around the corner, I have to wonder if this time it might be worth it.

Ten

JUNIOR YEAR

I gather the pleats of my uniform skirt in my hand to soak up some of the clamminess.

I finally convinced Joel to join us for Friday Night Eats. And even though I keep telling myself that it's stupid to be nervous about it, I'm lingering by the diner door, mutilating my skirt, ready to whisk him off to a free seat the minute he sets foot inside. I'm determined to make him see that life at Ridgedale isn't all that bad.

And if I'm wrong, at least I'll be close enough to protect him.

I wave frantically when I spot him, then guide him toward the counter, where Ben greets him with a high five.

"Hey, man. Good to see you here. Heard you made an awesome play tonight."

"Yeah, followed by a not-so-awesome play, which apparently negated any awesomeness that came before it."

"Bull," Ben says, waving off the comment. "I saw Macy's pictures of that pass you caught last week. If anyone's still talking smack, it's because they're jealous. You've been killing it out there."

Joel looks at me. "You got a picture of that? Can I see it?"

I groan internally at my decision to delete last week's pictures after saving them to my laptop. "I don't have it with me, but if it's okay with you, I'll post it to the Ridgedale's Finest page when I get home tonight. I think everyone should see it."

"Ask her to show you some of her other pictures too. She's a really good photographer," Ben adds, wiping the counter next to my elbow with a rag. "You should enter contests and stuff, Mace. I bet you could be a professional someday."

The same embarrassment I felt the last time Ben talked about my photographs turns my cheeks warm. Which is the first warning that I'm about to say something moronic. "It's just a hobby. Cheering is my passion."

Yep.

Both boys chuckle. "It's possible to have more than one passion, you know," Joel says.

The way he fixes those blue-green eyes on me when he

says the word "passion" makes me wish we were somewhere way less public.

The bell on the door jingles, snapping me out of my hormonal haze. A big group files in, including Meredith. She bounds over and hops up onto the stool next to mine. I ignore the way her eyes rake over Joel as she does it.

Soon almost every seat is full and the scent of hamburgers on the grill mingles with the sounds of chatter and music in the air. The football players alternately high-five Ben and rib him for his getup. Until Ken Davenport walks in with Tyrell. The second Ken spots Joel, he stops, cups his hands around his mouth, and yells "TROJAN HORRRRRSE" for the entire restaurant to hear.

Tyrell flips Ken the middle finger, but Joel ignores him and hunches over the counter like he's trying to hide inside his own skin.

"Who gave him the idea that he's funny?" I bark. "He's like a two-year-old with 'roid rage."

Meredith rolls her eyes, her pink-glossed lips pursed around her straw. "He may be a scrotum, but no one likes intruders on their turf."

My jaw drops. She said it quietly enough that I don't think Joel heard, but I can't believe she said it at all in front of him. Before I can strike back, she crooks her finger at Ben.

"Grab a straw, Benny. You've gotta try this."

Ben frees a straw from its wrapper and drops it into Meredith's root beer float. Meredith points to my camera and says, "Mace, how about a picture of me with Ridgedale's finest float maker?" She winks at the double entendre, without a trace of the attitude from two seconds ago. I have to wonder if I imagined what I heard before.

I snap a couple of shots of her and Ben, their faces pressed together as they sip from the same glass. And as I'm about to take a third, Meredith turns her head and plants one on Ben's cheek. He pulls back, blushing to the roots of his hair. Tyrell and a couple of the other guys make a raucous show of clapping him on the arms and shoulders.

Then Tyrell leans in to me, his tone hushed. "You might want to keep that camera handy." He waves in the direction of the booth where Ken has made himself at home. "I'm about to show those dipshits how it's done." He nods at Joel, and Joel nods back, holding up a cell phone as if to say, *Ready.*

Tyrell heads over to the jukebox, which contains music choices from the fifties all the way up to the present. He slips some coins inside, and a few seconds later "Marry You" by Bruno Mars blares through the speakers.

Tyrell and Bruno start to sing at the same time, and even though I've never considered myself attracted to Tyrell, my knees go a little weak. His voice is a-freaking-mazing. The entire diner stops to watch him, and next to me, Joel is recording it all on a cell phone. "*We're looking for something dumb to do/Hey, Jadie/I think I wanna dance with you.*"

The minute he says her name, cheers go up throughout the room. I'm glad Tyrell gave me a heads-up, because I get the cutest picture of Jadie in her booth next to Anna Chen, and Tyrell across the way at the jukebox, the two of them looking at each other like there's no one else in the room. Her cheeks turn the most adorable shade of pink, and she buries her smiling face in her hands. Tyrell continues to sing, belting out the lyrics he's changed to correspond to the homecoming dance as he slowly strolls over to Jadie's side. He kneels down next to her, saying something the rest of us can't hear. She covers her glowing cheeks with her hands and nods, then throws her arms around Tyrell's neck.

"You were in on this?" I yell over the commotion to Joel.

"I got recruited to record it. Tyrell's one of the few people who doesn't treat me like a criminal."

Maybe I'm wrong, but I swear he looks at Meredith then.

"For the record," I say, "I think you're pretty great."

"You'd testify to that?"

"Passionately."

We smile at each other, and I think, *We are totally having a moment*. Except that's also the moment when a handful of sundae spoons slips from Ben's hands and clatters to the floor.

And the moment when loud, obnoxious jeers ring out from Ken Davenport's table.

"Boo!" Ken shouts. "Boooo!" He stands up, holding his glass, and from the way his unsteadiness makes the contents slosh, I'm pretty sure there's more than Coke in it. "What is there, something in the fucking water in this place?" Never mind that he's holding a glass of soda. He points to Tyrell and bellows, *"Downgrade."* Then he reroutes his finger toward Meredith and says, "Total downgrade. What the hell happened, Kopala? You're really gonna drive a Prius after you've ridden a Bentley?" He points to himself, apparently the Bentley in question, and smirks. "Or in Davis's case, a Toyota."

I hop off my stool, anger pulsing in my veins. "Toyotas are Japanese, you moron, not Chinese. Do you even know the difference? Or are you mad because everyone here could take blow-up dolls to homecoming and their dates would still have more class than you?"

Ken's lips form a sloppy, condescending smile. "Interesting that you wanna school me on class while you're over there trying to bag some Pirate dick, Macy."

There are a few defensive outcries, but the rest of the room rustles with whispers and snickers. My fist curls so tightly that my fingernails cut into my palm. For a second I actually consider punching him. But then Meredith shoots off her stool and says, "You don't know what you're talking about, Ken, so stuff a sock in it. And I don't mean the usual location in your pants." She storms toward the door. "I'm out of here."

Joel stands up next and strides after her without a word. I turn on my heel and follow him out. Meredith is already slamming her car door when I catch up and grab a handful of Joel's shirt to slow him down.

"Joel, wait. I'm so sorry."

"You don't have to apologize for other people being pieces of shit."

"Please don't pay attention to them. Ken's always needed to take a tuning fork to his personality, but going after Jadie was beyond his normal brand of rotten. I think he was drunk."

"I wish I could be as surprised as you are, Mace." Joel snorts. "But people suck." As he walks away, he pounds the side of his fist against a handicapped parking sign, sending a metallic ripple through the night that makes me jump. "People fucking suck."

Eleven

SENIOR YEAR

Noah is prompt, if nothing else. He pulls up at four on the nose, and I run out to the driveway to avoid inviting him in. But there's no deterring my mother from following me out.

My mom thinks she's some kind of one-woman equivalent of a Myers-Briggs personality test. She claims to be able to sniff out a tool in less than five minutes with a few strategic questions. It's snap judgment at its best, but even I have to admit she's uncannily on the mark most of the time. She's right on my heels as I approach Noah's bright blue Mazda.

Noah sticks his head out the window, and Mom holds out her hand as I climb into the passenger seat. "Bonnie Atwood," she says. "You must be Noah."

"Yes, ma'am. Nice to meet you."

Strike one. That's another thing about the South that Mom's never gotten used to—young people calling her ma'am. It's meant to be respectful, but Mom says it makes her feel old.

"I hear you're new in town?"

I don't know why she'd ask him that when I already told her. It's like she prides herself on embarrassing me.

If Noah is aware that he's under scrutiny, he doesn't seem to care. "That's right. I came to live with my dad this summer. We're in Arbor Creek, not far from here."

"Oh, Arbor Creek! I have some friends there. And Jadie lives there too, right, Macy?" I nod, and I can almost see her making a mental note to put her spies on alert for Noah-related gossip. Another by-product of junior year: Mom's "mama bear" mode is a grizzly on steroids. She continues the cross-examination with, "And do you have any brothers and sisters keeping your mother company? Or is she on her own now?"

"No, ma'am, it's just my dad and me."

Strike two. Abandoning your mother is the filthiest of all sins in my mom's book. She's only in her forties, but she threatens to cut my brothers and me out of her will on a regular basis if we ever try to stick her in a nursing home.

"He was diagnosed with multiple sclerosis not long ago," Noah continues. "So I think it worked out for the best with me moving in."

And there's his redemption. Mom practically coos at his willingness to take care of an ailing parent. She makes sure I have my cell phone before ending the interrogation with, "You kids have fun. Remember, the park closes at dark."

She waves as Noah backs down the driveway, and I sink into my seat. "Sorry about that."

"For what? Your mom?" Noah glances over, his eyes alive with amusement "I have that effect on them."

I raise an eyebrow. "I take it you've met a lot of girls' parents?"

He shrugs. "I'm a friendly guy."

"I bet."

Our eyes meet, and it's there again—that flickering in my chest, the ripples of heat that have become part of my daily life. It hits me then that despite my best efforts, I'm attracted to him. That I could definitely see myself kissing him.

If I haven't already.

When we get to Old Mill, I direct Noah to the parking lot. It's only when we're both out of the car and he's slinging a backpack over his shoulder that I notice he's wearing flip-flops.

"I hope you brought sneakers," I say, pointing to his feet. "You can't hike in those."

He glances down and wiggles his toes. "Guess we'll have to skip straight to the swimming." He produces a wadded-up plastic shopping bag from the pocket of his shorts, which I realize are swim trunks. "I brought this to protect your brace."

I shake my head. "At least I know you didn't bring me here hoping to get an edge in the flag hunt."

He puts his hands in his pockets as we start down the hill, past the red brick and floor-to-ceiling windows of the Mill Club, and head toward the trail. "I guess I don't really get the point of it, to be honest."

"It's a team-building exercise. Coach Tori is big on the squad interacting with the football players outside of the games."

Noah feigns indignation. "What, the keg parties and hookups aren't enough?"

"Guess not."

"And what does the winner get?"

"Losers buy the winners milk shakes at the diner during Friday Night Eats." At least, they're supposed to. I have a feeling Tyrell ended up spotting everyone on his team last year. "And, uh, bragging rights?"

Noah stops and gives me a look of disbelief. "You go through all this trouble, and there's no infamy? No notoriety? Not even beer?" He shakes his head. "Mace, you guys are going about it all wrong."

"You might have a point. Come on." I nod in the direction of the wood steps that lead down to the rock-and-tree-lined creek.

"So why'd you quit the squad?"

"Long story. Here, we'll take the stairs, since you didn't bring appropriate footwear."

Noah ignores me, heading instead for the steep footpath to my right. He looks over his shoulder and winks at me. "I never take the easy way out."

"Suit yourself. But *I* don't enjoy breaking bones." I turn in the opposite direction and bound down the stairs, then jog over to where Noah is trying to hold his bag on his shoulder while negotiating a ninety-degree incline in brown leather flip-flops. "It's not too late to turn around," I call up to him.

No sooner do the words leave my mouth than his footing slips, and he doesn't so much slide down the hill as surf it. It's a wipeout, though, and he lands in a heap at my feet. I crack up laughing.

"So what did you prove by riding that hill like a wave?" I ask as I help him up, still trying to catch my breath.

"That I'm smooth as hell in every situation?" He dusts off his shorts.

"You already have a bad knee. You're lucky you didn't make it worse."

He flexes the leg that had a brace around it at the last football game. "No risk, no reward. Admit it; that was pretty badass."

"More like dumbass," I say through a fake cough.

He chortles, and as we head upstream toward the sound of the waterfall, he takes my hand again. It's starting to feel strangely comfortable, and I don't know what to think of that.

"Wow, so what are these pipes?" Noah asks, pointing to the huge snake of iron tubing that lines the path. It sits on concrete supports that are almost as high as his ribs and runs the length of a portion of the river.

"This is part of the old water power system. It carried the water from the dam to the waterwheel. The original was made of wood, but this one replaced it in the early 1900s."

Noah raises an eyebrow. "You're a history nerd?"

"If you count reading the placard at the observation deck."

We round a large tree, and when I see Noah's face, I know he's no longer concerned with the metal pipes.

"Wow," he says, except it's about ten syllables long. "This place is awesome." He steps up onto a rock to get a better look at the waterfall, staring appreciatively. "Forget hunting flags. If Meredith reschedules, I'm hiding out here and letting everyone else do the dirty work." He turns to me and flashes a grin. "Especially if I'm not getting a prize out of it."

He starts to step down, but something on the ground catches his eye and his mouth drops open. "What the—is that a chunk of the old building? A piece of history, just lying there on the ground, in the same water where we're about to swim?"

I have to giggle, because Noah geeking out over the mill ruins might be the cutest thing I've ever seen. Not that I can blame him. Being here always makes me feel like I've traveled back in time. I picture the mill rotting away like a flower, except the petals that scattered were made of brick and metal and concrete and were left here for us to discover.

"Who's the history nerd?" I tease.

He stretches a hand out to me, and I take it, letting him help me over the rock and down to a smooth patch of sand at the base of another tree. "You can't have a dad who's an air force veteran and not develop an appreciation for history. Let's set up here."

Noah spreads the blanket over the dirt in one quick motion, and then, without warning, grabs a fistful of his shirt from between his shoulder blades and pulls it off. That's when I forget what we were talking about, where I am, and what my name is.

My imagination did his naked torso no justice at all. Good God in heaven, are those nipple rings? Yep. Yes, they are. I'm going to drop dead on the spot.

Or, I'll do what I usually do when drowning in my own overheated blood: babble.

"There is kind of a prize for the pennant hunt, you know. Or there could be. I could feature the winner on the school blog."

Noah kicks off his shoes and steps onto a smooth, rounded rock at the water's edge. "For that picture thing? I heard about it, but I haven't checked it out." He balances on one foot and drags his other through the water. "Perfect." He pulls the plastic bag from his pocket again and brandishes it. "You coming in?"

I have my bikini on under my clothes, which is probably obvious from the straps tied around my neck. But the idea of getting undressed in front of Noah makes me squirmy. He steps closer to me as if he read—or maybe misread—my mind. "Do you need help taking your clothes off?" He eyes my brace and holds up his hands. "I swear that wasn't as creepy as it sounded."

I don't know who's more surprised when I lift my hands over my head. He takes the hem of my shirt and peels it up off my body. Suddenly I can't tell if the sound I'm hearing is the rush of water or the crackle of charged air between us.

How I thought that letting him take my clothes off could ever make things *less* awkward, I will never know. So I pull my cell phone from the back pocket of my shorts instead and start yammering again.

"Here," I say. "Let me show you the share site." I swipe the screen and pull up the Ridgedale's Finest page. "Everyone posts their photos here, and I write up a little feature on one picture for the blog each week. Well—I've only done a few so far. See?" I click the link and let him take a look.

He makes a face. "You highlighted some junior who got her first car? How was that the most worthwhile thing happening at Ridgedale last week?"

"Hey! She's been saving for that car since she was seven. I thought it was a cute story. Just like it'll be fun if I spotlight the hunt winners. I'll be covering it for the yearbook anyway."

Noah takes the phone from my hand. "Wow. You post a lot to this thing, huh?"

I shrug. "I like pictures."

"I don't get the need to document every second of your life and make sure the whole world sees it." But for feeling that way, he's scrolling pretty intently. "Hey, wait a second." He stops and clicks on a picture. "Is that you and Hargrove?"

"Oh." I try to pull the phone from his hands, but he holds firm. "That was taken last year. I've been meaning to delete it."

"Why?"

"Long story."

Noah glances up from the screen. "You can't use the same cop-out twice. We've got time."

I give him a sly look in return. "Then we also have time to talk about why you two are always at each other's throats."

He touches the screen of my phone again, making the picture larger. "Joel uses people. He's got your back for as long as you serve a purpose. After that, good luck." I wait for him to elaborate, but he hands the phone back to me and turns the tables with a question of his own. "Your friends don't approve of you hanging out with me, do they? Can I assume Hargrove's at least partly to blame for that?"

My mind flashes back to Meredith and the confused look she tried to hide when I brought up Joel starting the fire. "I used to know where my friends stood when it came to Joel. Now I don't know what to think except . . ." I don't know why my resolve is gone in that moment, but I blurt it out: "I think Joel kissed me the other night."

"You *think* he kissed you?" Noah says with a laugh.

"At the game. When the lights went out. Someone came up to me and kissed me, and I thought it might've been you, but it makes more sense that it was him. Except he hasn't copped to it, and I don't understand why he'd do that and then just walk away."

Noah snorts. "Walking away is something he's good at."

I ignore him, swiping my phone until I come to the picture of the photograph I found on the football field.

"I even went back the next day looking for clues, but all I found was this."

He takes the phone, and his lips settle into an unreadable line as he studies the black-and-white image of the tattoo. He stares in silence for so long that I wonder if he sees something I didn't.

"Do you know what it is?" I ask.

"Snake tattoo," he murmurs.

I roll my eyes. "That much I gathered. Do you know what it means?"

He hands the phone back to me with a shrug. "A lot of Native American tribes use snakes as symbols of defiance." When he sees my eyebrow arch, he adds, "I'm a quarter Comanche, according to my great-grandfather." He takes the phone again and gently tosses it and the plastic bag onto the blanket behind me before threading his fingers through mine. When he looks into my eyes, his have gone dark.

"So why does it make more sense for Joel to have kissed you, and not me? I'm assuming you've kissed him before?"

"Well, no, but—"

His thumb traces the inside of my wrist. "Then what makes you so sure it wasn't me?"

"I—because you haven't said anything. You haven't acted any differently. And don't take this the wrong way, but you seem like the kind of guy who, if you kissed a girl, would take the credit for it."

"How do you know that's not why I brought you here?"

My breath catches in my throat. "Is it?"

One of his hands moves to the small of my back. He doesn't respond—at least not with words. In the next breath his mouth is against mine, and I know this is supposed to be the answer to my question.

It's sweet and it's sexy, and unapologetically thorough.

It's also not even close to the answer I've been searching for.

It's not that Noah isn't a good kisser. But I know after only a few seconds that he's not *the* kisser. The way we fit together, the way he tastes, the way my body reacts—it's not that it's wrong. It's just that it's not *right*.

He pulls back, tugging my lower lip between his. "I lied," he says. I'm about to tell him I know, when he adds, "I brought you here to talk about something else." He pulls me closer and winds his arms around my waist. "But I guess confessing worked out okay."

What?

I push out of his arms and start to gather my things. "I don't know if this is a joke to you or what, but it's not funny."

"Whoa, hang on." Noah is at my side in a single leap and grabs my arm. "What did I do?"

"You're taking credit for something you *didn't* do. I'm not saying you don't know your way around a kiss, Noah, but it wasn't you on the field the other night. So if you're only saying it was because Joel's name came up, then you can count me out of whatever twisted game you're playing."

I try to jerk out of his grip, but he takes hold of my other arm. "Wait, Mace, listen to me. We were in the dark before, and now it's broad daylight. There are people around, and—I'm nervous, okay? Because I have to ask you something."

"Ask me what?"

He takes my phone from my hand and sits down on the blanket, patting the ground next to him. I hesitate before settling into the spot he indicated. When I do, he puts his arm around me and brushes his nose against my temple, his long hair tickling the side of my face.

Did I feel hair tickling my face that night in the dark? Why are those damn lips the only detail that's crystal clear? My anger crumbles away with my conviction. Maybe Noah is telling the truth.

"I'm sorry if I didn't live up to your expectations just now," he says. "But I hope this makes up for it." He holds my phone out with his other hand, and I see he's turned the camera on. "Since you like capturing important moments in pictures, you can call this one . . . 'When Noah asked me to homecoming.'"

My head snaps toward him as the phone clicks. I don't even have to look at the picture to know that what he captured is proof that this day hasn't gone as expected for either one of us.

Twelve

SENIOR YEAR

Meredith and Ben are still heavy on my mind when I get down to the football field the next afternoon. Joel is already sitting toward the top of the bleachers. I hope he doesn't ask for details on why I had to bail yesterday. I'm also hoping he has a plan for how to start this conversation, because I'm drawing a total blank.

"Hey," I say as I slip into the row of metal seats. He's staring out at the field where practice is in session with a sad, far-off look in his eyes. When I sit down, he doesn't say anything.

Joel quit the team after last season. He'd told me he planned to, but I never thought he'd actually go through with it. Football was something he loved and was genuinely good at. And from the look on his face, it's something he regrets giving up.

"Do you miss playing?"

He jumps a little, like I've caught him red-handed, then rubs the knee of his jeans and shakes his head. "Nah." He glances up, and even though I'm pretty sure my expression is neutral, he backpedals. "Okay, sometimes. But quitting was the right thing to do."

It seems more like he's parroting something that was told to him rather than stating his convictions. Especially when his eyes dart back to the field, and I catch a glimpse of that same wistfulness before he says, "Do you miss cheering?"

"Yes and no. I miss the games. I miss being in the center of everything. I miss being part of a team. But I don't miss feeling like I was under a microscope all the time."

And I'm not sure I even knew I felt that way until right now.

"I hear you. Sometimes you're so busy trying to keep everyone else happy that you end up making yourself miserable in the process." He takes one last look out at the field before sitting straighter and flipping his preoccupied expression off like a light switch. "So I thought you'd chickened out when you didn't show yesterday."

"Chickened out? Should I be scared to have this conversation?" I am, but I don't want him to know that. Of course, if the way I'm perched on the bleacher like I might take flight at any second is an indication, he can already tell.

"No, definitely not. I'm glad we're finally going to get it all out there. This should've happened a long time ago."

"Then why didn't it?"

"Might have had something to do with the fact that you said you were done with me."

"Oh, that." We both chuckle nervously, and I sneak a sideways glance at him. "So all joking aside. What happened that night?"

Joel draws a breath and looks at the ground. "I really don't know, Mace. I guess I just . . . lost my nerve."

"About taking me to the dance?"

"Not so much taking you as going, period." He picks at the fraying denim near his knee again. "I had a lot going on last year, things that I never talked to anyone about. No one here trusted me, my dad was gone, my mom had her hands full with work and my brothers, and I was basically the default father in the house. It was a lot of pressure. And I guess I did a pretty shitty job of dealing with it."

"I get all that, Joel." I stop, trying to figure out how to forgive him without excusing what he did. "But I bent over backward trying to prove to you that some people didn't care what school you came from or what team you used to play for. I always had your back. And you slapped me in the face for it."

More than that, he made a fool out of me. Betrayed my trust. The hurt has lingered like a phantom limb ever since.

"You're right. And you have no idea how sorry I am for that. But if you think it didn't hurt me that you turned on me so fast, you're wrong."

"Turned on you? The night started with you pulling a disappearing act and ended with Meredith's house almost burning down. How was I supposed to react?"

Joel's voice sharpens. "You really think I'd do something that petty? I mean, I know everyone else believes it, but really think about it, Mace. What the hell does it prove to destroy your homecoming float? How does it make a shit ton of sense to put on some douche bag display of loyalty to Mortonville when I still had to show my face *here* for the next two years?"

His anger is so real and his response is so logical that I don't even know what to say. It would be frightening to think that anyone could lie this convincingly.

"Who else could've done it?" I ask softly.

Joel rubs at his eyebrow, looking both agitated and tired. His tone softens. "I honestly can't tell you."

"Okay. Then maybe you can tell me this." I swallow over the sudden dryness in my throat, debating whether or not I want to know the answer to my next question right up until it leaves my mouth: "Did I tell you where the float was hidden?" Joel looks at me like I've grown a third eye, so I elaborate. "In the parking lot at the slushie stand that night. I was . . . pretty drunk."

To my surprise, Joel laughs. "So was I. You could've told me where to find the Holy Grail, for all I know."

"Oh."

I don't know what else to say. I feel like I should be relieved. Yet I'm not. Because even though my memories of that night are hazy, the feeling of dread that I woke up with had little to do with a hangover. The feeling that I said something I shouldn't have—*to* someone I shouldn't have— has been following me like a shadow ever since.

"You look upset," Joel says.

"I guess I'm disappointed that I still don't know who set the fire."

To my own ears, the words sound uncertain. But Joel's whole face changes. It's like I lifted a year's worth of storm clouds off his shoulders, and the smile that lights his face is brighter than a summer sky.

"You believe me, then?"

After a moment, I say, "If Meredith does, then why shouldn't I?"

Joel must not realize the question isn't entirely rhetorical because he looks positively giddy. He must know it too, because he clears his throat and takes his cell phone from his pocket. "Well, I can't give you any leads on the fire, but there's at least one mystery I can solve for you." He taps the screen of his phone a few times, and the next thing I know, I'm looking once again at the picture of him, me, and Ben from junior year.

"*You* posted that?" Blood starts to pound in my ears. What else is he going to confess to about the night that picture went online?

"Guilty as charged."

"But why?"

Joel flips the phone between his hands. "Because I know you're into pictures, and I feel awful about the way things happened. I was a huge jerk to you, and you didn't deserve it. I wanted to make things right. And I thought it would help if I reminded you that things were good once."

Did you also think it would help to ambush me on a dark football field and kiss me until I couldn't remember my own name?

I don't ask the question out loud. If he felt what I felt, why should I have to pull a confession out of him?

Simple. Because he either didn't do it . . . or he didn't feel it.

Joel fidgets under my expectant stare. "I'll delete it, though," he continues. "If it bothers you."

I sit on my hands, trying not to look disappointed. "I don't think it bothers me as much as it bothers the other person in the picture."

"Oh." Joel stays quiet for a few beats, turning his phone over in his hand. "Guess I didn't appeal to Ben's nostalgic side?"

"Not exactly."

"I won't do it again. I can't keep up with all these people trying to make it look like their lives are perfect, anyway."

I'm taken aback by his comment. "That's not what the site's about at all. People use it to share pieces of their lives. It's a way to capture memories, not a competition."

"If that's the real reason people use it, then you and Jadie shouldn't need to moderate the content and the comments. Right?" He taps his temple. "Memories are up here."

Now he taps his phone. "Putting them here is about other people's reactions to them." I don't get a chance to argue before he pulls up something else on the screen of his cell. "But I do have one more picture to show you."

He holds up the phone. When I squint against the afternoon brightness, he hands it to me instead. I'm totally confused to find myself looking at a picture of a silver heart-shaped necklace in the palm of what I'm assuming is Joel's hand. My own hand goes instinctively to my neck, even though the locket I used to wear, so similar to the one in the photo, is long gone.

This picture isn't posted to the RF page. It's in his photo gallery. And there's a simple, one-word caption scrawled in editing pen at the bottom: *Homecoming?*

When I look up, the necklace from the picture is dangling over the back of Joel's hand. And while the curve of his mouth says he's super-pleased with himself for pulling this off, the slight bounce of his foot against the concrete gives away his uncertainty.

My hand lingers at my collarbone as my eyes drop to the necklace. "Is that for me?"

Commence the asking of dumb, super-obvious questions.

"It's for you." He chuckles and lays the pendant in my hand. "I noticed you never got another one after what happened last year. That day that I ran into you and Ben at the—"

"I remember," I say.

It's the fact that *he* remembers that has me totally confounded.

Thirteen

Bad luck or not, I don't have a choice about going to my brothers' next soccer game. It's my parents' twentieth wedding anniversary, and their friends offered them a stay in their time-share on Tybee Island for the weekend.

My mother was hesitant, but between Aaron's new medication, his guitar lessons with Ben, and the heart-to-heart we sat him down for after the last game, we felt we'd covered the bases for getting through one weekend without incident. Plus Mrs. Milton, one of the other soccer moms, offered to let the boys sleep over on Friday night, so that I'd be alone with them only on Saturday before my parents come home on Sunday afternoon.

So far, night one is in the bag. I cheered at the football game, then went to the diner and slept at Meredith's afterward. As I start my car in preparation for heading to the soccer field, I can't help but think, *How hard can this be?*

The coaches are leading warm-up exercises when I arrive. I spot a silver-haired woman on the sidelines waving me over, sparing me the awkwardness of having to admit that I didn't quite remember which one was Mrs. Milton. "How did they do last night?" I ask, taking a seat on the bleacher below hers. "Did they drive you crazy?"

"No. They were very well behaved. The boys can stay over anytime," Mrs. Milton says warmly, and I wonder if she's just being polite. They're not bad kids, though Aaron has his moments. But they both have more energy than the sun, and it combusts often and much.

"My parents threatened to take away their comic books for two weeks if they weren't angels. I guess it worked."

"That would do the trick for me," says a voice on the other side of me. I turn to find Ben taking a seat next to me on the bleacher. "So what did you try today? Real four-leaf clovers for breakfast?"

I point to my mother's camera hanging around my neck. "I promised to pretend I'm shooting them for *Sports Illustrated*. And—" I hold up my arm to show him the gold charm dangling from my bracelet. "I broke out my grandmother's good luck horn from Italy. We're totally covered."

Ben squints and leans closer. "What is that? A chili pepper?"

"It's supposed to be an antelope horn. According to my grandmother, it wards off the evil eye. I normally never wear it. It makes me feel like I have a sperm dangling from my wrist."

Mrs. Milton snorts, and I realize that probably wasn't the most appropriate thing to say, especially since we're on church grounds. I turn to Ben, giggling behind my hand.

"Like I said before," he says. "Whatever works."

And this time it actually does. I spend most of the game squatting on the sidelines snapping pictures, and maybe something about the fancy camera inspires the kids to play like professionals, because the Blue Dragons win the game by six points. My brothers are so excited that they run over to slap me sweaty high fives, and Aaron even gives me a hug. I text my mother a picture of the three of us with our grinning faces squished together as proof of how much ass I'm kicking at this babysitting gig.

One of the coaches brought a cooler full of ice cream bars, and I give the boys permission to eat theirs on the playground behind the church before we head home. Ben's brother gets the okay from their mom to do the same, and Ben and I stroll together to where the boys are darting around as if they hadn't spent the last hour in constant motion.

"So will you be at Mer's working on the float today?" Ben asks.

"Yep. Will you?"

"I'm not so sure she wants me there."

My face scrunches in confusion. "Ben, you know she does."

"But does she want *me* there, or my magical hands?"

I snort-laugh. "Both."

Ben pauses by a green-painted bench, looking uncomfortable all of a sudden. His hands are restless at his sides. "Then what was up with her the other night? She acted so weird when Ken called us out at the diner."

I tug at the hem of my shorts, not sure what to say. I was so preoccupied with the way Joel stormed off, I haven't given much thought to Meredith's reaction. "One too many public disagreements in a short period of time, I think. First with Jadie and then with Ken. And I'm sorry, by the way, that he was such an asswad. It took all my restraint to keep my fist out of his nasal cavity."

Ben waves off the comment. "Davenport doesn't bother me. I felt a lot worse for Jadie and Tyrell. But I have to wonder if maybe it's not such a good idea for me to"—he shifts on his feet—"you know."

"Ben, no. First of all, when you ask Meredith to homecoming, you don't have to create some big, elaborate proposal for the whole school to see. I mean, you can if you want to, but she'd be happy with any way you asked her. And as far as the diner goes, I'm ninety-nine percent sure she was having an off night. I wouldn't take it personally."

"I'm trying not to, but it's kind of hard. I feel like if this—if I—was something she really wanted, then she would've reacted . . ." He falters. "Not like that."

He plunks down on the bench. I sit down next to him just in time to see it happen.

Aaron is paused on the catwalk at the top of the jungle gym, taking the last bites of his ice cream before another run down the spiral slide. Michael and two other boys come barreling up the steps at the speed of light, their footfalls clanging against the aluminum. They're oblivious to everything except beating one another to the top.

Even though I can see what's going to happen before it does, all I can do is shoot to my feet, my hands outstretched in useless horror as three bodies collide with one another and ram into Aaron. His limbs flail and he flies backward. Right through the opening in the safety rails, where there's a gap for climbing up the fake rock wall.

It's at least a six-foot drop. I watch him fall like I'm stuck in a dream, seeing everything in slow motion and knowing I'll never get to him fast enough, because the bones in my legs have turned to lead.

When he lands, his head slams against the graying railroad ties that surround the play area, and he splays across the wood chips. He doesn't scream. He doesn't cry. He doesn't move a muscle. All I can think is, *My brother is dead.*

Time starts to move again. I don't even remember covering the distance between where Ben and I were sitting and where Aaron is lying, as I drop to his side, wood chips cutting into my knees and sticking to my skin. I scream his name, patting the sides of his face. I've seen and sustained enough sports-related injuries to know I shouldn't move him, but his stillness is so terrifying that I can't stop myself from squeezing his arms, his legs, his hands, trying to make him respond.

"Ethan, go get Mom!" Ben yells, grabbing his cell phone from his pocket. "Stay back, guys. I'm calling an ambulance." He places himself between me and the other kids who've gathered behind me. I know without looking that the sobs I hear are coming from Michael.

They say your life flashes before you in times of crisis. But as I plead with Aaron's motionless body, it's scenes from Aaron's life that surface in my mind like coins from the bottom of a wishing well. I remember how he and Michael were so small when they first came home from the hospital that they could both fit inside the same horseshoe-shaped opening of one Boppy pillow. I remember the way I totally dropped my jilted only-child attitude the first time Aaron fell asleep on my chest, and wishing that I could snuggle his little body like that forever. I recall the way he hugged me only a few minutes ago, even though he and Michael make fake retching sounds if our parents so much as hold hands in public. I haven't asked for a hug in a long time because of it. Only now that I know there's still a part of him that doesn't mind me holding him close, I wish I'd asked more often.

Soon I'm surrounded by mothers and fathers and grandparents of kids on the soccer team. It's a scary, isolating feeling to know that I'm all my brother has right now.

But the thought flies to the back of my mind when Aaron's eyelids start to flutter open.

"Hey. Hey, buddy," I say, frantically patting his hand. "Can you hear me? Are you okay?"

"Macy?" The grogginess in his voice doesn't disguise the pitch of terror. "I can't see you."

My heart drops into my stomach. "Look at me, buddy. I'm right here. Can you look at me?"

He doesn't. His gaze stays somewhere over my shoulder, unfocused and vacant.

"I can't see," Aaron says again, his chin trembling. "Mom? Where's Mommy?"

"Aaron," his coach says, kneeling next to the railroad tie. "It's Coach Harvey. Can you tell me where you are?"

"It *huuuurts*."

He's crying, and my mouth goes bone dry. "Why can't he see?" I croak.

"He must've hit his head pretty hard." I follow Coach's eyes to the spot they keep darting down to. It's only then that I notice the red stain on the gray wood beneath Aaron's head.

Blood. A lot of it.

"Don't worry, kiddo," Coach Harvey says as my own head starts to swim. "We're gonna take you to the hospital and get you fixed up in no time."

"Macy," Ben says, kneeling down next to me and putting a gentle hand on my shoulder. "My mom is calling your parents. Give me your keys so you can ride in the ambulance with your brother, and I'll drive your car to the hospital. I'll take your camera, too. Mrs. Milton is going to bring Michael home with her."

Michael immediately shrieks in loud protest, and several of the adults rush to reassure him as the wail of sirens draws closer. I look at Ben, and he nods calmly at me. It's a small, simple gesture, but it's achingly genuine. When I realize that his is the only face not pinched into a mask of barely disguised panic, it makes me wish I didn't have to look anywhere else. Knowing he's calm makes me feel grounded.

When he touches my shoulder and says, "Everything's gonna be okay," I almost believe it.

When I was younger, I was really into soap operas. Well, my *mother* was really into soap operas, and by default, so was I. Every summer, activities and outings came to a grinding halt at noon so we could glue ourselves to the screen, because God forbid if someone else knew what happened before we did. And I don't know why, but all I can think as I'm standing behind a glass window, chewing at my cuticles as Aaron disappears into a CAT scan machine on the other side, is how infuriatingly inaccurate soap opera hospital scenes are.

On TV, there's no waiting. You never see anyone filling out piles of paperwork, or frantically trying to find a spot in the ER with enough cell service to let them take down insurance info from worried-sick parents who are running stoplights to get home. They'd never show someone struggling to hold down the contents of their own stomach while stuck in a room with only a thin blue curtain separating them from the girl vomiting violently on the other side. And the patients? They always look like they're sleeping peacefully, their hair glossy and styled despite being unwashed and mashed against a pillow.

My poor brother looks like he's been through a war.

"What a crock of shit," I murmur under my breath. It's not until Ben appears at my side that I even realize I said it out loud.

"What's wrong?" he says. "Did Aaron wake up?"

I hadn't realized, possibly another result of too much TV, that it was okay for Aaron to fall asleep while we waited. I kept poking and pinching him to keep him awake, even after he landed a nice wallop to the side of my head. But then one of the doctors gave me the thumbs-up to let him drift off and assured me that irritability came with the territory of head injuries.

"No. He's still passed out." He barely stirred when they came to collect him for the CAT scan, but his movement was enough to keep the nurses from being too concerned with his lack of consciousness. I rub at my eyes, which are burning with their own exhaustion. "But it's times like these when it would be really nice if the rest of my relatives didn't live seven hundred miles away."

"I know. But I'm here." He holds up a white Styrofoam cup. "And I brought you some tea."

I reach gratefully for the cup. "God, thank you so much."

Ben looks sheepish as I take a cautious sip of the steaming liquid. "It's not Mugsy's, but I thought it would do in a pinch."

"How did you know I like Mugsy's?"

"I've seen you come into school holding their cups." His eyes widen. "Wow, way to sound like a creeper, Ben."

I smile. "Not at all. Do you like their coffee? I'll bring one for you the next time I stop before school. Or maybe we can do a study date, my treat. It's the least I can do." He's been amazing today. But I don't trust myself not to choke up if I tell him, so I take a purposeful sip of tea before adding, "Can I ask one more favor?" I motion to the sign on the wall that shows a cell phone with an X over it. "Can you go call Meredith and let her know what's going on?"

"Good idea. Don't want her thinking we skipped out on her."

"No, Ben, you go. I really appreciate you being here, but you and Coach Harvey have given up enough of your day. Please let him drive you home. There's nothing that either of you can do."

"I told you, we'll head off as soon as your parents get back. I'm not gonna leave you here alone."

He means it. Coach Harvey, on the other hand, has to get to his daughter's birthday party. He gives me his cell phone number before he leaves so I can update him with the results of Aaron's scan when we have them. Ben waits with me until my parents arrive, and while it certainly feels like I've been at the hospital for an eternity, I'm pretty sure they had to break the time-space continuum in order to get there as quickly as they did.

My mother is sobbing and my father is the same washed-out color as the hospital walls when I run into their arms in the hallway. They look like a cyclone swooped them up off the beach and transported them here, Mom still smelling faintly of sunblock and Dad wearing a T-shirt that doesn't match his swim trunks. I can only imagine the state of their suitcase.

"Is he okay?" Mom sniffles, swiping at her tears and the stray strands of dark hair falling in her face.

"He will be, Mom." I make an attempt to smile, but I'm so drained that the result is pretty pathetic.

"Oh, Macy." Mom squeezes my shoulders. "You look exhausted. Have you eaten anything?"

I motion to Ben, who's leaning against the wall a few feet away. "Ben got me some peanuts from the vending machine."

My mother sidesteps me and envelops Ben in a crushing hug.

"Thank you so much for staying with them," Mom whimpers. "I'm so sorry we weren't here." Ben looks like he has no idea where to put his hands, and I almost giggle at the relief on his face when she releases him and turns to me. "You two go home and get some food and some rest. We're here now, and we'll call you as soon as we know something."

I protest, but between the heaviness of my limbs and

the insistent grumbles of my stomach reminding me that I'm running on fumes, I let her convince me. But not before I make both of my parents swear that someone will call me the second they have any kind of news.

"Meredith wants you to text her," Ben says as the elevator doors close. "She's really worried."

I take out my phone and pound out a message: LEAVING THE HOSPITAL NOW. PARENTS ARE WITH AARON. WAITING ON CAT SCAN RESULTS.

She answers before we even reach the lobby: I'LL KICK THE GIRLS OUT EARLY. BE THERE SOON AS I CAN.

I write back: I'LL LEAVE THE DOOR UNLOCKED.

The elevator doors part, and I've taken only a few steps when I stop short. I must be more tired than I thought, because why else would I hallucinate Joel Hargrove, wearing black dress pants and a white button-down shirt, at the hospital on a Saturday afternoon, leaving the coffee shop across the hall with a black-lidded Styrofoam cup in hand?

"Hey, Joel," Ben calls. Okay. So this actually *is* happening. "How's your brother doing?"

Of course. I forgot that Peyton is here for his tune-up. We meet in the carpeted space between the elevators and the coffee shop, and the stress of the morning doesn't grant my nervous system one bit of immunity against how hot Joel looks right now.

"He's good," Joel says as he and Ben exchange a bro handshake. "Going home tomorrow." His eyebrows draw together. "What are you guys doing here?"

"Macy's brother took a bad spill at the playground," Ben answers, and I'm grateful that he seems to sense how useless I am right now. "I was about to drive her home. Did you need a ride?"

"Thanks, but I'm waiting for my mom to switch with me. She's taking Peyton duty when she gets off work, and then I have to go clock in. She got me a job busing tables at the club where she works. Hence the penguin duds." He runs his hand over the pleated button plate of his shirt and flashes a megawatt grin. A rush of heat races up my neck in response.

My hand flies to my throat, though if I'm trying to draw attention *away* from the splotchy colors my skin is turning, playing with my necklace probably isn't the smartest move.

Not that it matters, because my locket is gone.

I gasp when my hand comes in contact with bare skin instead of a rounded silver heart. The warmth that already flooded my face intensifies as I touch my throat and chest, hoping that I'm somehow wrong. But when I look down, a nervous prickle of sweat breaks out over my skin. There, stuck between the V-neck of my shirt and the tank top underneath, is a messy pile of thin silver links.

"Oh *no*." The words escape in a panicked moan as I pull the delicate strand free from my clothes. The pendant containing my brothers' picture is nowhere to be seen. "My necklace."

"You lost your necklace?" Ben says, alarm rising in his voice as my face threatens to crumple. But then he's as resolute as he was on the playground. He places a firm but gentle hand on my arm and says, "Don't worry. We'll find it. Let's retrace our steps, and if it's not here, we'll go back to the soccer field before I bring you home. Okay?"

I shake my head. "I still had it in the ambulance," I whimper. "I kept trying to make Aaron focus on it."

"All right, we'll divide and conquer instead," Joel cuts in. "I'll walk the hospital with Macy, and Ben can ask around the ER."

"Perfect," Ben says, already jogging toward the emergency room. "Call or text me if you find it, and I'll do the same. We'll meet back here."

As many times as I've thought about getting Joel alone, I did not imagine it like this. I'm red and sweaty and on the brink of tears, and as we revisit every step I took since leaving the ER, I'm grateful that we're too busy staring at the floor to do much talking. I don't think I could be witty or flirtatious right now if someone offered me an all-expenses-paid trip to Hawaii.

Aaron must have been moved to a different part of the hospital, because my parents aren't in the CAT scan waiting room when we get there. Neither is my necklace. My dread increases as we run out of places to look. And when we get back in the elevator empty-handed, I feel like I let my brothers down all over again.

"It's not your fault, Macy," Joel says, putting a tentative hand on my shoulder. "But I know how you feel. The last time my dad got deployed, he gave me and my brothers each something of his to hold on to while he was gone. So Peyton had to be about four years old then, and he got my dad's watch. Mom told him he couldn't wear it out of the house, but I let him sneak it out to a carnival one night. We never saw it again. Poor kid cried for weeks, and I felt like absolute shit."

"That's so sad."

"I know. I ended up handing off what my dad had given me, to make up for it."

"What was it?"

"Oh. Uh, my grandfather's wedding ring. My father wore it on a chain around his neck."

I touch the bare spot on my chest again. "Guess we both lost our necklaces."

"I didn't mind getting rid of mine."

And then it happens. All the emotions I switched off earlier slam into me full force as I realize I'm going home without my necklace or my brother. I was levelheaded and strong for as long as everyone needed me to be. Now that no one needs that, it isn't even an option.

When Joel realizes I'm crying, he looks mortified. "I'm sorry," he says, leading me out of the elevator by my hand. "That was shitty. I shouldn't have said that."

To my surprise, he pulls me into a hug. In the back of my mind, I pray that my deodorant is strong enough for what I've put it through today. It's bad enough that I'm bawling in front of him, but doing it crushed against his body isn't helping the frantic rate of my pulse.

Joel envelops me tighter in his arms, and the way he's holding me makes the panic subside. He rests his cheek against my hair, rocking me gently. When I press my hand against his back, he sighs. I put my arms around him and hold fast. His body relaxes into mine.

It's almost like he needs this as much as I do.

Fourteen

SENIOR YEAR

All too aware of Joel's expectant eyes on me, I run my thumb over the featherlike designs engraved in the surface of the locket. When I press the tiny latch on the side, the heart springs open, revealing its center. It's empty.

"There's no picture in it."

He half smiles. "Pretty sure I haven't earned locket-worthy status. Yet." He scoots a little closer. "So what do you think?" he asks, his voice low. "Will you let me make it up to you and take you to homecoming? For real this time."

My mouth won't work, and forming words for an answer feels like trying to lift Thor's hammer. I couldn't bring myself to accept Noah's invitation to homecoming, but I haven't rejected it either. If everything Joel said about the night of the fire is true, then there's no reason I can't say yes to him. But that's a big "if." I'm not sure it's really that simple to sweep a year's worth of mistrust under the rug.

Coach Simmons's whistle shrieks through the air, and Joel's head snaps toward the field. When he turns back to me, his brow is furrowed. "Listen, Mace, I know it's a lot to digest. So you don't have to give me an answer right now." He takes his phone from my lap and stands up. "But think about it, okay?"

He starts down the steps, telling me he has to go pick up his brothers. At least I think that's what he says, because I'm only half listening at this point. I'm too busy replaying everything he said before it.

But as I sit there with the silver locket still resting in my palm, it's what he *didn't* say that's bothering me the most. And that's not one word about the kiss in the dark.

In my peripheral vision, someone is approaching my locker. I'm praying it's not Noah or Joel. I purposely got to school early to avoid bumping into them, and I'm not ready to pick up where I left off with either one.

Trying to come up with an excuse for why I couldn't immediately accept Noah's homecoming invitation was right at the top of my Most Awkward Moments list, or at least a solid top-ten contender. My guard had gone flying back up once I'd suspected he'd lied about kissing me on the football field.

What I didn't know was how to explain to Noah that history is repeating itself. And now that Joel's asked me to homecoming, it's repeating itself twice.

I am a moron.

To my surprise, it's Ben who stops and leans against the wall of metal doors next to me. He shoves his hands into the pockets of his jeans. "I wanted to apologize if I was kind of a d-bag at Mugsy's the other day."

I shake my head. "No, you were fine. I know things are still weird."

"The thing is, Meredith and I talked about everything a long time ago." He plows ahead like he didn't even hear me, like he really needs to get something out. "I know where I stand with her, and she knows where she stands with me." The way the words tumble out of him tells me he's nervous, which makes *me* nervous. I didn't plan to take my windbreaker off, since our school is always freezing. But anticipating whatever Ben is working up to is making me overheat, and I reach for the zipper at my chin. "You and I, though, we never spelled things out. And I meant it when I said we should tal—" My zipper parts, and Ben's eyes bulge as they fall on my locket. "Where did you get that?"

"This?" I close my hand over the silver heart. The horrified way he's looking at it makes me want to hide it, even though it's way too late. My voice is unusually small when I say, "Joel gave it to me. Because of the one I used to wear. The one my brothers gave me."

I sound like I'm making excuses, even though I have no reason to.

"Where did *he* get it?" Ben looks furious, and even though I want to ask how I'm supposed to know or why it matters, I simply tell him I don't know. "He just gave it to you?" Ben's hand curls into a fist at his side, and I'm half wondering if he's going to punch a locker. "Like, handed it to you and said, 'Here you go'?"

"He gave it to me yesterday"—I wind the chain around my fingertip so tightly that it goes numb—"when he asked me to homecoming."

Ben's expression goes slack, and for a moment he stands there like I'm the one who's punched something—him. Then a humorless bark of a laugh bursts from his throat.

"Nice," he says. "That's fucking perfect."

And then he's gone, leaving me with the all-too-familiar feeling that I've done something very, very wrong, except I have no idea what.

Fifteen

JUNIOR YEAR

It's strange being a passenger in my own car. But it's even stranger that I'm leaving the hospital without my necklace and that Ben doesn't seem to know what to say to me since retrieving me from Joel's arms in the hospital lobby.

So after a few minutes, I break the silence. "Thanks again, Ben. I'm really grateful that you stayed with me."

His posture relaxes, like he's relieved I spoke first. "It would have been a lot to handle by yourself." He sneaks a sideways look at me. "Do you want me to stick around? I mean, instead of going home. I could keep you company for a while."

"You don't have to."

"I asked if you *wanted* me to."

I'm not the kind of person who needs constant company, but the thought of a silent, empty house amplifying the noise inside my head makes me fidget with anxiety.

"Maybe . . . maybe just until Meredith gets there? We have homemade lasagna," I offer.

My mother forbade me to do any cooking while she was gone, though I'm sure I could've handled boiling water for mac and cheese without burning the house down. Then again, I also thought I could handle babysitting my brothers for a day, and look how that turned out.

At any rate, Mom left a whole roasted chicken and a lasagna the size of a picnic bench in the fridge, as if we were about to hibernate for the winter rather than survive two and half days.

"*Worth it.*" Ben pumps his fist in victory and then looks over at me. "Kidding. I would've come with or without the lasagna."

But he still devours a brick-sized piece when we get back to my house. I pick at mine, more nauseous than hungry. I'm not sure if it's because my stomach has been empty for so long, or because I keep touching the spot on my neck where my locket used to lie, or because every minute feels more ominous each time one passes without a call from my parents.

Ben follows me into the living room when I give up on trying to enjoy my food. I collapse onto the couch, but he stands next to the coffee table and picks up the oversized sketch pad that Michael left lying there.

"Did Aaron draw these?" he asks, clearly impressed at the superhero renderings inside.

"No. Michael's the artist. They make their own comic books. Michael draws the pictures and they collaborate on the story and dialogue. Half the time they end up fighting and trying to color each other's faces, though."

"Typical. The face coloring, not the drawings. These are *really* good. I used to do the same thing, making up my own comics. I had one where Superman and Lex Luthor were both exposed to red kryptonite and it turned Superman evil and Lex good. Which probably couldn't happen because Lex isn't Kryptonian, but—" He cuts off when he glances up at me, and his brow furrows. "Are you feeling okay?"

I'm really not. I hate that I've made such a huge mess and that Ben squandered the majority of his day helping me clean it. I hate that I had to bail on helping with the homecoming float. I hate myself for not doing a better job of watching my brothers and for losing the gift they gave me, without even noticing.

And I especially hate that I'm going to cry again.

I cover my face, because there's no stopping it. "Why haven't my parents called yet?" I wail behind my fingers.

I hear the sketch pad hit the coffee table, and then the cushion next to me dips. Ben gingerly puts his arm around me. "Aw, Macy, don't be upset. They probably haven't heard anything yet. And don't forget they have to call Michael and everyone else who's worried too. Maybe no news is good news."

"But what if it's not? He fell so hard, and his head was bleeding and he kept saying he couldn't see. What if no news is bad news?"

I wipe away the wetness on my cheeks with the back of my hand. Ben dashes into the kitchen and reappears a second later with a tissue, returning to my side as he hands it to me.

"It was scary as hell, I know," he says. "But you handled everything like a champ, and Aaron is exactly where he needs to be so he can get better. That's what you need to concentrate on right now."

I nod. When I go to dab my eyes, my bracelet catches my eye. "The boys were right," I say, holding up my wrist. "I am bad luck."

Ben flicks the dangling horn with his fingers. "Maybe it is just a sperm after all."

I can't help cracking a smile.

"Here," he says, stretching toward the coffee table. He grabs a red marker that's lying next to the sketch pad and uncaps it. "Forget lucky chili peppers. Let me give you something way better." He takes my hand and holds it so that my knuckles are facing him. The marker tickles my skin as he starts to draw, biting his lip in concentration. When he finishes, he tosses the marker back onto the table, still holding my hand.

"See?" he says.

"The Superman *S*?"

One side of his mouth turns up. "It's not an *S*. On my world, it means 'hope.'"

I want to tell him he wins everything for that quote. I want to hug him. I think maybe I *do* hug him. I'm not entirely sure, because the next thing I remember is waking up with my face smooshed against Ben's shoulder. Only, now we're not alone.

Meredith is standing over us, staring at my and Ben's bodies slumped against each other on the couch. And more specifically, at the spot where my hand is still nestled on top of his.

Sixteen

SENIOR YEAR

I know I can't avoid Joel and Noah all day. My plan is to talk to Noah at lunch, but he materializes from nowhere as I'm heading to my first class and tugs me into an empty hallway.

"You got a second?" he says.

"Listen, Noah, about yesterday—"

"Yeah, about that. You seemed kinda shaken up by the whole thing, so if I came on too strong, I'm sorry." He glances up and down the hall. "I wanted to tell you there's no pressure for homecoming. If it's easier, you can pretend I never asked."

I must look taken aback, because I am. And if I'm being honest, maybe a little relieved, too. "Are you rescinding your invitation?"

"No, not rescinding. I'd definitely like to go with you. But if you want to go with *me*, I'll leave it up to you to say so. Even if it's as friends, I'm cool with that. Otherwise, we'll pretend it never happened."

"So if we go together, I have to be the one to ask you?"

Somehow this feels like *more* pressure, not less.

Noah takes my hand. "Mace, I'm not gonna lie to you. I like you a lot, but I had my own, uh, less-than-honorable reasons for asking you to homecoming." He threads his fingers through mine and takes a step closer. "I'd really like to see where this goes. But I don't want to start off being a prick."

I swallow hard. "So you admit you asked me because you're trying to piss off Joel?"

"It's not—it's not all that simple. But that might've been part of it."

My lips press into a hard line. "And the kiss?"

To my own ears, my voice sounds razor-sharp. But Noah doesn't seem to notice. He brings our joined hands up to his face. "That's up to you too." He traces my fingertips over his bottom lip. "I'm willing to try again."

That's so not what I meant. I'm trying to give him a chance to say once and for all if he was the one to kiss me on the football field, and his response is to ooze sex appeal all over the floor. If he's expecting me to giggle and melt into the linoleum, it's not going to happen.

In the split second when I hesitate instead of ripping my hand away from his mouth, I hear the squeak of sneakers at the mouth of the hallway. I turn in time to see Ben's disgusted face, a second before he bolts out the door.

I head toward the Yearbook Club room with my lunch, because I am so behind on my assignments for the week.

Definitely not because I'm avoiding anybody.

My phone starts to ring, and I'm puzzled to see it's Jadie. When I pick up, she squeals, "I just ran into Fielding. Guess who won the bid to design the homecoming bulletin board."

"Oh my God, please say we did."

"WE DID!"

I do a little celebratory jig in the empty hall. Each year, two members of the yearbook staff are chosen as lead decorators of the bulletin board outside the gym, the first thing people see as they enter for homecoming. We had to present our ideas in a report, and Principal Fielding personally chooses the winning concept.

There's an extra bounce in my step when I arrive at the empty yearbook room. The first thing I do is pull up the Ridgedale's Finest page to see what's worth highlighting. It's mostly the usual fare: students' selfies, shots from club meetings and sporting events, groups of friends cheesing for the camera, a few attempts at snaps made to look candid when they're definitely not.

A lot of homecoming-centric pics are starting to pop up too. Guys posting "she said yes" photos, girls showing off their bouquets of roses, or in one case, a giant heart made of flower petals in the middle of the hall with "Homecoming?" spelled out with stems and more petals in the center.

It's cute, and yet I frown at the screen. I've posted to this page tons of times, because I've always thought of pictures as a method of preserving the moments you can't get back, a way to hold on to something beautiful. And I still think I'm right. But after talking to Joel and Noah, I have to wonder about how much of what people share is for attention. And how big the disparity is between what's real and what passes for reality.

I plug in my flash drive with a sigh. A second later, my sigh turns into a gasp.

Somehow, I managed to throw the wrong Cruzer into my bag this morning. Because the folder I clicked has opened into hundreds of tiny scenes from junior year.

I scroll through silently, my lips parted in awe. It's amazing how memories can hide in the corners of your mind, like a favorite old pair of shoes waiting to be unearthed from an overstuffed closet. Treasured but forgotten, until they're stumbled upon again.

There's Meredith and me with my brothers at Stone Mountain Park. Some of my first sunset pictures, many of which now hang on my bedroom wall. Joel, mid-leap on the football field, seconds before catching the ball spiraling toward his waiting hands. Jadie in her cheerleading uniform, hands cupped around her mouth, cheering for Tyrell. The promposal at the diner. Ben sitting between my brothers on Aaron's bed, a guitar across his chest. Ben and Meredith, their cheeks sucked in around their straws in Meredith's float.

I stop scrolling when I get to a series of streetlamp-lit photographs taken in the parking lot of Snow in Georgia, the slushie stand where everyone congregates before the weather gets too cold.

I let the pictures run in slideshow mode, and can't help but smile as the images flash by. I've barely touched alcohol since that night, and for good reason. Since the photos are sorted from oldest to most recent, it's like watching the night devolve all over again. But as the frames fade in and out, my smile fades too.

The last pictures of the night are off-center selfies of Joel and me sitting on the hood of his car. My grin is sloppy and unbridled, and both our eyes are bleary. His are bloodshot, almost like he'd been crying.

I hate him.

The words ring through my head again, the same way they did right before the blackout on the football field. Something contracts in my stomach. Because as I study the picture again, I'm certain now that I *do* remember Joel crying—not before we took this picture, but after.

I let it sink in for a minute, trying to dredge up more details from the sea of booze I drowned them in. There's so much more that I need to know about that night. I sit perfectly still, afraid the memories will scatter like spooked birds if I move a muscle. I stare for so long that the screen goes dark.

As I'm about to reach for the mouse, a voice says, "Can

we talk for a sec?" and I almost hit the ceiling. Meredith is standing in the doorframe. I do my best to look collected and motion toward the empty chair next to me.

"Of course. I'm just working on something for year-book. Grab a seat."

Meredith settles into it and crosses her long legs. "So I heard Joel asked you to homecoming."

"How did you—" I start to say, but then I realize. "Ben told you."

She nods. "Did you accept?"

"Not yet. He said he wants to make up for what hap-pened last year, but I don't know." My hand moves absently to the locket Joel gave me. "He's still adamant that he had nothing to do with the fire." I look at the floor. "But I guess I don't need to tell you that."

"Fire or no fire, you don't have to justify it to me, Macy. It's your decision."

Okay. That wasn't the response I expected. Meredith shifts and sits on her hands. It hits me that she's not act-ing agitated and aloof the way she did when I cornered her in the courtyard. She seems uncomfortable, nervous about something. "And as far as trying to make up for last year . . . I think Ben is doing the same thing. Which is why I wanted to talk to you first."

"First? As in . . . ?" I leave the question open and wait for her to fill in the blank, even though I have a feeling I know what's coming next.

"He asked me to homecoming." Yep, I knew it. There's

an odd heaviness in my chest, like someone punctured my lungs with a pin. "I totally didn't expect it, but I think he feels bad too, about the way the last one ended, and it sort of happened." She smooths a piece of hair behind her ear. "But I didn't want to say yes without talking to you first."

"Why is that?"

She fixes a hard stare on me. "Macy. You're sure nothing happened between you and Ben last year?"

The look on Ben's face when he saw Noah and me in the hall flashes through my mind, and so does the way he reacted to my locket from Joel.

I think we should talk about what didn't happen that night, he said.

And yet he asked Meredith to the dance. It's the same as saying that the window of opportunity for that conversation is closed, locked, and boarded up. It doesn't matter anymore.

"Nothing. I swear."

"See, that's the part I'm not so sure about. Even if it was nothing to you, I think it *was* something to him."

"I don't get it," I say softly. "If that's what you thought, then . . . why is he the one you forgave?"

Her shoulders slump, and she's quiet for a few beats. "Because it was easier to blame you than to admit I didn't have a chance."

I start to reach for her arm, but think better of it.

She shakes her head. "It's fine. We're friends, Ben and I, and I'm learning to be okay with it." She turns a shaky smile on me. "I guess there are some people I'd rather not live without."

I don't bother to ask if she's saying what I think she's saying. I practically jump into her lap and wrap my arms around her. She laughs, and the sound is like slipping on a comfy old sweatshirt. I love it. She must be thinking the same thing, because she wraps her arms around my shoulders and squeezes.

"I got into UNC," she says.

"So did I." I detach myself from her, my long-abandoned visions of us taking UNC by storm together coming back to life inside my head. Maybe things *can* change.

Which reminds me: "I have to know, though," I say. "Why the change of heart about Joel?"

"Well, this might be hard to believe, but . . . I'm not always right about everything."

I laugh, even though it's a non answer. There's something she's not telling me, but I'm not about to rock the boat when the water might finally be settling. "And whether he set the fire or not, the school still isn't going to bring back the parade this year. Even if they did"—she gives me a meaningful look—"it wouldn't be the same."

I can't meet her eyes when I answer. "You guys seem fine without me on the team."

"Macy, how could you think that? You and I have been cheering together since we were kids. It was like the start of an institution."

"Exactly. An institution I didn't know how to be part

of without you. Let's face it, Meredith; we were a team, but the squad was always yours. There was no place for me after . . ." I trail off, not wanting to say *after you shut me out*, even though it's the truth.

"But don't you miss it?"

I falter under her expectant stare. For a long time, cheerleading was my world, and Meredith was like the sun it revolved around. But things have changed, and to be honest, it hasn't all been terrible. I don't know how to tell her that I'm not sure how much of *me* is still wrapped up in *us*.

She stands and slings her bag over one shoulder. "It's okay. I get that you have a new thing. I'm just glad we talked." She hesitates a second. "And, Mace? Seriously. Go to the dance with whoever makes you happy. If there's anything I learned from last year, it's that you can't let other people's bullshit drag you down." She taps her fingers against the strap of her bag, like she's trying to choose her next words, or debating whether to say them at all. "But be careful, okay?"

When she steps back, the bulk of her bag knocks against my mouse. The screen comes to life as the slideshow lands once again on the picture of Meredith and Ben sharing the float at the diner.

Meredith's eyebrows lift, then pull together. "I thought you were working on stuff for the yearbook."

"Oh." I wave my hand at the screen. "I brought the wrong flash drive and ended up taking an unexpected trip down memory lane."

I give her a *No big deal* look, but the sad, far-off way she's staring at the computer is so intent that I wonder if she's still aware that I'm here.

"I remember that day," she finally says. "Ben talked about you a lot after that." She readjusts her shoulder strap, and the smile she attempts doesn't hide the sadness in her eyes. "I'll see you later, Macy."

She turns and heads out the door, face turned toward the floor. That picture shook her way more than I would've expected. Maybe putting the past behind us isn't going to be as easy as I thought.

Seventeen

JUNIOR YEAR

"I'm thinking about quitting the squad," Jadie blurts out of the blue as we're walking to class.

I stop so fast that my shoes screech against the floor. "What? Why? Is it because of what happened at the diner the other night? Jadie, you can't let a handful of drunk assholes ruin your life."

"Is it really ruining my life if I'm not a cheerleader anymore, Macy? Think about it. Of every girl on the team, you were the only one who stood up for me. Meredith didn't even bother to defend me, or Ben, for that matter, before she ran out. And the guys? I practice every day and get out there every Friday night and have wasted how many weekends erecting a damn monument on wheels in honor of those doofuses, and then I find out half of them don't even think I'm worth treating like a real person. They *laughed* at me, right to my face, while someone made fun of me."

"I know it was awful." I put my hand on her arm like I'm trying to calm her, even though she seems perfectly collected. "But I think Ken was jealous because Meredith turned him down for homecoming, and then she was draped over Ben right in front of his face, and you got caught in the line of fire. None of them actually have a problem with you. They just don't know how to think for themselves."

She gathers her petite body into a ramrod-straight line. "If they don't have a problem with me and they laughed anyway, then they can follow Ken right into a pit of venomous snakes. And unlike them, I do know how to think for myself, and we both know Meredith hates it." She shrugs, letting her posture relax. "Maybe it's time to fly solo."

"But . . . but I'd miss you."

Jadie rolls her eyes. "I'm not talking about kicking the bucket here, Macy."

I try to smile. "Okay. But promise you won't make any snap decisions. Give yourself time to think about it."

She promises. But as she turns to leave, I have the awfulest feeling that I'm standing at the edge of an era's end.

I'm still not used to hearing Ben's voice coming from my brothers' room. We decided to keep up the guitar lessons during Aaron's recovery, since music is therapeutic not only for behavioral problems but for head injuries as well. His official diagnosis was a fractured skull and a concussion. His vision came back, but it's been blurry. He gets dizzy when he stands. Not to mention that he's crabby and irritable almost 100 percent of the time, especially since he can't watch TV or play video games. But because his lessons are one of the few things he looks forward to, Ben walked over after school, and when he's done teaching, I'm driving us to Meredith's to work on the homecoming float.

"Hey," my mother says. "You left practice early?"

I hold up my injured arm. "Still not a hundred percent. I got bored sitting out, so I thought Ben and I could get a head start on the float."

My mother glances toward the second floor, where halting but recognizable notes of "Smoke on the Water" clunk through the air.

"Here," Ben's voice says. "Hold your hand a little more like this and put your finger here and—yeah, like that."

"I'm trying," Aaron replies. He sounds frustrated, but it's a controlled frustrated. Like the angry pod alien who's been inhabiting my brother's body is finally losing its grip on him.

"Perfect. See how much easier that makes it?"

Mom's eyes shine with pride. "Ben is so good with them. So patient. This is exactly what Aaron needed."

I get myself a snack before heading upstairs to collect Ben. But when I see him on Aaron's bed, sandwiched between the boys with a guitar across his chest, I sneak into my room to grab my camera and snap a quick picture.

"Sorry," I say when the twins groan. "It was too cute to pass up." I snap another before Aaron dives facedown into the comforter and Michael buries himself in a pillow. "Ready to go, Ben?"

He tells Aaron to call him if he has any questions, and then we pile into my car.

"So 'Smoke on the Water,' huh?" I say. "And here I thought you'd be teaching him 'Twinkle, Twinkle, Little Star.'"

"Nah. I could, I guess, but 'Smoke' is a really easy one to learn. He's catching on pretty quickly."

"He has a good teacher. In case my mom hasn't told you a trillion times."

Ben grins. "It makes me want to pick up lessons for myself again. I should, now that I can pay for it. I always wanted to start a band."

"Maybe you should follow Joel's advice and pursue your passion."

"Um, that was my advice, actually."

"Oh." Now that I think about it, Ben *was* the one to bring it up. I forgot everything other than Joel saying the word "passion" as his eyes x-rayed my soul. Oops.

There's an awkward beat of silence as Ben turns toward the window. It's only a second, and then he turns back and motions toward my arm. "You healing up okay?"

"Getting there." I rotate my wrist a little, dismissing the odd blip from a moment ago. "I think I might be back in the game by Friday."

"Good. Uh, hopefully the after-party will be a little less *eventful* this time."

"It better. I'm guessing that was Joel's first and last Friday Night Eats."

"Probably."

When he doesn't say anything more, I reach over to change the radio station. "What about you? Can you at least get the night off?"

"I thought about switching with someone, but what good is it to run away from an overgrown baby like Ken? Next time I'll hand him a diaper and be done with it."

I laugh. "Maybe I should supply the Butt Paste. I don't think he appreciated me telling him off."

"It was awesome, though. Those were some serious cojones, Macy. You should be proud of yourself."

He gives me a look that is full of such genuine admiration that I *do* feel proud of myself.

We pull up to Meredith's house, and Ben's little brother is outside playing across the street. He runs to retrieve a baseball glove when he sees us, and waves it in the air as we get out of the car.

"Hey, Ben! Wanna play?"

"I will, buddy," Ben calls back. "As soon as I'm finished helping Macy and Meredith with some stuff."

"You're ditching me for a *girl*," the boy says, clearly agitated.

I wave my arm over my head. "Hi, Ethan!"

His expression stays stony. "My name is Edgar."

"That's what he likes to be called since our grandfather passed away," Ben explains.

"It's my middle name," Ethan-Edgar cuts in. "But it was his first name. So now it's my first name too."

"I think it's a great name."

"Because it is." He throws his glove down, announces he has to pee, and then jogs off toward the house.

"Sorry," Ben says, scratching his head. "Thinking before he talks is not his best talent."

"I have that times two at home. It's okay if you want to go."

"Nah." Ben darts over to retrieve Ethan's glove and throws it closer to the house. "Ten bucks says he's already plugged into a video game and glomming down a bowl of cereal. Let's go."

I open the garage door with the remote Meredith gave me before I left practice, and we duck under as the door rolls parallel to the ceiling. I poke my head inside the house to let Mrs. Kopala know we're here. Then Ben and I climb up onto the trailer, which is slowly but surely starting to take shape. The oversized stereo has been spray-painted and, thanks to Ben's handiwork, is standing sturdy. Now we need to make oversized musical notes; cut out tile-sized squares of shimmery, colored paper that will serve as the nightclub dance floor; paint the Ravens logo on the stereo; douse everything in glitter . . . Yeah. There's still a ton of work to be done.

"This came out nice," Ben says, running a hand over the

top of a cardboard speaker. "I wish it actually played music."

I nod toward the far corner of the garage behind him, where Mr. Kopala's workbench sits. "There's a radio over there. Go ahead and turn it on."

A few seconds later, the sound of music fills the room, and Ben hops back up onto the float. He takes the task of building a makeshift turntable for the top of the stereo, and I set to work on some of the crafty jobs. We sing along to the radio, even though neither of us is very good. What we lack in vocal skills we make up for in love for nineties music, and the ability to laugh at ourselves. Which we do a lot over the next few minutes—especially when Ben attempts to mimic one of Steven Tyler's screeching high notes in an Aerosmith song and ends up sounding more like a cross between a hyena and a dying dog.

I'm laughing so hard, I'm practically crying, and I have to stop and catch my breath. "Okay. A word of advice? Maybe don't do that at homecoming."

"Don't worry. I dance better than I sing." His face screws up in thought, and his hands still. "I think. Crap. I hope."

A series of slow, mellow notes replaces the drums and guitars of the Aerosmith song, and I set aside my stencils and scissors. "Do you want to practice a little? We have some time before everyone gets here."

"Like, right here?" He indicates the float.

"Yeah. Why not?" I stand up, take his tools, and leave them on one of the speakers as I tug him to the center of the trailer. "You said you wanted help untying your tongue, right? Well, pretend I'm Meredith and this is our first slow dance at homecoming. The perfect opportunity to take things to the next level. What do you want to say?"

His eyes drop, and he fidgets. Amid the craziness of Aaron's accident, I almost forgot that Ben was having second thoughts about asking Meredith to the dance.

"You're still going to ask her, right?"

"I—yeah. I think so. I guess." He rubs at his temples. "I don't know."

I have no idea what to say. But then a package of markers on top of an overturned crate catches my eye. "Hang on. I know what you need."

"What are you doing?" Ben asks as I step close to him, uncapping a red marker.

"Returning a favor."

I lift up on my toes and tug down the collar of his T-shirt, placing the tip of the marker on his newly revealed skin. The garage goes quiet as I sketch, with the exception of the music and the rhythm of Ben's breathing. I step back when I finish, replacing the cap. Then I turn him toward the cracked mirror from Meredith's old vanity, which hangs on the garage wall.

He laughs, the tension easing out of him, when he sees my shoddy artwork. "My very own Superman S, huh?"

"Not an S. Hope, remember? You look like you could use a little encouragement."

"Fair enough." He studies me, then reaches for the black marker. "You need something too."

To my surprise, he presses the marker against the top of my sternum, the same spot where I still feel the phantom weight of my locket every time I forget that it's gone. He draws one side of a heart, then the other. In the center, he connects them with a familiar, angular S shape.

"Since we never found your other one," he says.

This time, I don't hold back. I throw my arms around his neck and hug him. "Thanks, Ben," I whisper into the linen scent of his shirt. He hugs me back, and it's only when neither of us pulls away that I remember what we're supposed to be doing. I reposition his hands at my waist. Then I drape my arms over his shoulders and start to sway to the music. "Ready? I'm Meredith."

Ben groans. "This is way too much pressure."

"*Practice*, not pressure." I stand on my toes to make myself taller. "Hey, Benny. So I'm super-glad we're here at homecoming together." We look at each other and burst out laughing. Ben starts to turn away, but I pull him back. "No, for real this time." I clear my throat and stand flat on my feet, and we start to sway again. "So I'm having a really nice time."

"Me too. Thanks for coming with me. I was nervous about asking you."

I put on my best Meredith-esque grin. "Nervous? Why? I like hanging out with you. And bonus that you're funny and super-cute."

Ben stops swaying. "You think so?" He looks confounded. It's almost like he's never heard the word "cute" used in reference to him before. Standing this close to him, I find that hard to believe. His skin is clear and soft-looking, and he has a ski-slope nose that's sprinkled with a few faint freckles. There's a perpetual mischievous curve to his lips, like everyone should be dying to know the things he's seen with those wide-set eyes. He's kind of . . . beautiful.

"Of course I do," I say softly. "Hasn't anyone told you that before?"

"No one who counts."

I study him curiously. "Do I count?"

Ben's gaze drops to the floor. "You count."

"Good. Because you *are* cute, and you are funny. And you have really pretty eyes."

"You have really pretty everything."

I'm not sure when we stopped dancing. And I'm even less sure of what happens next. I can't tell if it's the uneven footing of the trailer bed, but I know there's less space between us than there was two seconds before. I'm looking at Ben, and Ben is looking at me.

And then we're diving to opposite ends of the float amid the approaching sound of Meredith and the rest of the squad.

I zip my sweatshirt over the heart on my chest and pick up my scissors, studiously avoiding everything except my oversized music note. Not that we've done anything wrong. So I can't understand why my heart is beating like it's trying to kick a hole in me.

I glance over my shoulder at Ben. He grins back at me,

and a rush of relief calms my racing pulse. *Good*, I think. *It didn't get weird.*

Because for the briefest second, I couldn't tell if Ben meant that compliment for me as Meredith, or for me as *me*. For the tiniest instant, I almost thought we weren't pretending anymore.

Eighteen

SENIOR YEAR

Because my life hasn't been strange enough, Mr. Hargrove is now my algebra teacher. I knew this was going to happen, because a sub had been filling in until he could officially switch from military duty to teacher duty, but it's not helping the feeling that junior year is suddenly surrounding me on all sides like some kind of satanic spell circle.

Sitting in his classroom each day while he stands at the front—a live, in-the-flesh person and not just someone I've heard about—has made me think a lot about the night at the slushie stand. The one detail I want to recall—whether or not I flapped my gums about the homecoming float's location—is still eluding me. But other fragmented pieces of that night have been coming back to me. The problem is,

I don't know if they're real, or alcohol-drenched amalgamations of truth and imagination.

And worse, I suck at algebra.

It's the last period of the day, and I linger at my desk after the bell rings, packing my things with exaggerated slowness as I try to work up the courage to ask for extra help with the material I can't seem to grasp.

As if he read my mind, Mr. Hargrove says, "Were you comfortable with today's lesson, Ms. Atwood?" Before I can answer, he taps the board. "Factoring is fun, isn't it? It never ceases to amaze me that numbers can be so straightforward and so versatile at the same time. They never lie."

Math has never been my strongest subject, and Mr. Hargrove teaches it like he's simply offering a road map to the easiest, most self-explanatory stuff on earth. It's not that he isn't nice, but I can't shake the feeling that he might laugh in my face if I admit that I'm having trouble understanding.

"Maybe numbers don't lie, but sometimes I feel like they play tricks on me. Even when I think I'm doing the steps right, I still come out with the wrong answer. I don't think my brain is wired for this." I wave at the mess of red gibberish on the whiteboard.

Mr. Hargrove motions for me to take a seat. "Everyone's wired for this. It's a matter of making the wires connect."

That's sort of what I was afraid he'd say. Now I'm dreading letting him see how much sense numbers *don't* make to me. Although, if he's noticed my grades, it's probably not much of a mystery.

There's a knock on the door then, and Joel sticks his head into the classroom. "You ready to go, Da—" His eyes fall on me and he waves. "Sorry. I'll come back later."

"Nonsense. Come in. Ms. Atwood and I are going to take another stab at factoring." I've never wished for the ability to slip through solid matter—like, say, linoleum floors—quite as hard as I am now. Because I definitely don't want to do this in front of Joel

"Ooh, fascinating," Joel deadpans.

Mr. Hargrove wraps an arm around Joel's shoulders and squeezes. "Have you met my Joel Matthew? This kid's an ace at math." He ruffles Joel's hair. "And my pride and joy."

Joel smooths his hair, clearly embarrassed. "We're friends, Dad," he mumbles. Then he glances at me, silently asking if that's true.

I smile in response. "Joel Matthew, huh? That's a nice name."

"He's named after my father," Mr. Hargrove says. Joel rolls his eyes and shakes his head, and I get the feeling that his father has told this story more than a few times. Joel spins a chair backward and sits on it, looking up at his dad expectantly. "Joel's mother and I got married young, or at least what's considered young today. We wanted to start a family right away, but for whatever reason, it wasn't happening. After almost three years with no luck, we started to lose hope." He lays a hand on Joel's shoulder. "Around that time, my father got very sick. He passed away one month shy of his seventieth birthday, and I was devastated that he never got to see that milestone. On the day of his birthday, we found out we were pregnant with Joel."

"That's a pretty amazing story." I look at Joel, but he slings his forearm across the back of the chair and rests his chin on it, like an obedient dog waiting for his master.

"And then to think, three more followed after him. I'll never understand how people can say they don't believe in miracles," Mr. Hargrove continues.

Joel's head jerks up. "Dad," he barks. "We're not in church."

"I know. But I've seen humanity at its worst. I was dropped at death's door, and I got to pick up my bags and walk away. So to me"—he points a marker at the board—"the idea of God is every bit as concrete and logical as these numbers." He puts the marker down and walks back over to Joel. "And this kid is a miracle. Matthew, his middle name, means 'Gift from God.'" He runs his hand over Joel's hair, more gently than before. "And it couldn't be more appropriate. Because you can do anything you put your mind to, Joel Matthew. Don't you forget it."

Joel ducks from his father's touch and stands up. "I'll be in the library until you guys are done."

He doesn't wait for an answer before turning and hightailing it out of the room. I feel like I need to go after him.

"Um, on second thought, I should get going. My dad'll help me if I get stuck on the homework."

"Of course," Mr. Hargrove says as I head to the door. "We can go over it tomorrow if it's still not clicking."

Joel must've kept up his on-a-mission pace, because I see nothing but an empty hallway when I leave the classroom. I start in the direction of the library, and nearly smash my face into his chest as soon as I turn the corner.

"Sorry. Are you okay?" he asks, holding my arms to steady me.

"I was going to ask you the same thing."

"Me? I'm fine." He glances in the direction of his father's classroom. "I just hate when he gets like that. Yeah, he's been through a lot, and yeah, it's awesome if your beliefs got you through it. But he never stops to consider that some people might not think exactly the way he does, and maybe they don't want to be preached to."

"No, it's fine. I didn't think he was preaching. He seems really proud of you. It was a sweet story."

Joel leans against the locker, the side of his head hitting it with a soft *thud*. "A story's all it is."

"What's that supposed to mean?"

We start to walk again, at a slower pace this time, and I watch his profile in the pause that follows. He seems hesitant to explain, and his lips are set together like he doesn't trust himself to do it correctly.

"He gives me too much credit. The way he talks about me, I feel like I'm supposed to sprout wings and walk on water, or some crazy shit like that. I'm not a miracle in the shape of a kid; I'm a *kid*. But his expectations of me are so high, it's pretty much inevitable that I'm going to let him down."

"I don't know, Joel. You seem to be making him pretty happy just by existing."

Joel frowns, and suddenly his eyes are oceans of sadness. "He's happy because I let him keep his delusions." Before I can react, he turns to me with a wan half smile and touches a finger to my locket. "Have you thought any more about homecoming?"

My mouth goes dry and I clutch the silver heart. I know I need to tell him about Noah, but thinking about Noah reminds me of what I still think may be his false confession about the blackout kiss. If Joel is really the one who kissed me, I want him to tell me. Now. And if there's a reason he hasn't come forward, I want to know that, too.

"Is there something else you want to tell me first?"

"There are lots of things I'd like to tell you, Mace," Joel mumbles. He takes a step back and scratches his head. "But maybe . . . not right now. Okay?"

It's the same thing he said the night of the blackout, and I'm no less curious than I was then. But staring into his eyes, I know I'm not going to push the issue. He looks almost on the verge of tears. And there's something else beneath the sadness that makes the skin on my arms prickle with worry—something that looks a lot like fear.

"All right. Then I should tell *you* something. Someone else sort of asked me to the dance before you did."

Joel shifts on his feet. "Let me guess. Ben?"

"Ben? God, no. Why would you think that? Ben asked Meredith."

"Oh. I don't know." From the way he rubs the back of his neck, I get the feeling he wishes he'd said anything but that. "I guess I thought—" His arm drops and he blinks. "It was Granger, wasn't it?"

"It was," I say.

"Figures." Joel snorts.

"I haven't answered him," I rush to add.

"That's why he took you to Old Mill, right?"

"How did you know about that?"

He looks at me like he can't believe how dense I am. "I told you, I had to work." When my expression stays blank, he adds, "At the Mill Club? Where I've been busing tables for a year?"

I knew Joel had a job at a country club. Somehow, which one never came up. But I bet someone else knew all about it.

"So Noah asked me to go because you'd be there?"

He drags a knuckle across his eyebrow. "I guess—I don't know. I started that job after I left Mortonville, so maybe it's a long shot. Forget I said anything." I open my mouth to argue, but it's like an invisible cell door has closed between us. Joel's expression is unreadable when he cuts me off with, "You know what, Mace? Do yourself a favor and go with him."

"But that's not what—"

He starts to back away. I feel like I'm standing at the water's edge, watching him drift out of my reach.

"It's okay." He takes a few backward strides toward the math hall. "For real. You're better off."

His father appears around the corner then and puts an arm around Joel's shoulders. "Ready to go?"

"Yeah." Joel eyes me like I'm something he saw emerge from a swamp. "Let's get out of here."

Mr. Hargrove waves good-bye when they walk past. Joel does not.

I'm pretty sure my mouth is hanging open a little bit as they go. First, because in the span of one day, I've gone from having two invitations to homecoming to having none at all.

And second, because as I watch Joel retreat toward the main doors with Mr. Hargrove's arm draped across his back, the image feels all wrong. Because I'm more certain than ever that Joel did say the words "I hate him," and he said them about the man at his side.

Nineteen

I'm starting to think there's a snowball's chance in hell that Joel will ask me to homecoming. I shouldn't be thinking about it—shouldn't be hoping for it, even if it's only in the most secret corners of my mind. All of my friends regard him the same way, and it's the way I imagine the Amish regard certain types of technology. That is, fine to talk about, fine to admire from a distance, but strictly off-limits to anyone in our circle.

I can feel all eyes on me at Friday's practice when a freshly showered Joel waves at me as I'm straddled on a yoga mat while he's making his way out of the locker room. Some of the girls wave back, and Joel responds with a polite nod. But as I make my way over to him, I don't need to turn around to know they're whispering.

I'd also eat my own gross, sweaty sock before I'd believe that it doesn't have at least a little something to do with jealousy.

"How's the wrist?" Joel says, pointing to my naked arm.

I lift my hand and rotate it. "It feels a lot better. I'll be cheering at the game tonight."

"Awesome. See you there." Joel starts to turn away, then taps the cinder-block wall and doubles back. "What about tomorrow night? Do you have any plans?"

My heart skips a beat. If I do have plans, I can't remember what they are. And I'm pretty sure I'd cancel them anyway.

"I don't think so. Why?"

"Snow in Georgia is giving away samples of their new fall flavors this weekend. A bunch of the guys are gonna be there, and Ben and I are going together. You coming too?"

Oh, right. I did have plans this Saturday. Luckily, hanging out at the slushie stand *is* my plan. And the plan of half the people in school. Snow in Georgia's fall sampler night is a tradition in Ridgedale, the same way it is at Mortonville. It's located between the two towns, and it's a popular hangout for a bunch of the local high schools. There are always rumblings about who's going to start with who, but usually the night ends with nothing more than some harmless drunken taunting.

Usually.

"I'll be there with Jadie and a few of the other girls," I say, trying not to sound overeager. And ignoring the fact that Jadie insists she's not going. "I can't wait to try the apple pie flavor."

And fail at being casual.

Joel grins. "Ben's all pumped up for the eggnog flavor. I think that sounds freaking nasty."

I chuckle to myself. I've always thought of eggnog as the equivalent of runny-egg ice cream, and it grosses me out. Somehow, Ben being excited for it doesn't surprise me at all.

"Eggnog should be outlawed, especially since it's *fall* flavor night, not Christmas. That's cheating."

Joel shrugs. "As long as they're not asking us to show up dressed for an ugly sweater contest, I can live with it."

Another giggle bubbles up in my throat. "I can totally see Ben doing that, too."

"And winning."

We both laugh some more, and Joel tells me to let him know if I need a ride on Saturday. As he walks away, Jadie bumps against me, knocking me into the wall and out of my fantasy about what an apple pie slushie might taste like on someone else's cold, cinnamony lips.

"That looked promising," she says.

It doesn't surprise me that she came to find me. Even though she marched into practice the Monday after the diner incident with her nose defiantly in the air, the two of us have made extra efforts to stick close together. Watching each other's backs.

"He invited me to Snow in Georgia on Saturday. Sort of."

Jadie squeals. "See? He's so asking you to homecoming next. I'm calling it right now."

"Shh!" I pull her farther into the hallway. "You really think so?"

When my eyes dart toward the gym, Jadie's mouth gapes. "Ew, Macy, don't lower your voice because of them! Who cares what they think?"

"So you'll go on Saturday night, then?"

"Nice try, but if I never see Ken Davenport drunk again, it'll be too soon. Besides"—a dreamy smile floats across her lips—"Tyrell is taking me out to dinner and a movie." I must look crestfallen because she hastily adds, "But you can still sleep at my house afterward. We'll swap stories. And you can show me all the pictures I know you're going to take."

I bite my lip, trying to contain the dopey grin stealing over my face. "What if he does ask me?"

"Then you say yes, dummy. I like Joel, no matter what anyone else says." Her dark eyes glint with mischief. "I have a feeling you're going to see a whole different side of him tomorrow night."

TEXT ME WHEN THE WEDDING IS OVER. MAYBE WE'LL STILL BE AT SiG.

I hit send on my message to Meredith as I'm pacing in

front of my dining room window, watching for Joel's car. I decided to take him up on his offer for a ride to the slushie stand when I realized I'd be without my two sidekicks, and Ben volunteered to be the designated driver.

My phone buzzes. DOUBT IT. TEXT ME DEETS IF ANYTHING GOOD HAPPENS.

There's so much nervous excitement coursing through my veins that I can't be as bummed out about Meredith not being here as I should be. She, on the other hand, was none too happy when she realized she'd be spending fall sampler night serving as bridesmaid in her cousin's wedding.

"Nooooo," she moaned, giving the word about seventeen extra syllables as she clomped around the hall near my locker. "I've barely seen Ben since I flaked out at the diner, and now I have to spend fall sampler night in a green chiffon toga, debating whether to tell my aunts they have lipstick on their teeth." She threw herself against the wall and slid down to the floor.

"Have you talked to him about it at all?"

"I did, but . . ." She tugged her *M* pendant back and forth along the chain. "Has he said anything to you about who he's taking to homecoming?"

I didn't like the way she looked at me then. It made me very aware that there was something she *wasn't* asking. So I dodged the question with one of my own.

"Would you go with him if he asked you?"

"I guess I kind of assumed he would. But he hasn't."

"Maybe he thinks he's not your type." I gave her a pointed look. She ignored it.

"We can go as friends, you know." She pulled the *M* up against her lip. "I feel like things are getting weird between us. And not in a good way."

I ignored the second loaded look she shot me, and reassured her that Ben was probably nervous and looking for the right way to ask. I promised to do some digging and report back after the party.

In reality, I don't want to be the middleman. Trying to interpret the difference between what Meredith says and what she really thinks is getting old. And when Ben does share things with me, I don't repeat them, for the simple reason that I don't think it's my place. We might've bonded over Meredith initially, but now that we're friends, I don't want to lose his trust.

And aside from that, I honestly have no idea why he still hasn't asked her to homecoming.

A black Nissan Altima pulls up to my house, and my heart leaps into my throat. Joel is at the wheel in black sunglasses, looking smoother than a fresh jar of Skippy. He parallel parks against the curb in front of my house, and even though I've never thought of driving as sexy, I suddenly want nothing more than to watch him operate a vehicle for unspecified amounts of time.

"That's them?" my mother says, appearing behind me from out of nowhere. "You have everything you need?"

"Yep. I'll get the door."

I'm hoping she'll get the hint that it doesn't need to be a two-person job, but she's right behind me as I open the door to Ben and Joel.

Mom greets them and then turns an iron stare on me. "You're sleeping at Jadie's tonight, right?" What she's really asking is, *You know I'm not oblivious to the fact that you'll be drinking, right?*

I resist the urge to salute and say, *Yes, ma'am,* opting for, "Yes, Mom. I already dropped off my overnight bag and everything." I also leave out the part about having done it as a precaution against potential memory impairment later on.

"I'm well aware of what goes on in the Snow in Georgia parking lot," Mom says, turning the interrogation to Ben and Joel as I dig the heel of my hand into my forehead. "So I need your word that if you find yourselves unable to drive, you'll call me and wait to be picked up instead of doing something irresponsible."

"Don't worry, Mrs. Atwood," Ben says. "There's no way anything is happening to one of your kids on my watch a second time." He crosses his thumb to his pinky and holds up the three remaining fingers. "Scout's honor. Besides, I'm actually mildly allergic to alcohol, so I couldn't drink even if I wanted to. I mean, I could, but the blotchy skin and runny nose aren't really worth it."

I raise an eyebrow behind my mother's back, silently asking if he's telling the truth. He turns a lopsided grin on me in response. "I know. Just when you thought I couldn't get any cooler."

"So we're definitely coming back in one piece," Joel adds. He clamps a hand on Ben's shoulder and musses his hair with the other. "Because all of Ben's slushies will be virgin. Just like him."

The knot between Mom's eyebrows eases up a bit, even as Joel's and Ben's inner twelve-year-olds emerge and they push each other back and forth on the front step. "That actually makes me feel a little better." She pulls me close for a hug. "I'd never forgive myself if something happened to my girl." When she releases me, she points to the camera hanging around my neck. "And don't lose my camera trying to hide evidence."

"We'll be fine, Mom." I pull away, giving her arm a reassuring squeeze. "Nothing bad is going to happen tonight."

When we get to Snow in Georgia, the parking lot is already pretty packed. More so than I remember from past years, but when I say as much, everyone disagrees with me.

"It's always like this," Joel says. "You'd think they put hundred-dollar bills at the bottom of the cups."

One thing hasn't changed: People are spilling out of cars all over the lot, sitting on the hoods, bumpers, and even the roofs, with their cups of shaved ice. Parking is always a crapshoot, because no one wants to be the first to arrive but everyone wants the best parking spaces for their posse. It's sort of an unspoken rule that the first cars to pull in call dibs on that section of the lot for their school, and the row of spots that hugs the woods behind the building is always the most coveted.

The building itself is angular and white, with neon palm trees and hammocks alight in the windows, and a sign that looks like a JumboTron on the roof with the name of the stand spelled out in windblown snow, flanked by two palm trees. Digital snowflakes fall in a constant, uniform stream in the background, the most unrealistic snowfall imaginable. It's always struck me as funny, because there aren't many palm trees in this part of Georgia. But it does snow on occasion, enough that anyone who lives here knows better than to believe it looks like white pellets marching single-file from the sky.

"Sweet," Joel says as we inch around to the back. "Ridgedale got the back row."

A few of the football players whoop and thump the hood as we pass, and we all notice at the same time that Joel is wrong—Ridgedale's managed to claim only two thirds of the back lot. On the other side of the bike rack that sits on the small concrete path to the picnic table area is a line of at least five Mortonville-decaled back window occupying the rest.

Almost as soon as we see them, the kids get off the cars and start booing at Joel.

"Wow. Friends of yours?" Ben grumbles, glaring out the window.

Joel grimaces and cuts the wheel so hard that I grab the handle on the door before I can stop myself. "Sorry," he mutters. "Guess I'm a traitor no matter where I go."

I reach over to squeeze his arm as he pulls onto the small patch of lawn in front of the woods. Normally there are picnic tables scattered around it, but in anticipation of the night's unusual parking patterns, they've been lined up like guards against the tree line. Joel jerks away from my touch, and I jump again, immediately feeling stupid.

"Sorry," he says again. "They think they're funny. But I don't."

I feel so bad for Joel. It was no secret that he had a hard go of earning people's trust at Ridgedale, but I never stopped to think that his old friends might've turned on him for leaving.

"Dude," Ben says. "We can go if this was a bad idea."

Joel turns to him as he unbuckles his seat belt. "No, it's cool. They're harmless, even if they're peacocking like assho—" He chokes off midsentence, his eyes following something past Ben's head in the back window. A car pulls into my sight line before I can see what, and in those two seconds, Joel swallows and finishes with, "Assholes."

Ben swivels toward the window and then turns back to Joel. "You're sure?"

"Yeah." Joel frees himself of the seat belt. "Tell me what you guys want, and I'll grab the first round."

He's getting out of the car before we can protest. So we give him our orders and reconvene outside the car. I'm keenly aware of Jadie's and Meredith's absences, especially when I spot Ken Davenport eyeing me from a few spots over.

"I wish Jadie and Tyrell had come tonight," I say to Ben. "And Meredith."

He snorts. "Can you really blame them for not wanting to? I thought twice about coming myself, except it felt like agreeing that I'm not worthy to breathe the same air. And honestly? Things have been kind of weird with Meredith lately."

"I know she still feels bad about the diner. And she'd feel even worse if she knew you'd used the word 'weird' when you still haven't asked her to homecoming."

Ben's face falls, and I wish I could cut my own tongue out for saying that. So much for staying neutral.

"Oh." Ben's eyes drop to his red Converse sneakers resting on the bumper. "About that—"

"Collins," Joel's voice interrupts. "Come get your nasty eggnog slushies before they melt all over the good ones."

Joel is walking toward us hugging a Styrofoam tray, a tower of sample-sized plastic cups stacked between the three full-sized cups balanced against his torso.

"Full-sized? You don't mess around, do you, Hargrove?" Ben says, eyeing the mounds of shaved ice.

Joel sets the tray on the hood of the car between Ben and me. "I figured these would last longer than a bunch of ice shots. I guessed on the flavors, so you can switch if you want. But first." He hazards a quick look in every direction before pulling a miniature bottle of Captain Morgan from the pocket of his zip-up, unscrewing it, and slipping a generous splash over one of the snow cones before offering one to me.

"For Macy—"

"Butter Rum?" Ben cuts in, ribbing about my Life Savers.

Joel eyes the cup. "Uh, I didn't see that on the menu. I picked Wedding Cake, since Meredith had to skip out for a wedding. Did I mess up?"

I reach over to take it from him. "No complaints here."

If Joel saw a flavor called Wedding Cake and thought of me, this night might hold even more promise than I thought. But it also reminds me that Ben seemed on the verge of saying something important before we got interrupted, and I need to find out what.

"And for Collins." Joel holds a cup out to Ben. "Pickle Juice, because it was the nastiest-sounding thing on the menu."

"Dude, you suck." Ben swipes the cup and downs a mouthful. "I take it back. This is awesome."

I nod toward the slushie that Joel takes for himself. "What about yours?"

He makes another quick assessment of the parking lot before dumping three quarters of the remaining alcohol over his pink-and-blue ice. "Birthday Cake." He raises the cup. "Happy birthday to me."

I gasp, and Ben jumps off the car to give Joel a thump on the back. "Happy birthday, dude. Why didn't you tell us sooner? We would've treated *you* to the first round."

"You guys can get the next one," Joel says as I throw my

arms around his neck in a birthday hug. Ben and I agree to spring for round two, or we would, except for the loud cat-call that sounds at that instant. It's coming from the direction of the Mortonville cars, and Joel's head snaps toward it with a fierce glare.

"Hey, Hargrove," a boy in a gray hoodie calls out, flicking ash from a cigarette. "Pack up your threesome and get the hell out of here. No one needs to see that shit."

Joel's body goes rigid, and his arm pulls back like he's going to punch someone. "Then how about I jam that cigarette out in your eyes and that'll solve two problems? Class fucking act, as always, dickwads."

"Ignore them," I say, tugging Joel's cold fingers. "If karma's any good at her job, they'll choke on their own vomit tonight." When his hand curls around mine in response, the chill instantly becomes an electric charge that shoots through my body. I thread my fingers through his before I can talk myself out of it. I know there's something I'm supposed to be doing, some matter that I just reminded myself to take care of. But when Joel grins down at me, I cannot for the life of me recall what it was.

After that, it isn't long before the night gets a little blurry. Joel's pockets and trunk are both loaded with liquor, and the Wedding Cake ice in my cup becomes rum cake. And it's delicious.

Even in my compromised state, it's not difficult to see that the more he drinks, the more agitated Joel becomes by the presence of his old classmates. Ever since the threesome comment, he keeps laughing too loudly and stealing glances in their direction. He jumps every time someone addresses him, like he expects to be accosted any second.

Needing a breather myself, I take his hand and lead him away from the car where he's watching a game of Medusa and toward his own car. When I try to hoist myself onto the hood, I have all the coordination of cooked spaghetti and my foot slips, almost resulting in a face-plant into the black metal. Joel and I are both snickering, a tangle of sloppy limbs as he helps me sit, and he stands facing me.

"You okay there?" he slurs.

"I was going to ask you the same thing, Mr. Jumpy-pants."

Joel looks down at his jeans and stumbles a little. "My pants aren't jumpy. I'm just happy to see you."

I giggle and pull him closer by grabbing a handful of his jacket, though it's more of an effort to steady myself than to flirt. "You know what I mean." I nod toward the increasingly loud Mortonville crew. "It seems like you don't want them here. Like they're aggravating you just by breathing."

"Breathing, existing. Those can be annoying things."

I give him a *Be serious* look, though I'm not sure how serious I look myself with bleary slits for eyes. "You don't really believe you're a traitor, right?"

He leans against the hood with his hands on either side of my thighs. He's so close that I can pick out the flecks of green in his eyes and smell the alcohol on his breath. "What does it matter, if everyone else believes it?"

I sit up straighter. "*I* don't believe it."

The corner of his mouth pulls up, and there's an amused glint in his eyes. "Oh yeah? And what do you know about me?"

"Not as much as I want to."

Thank you, Captain Morgan, for your power to make me an ace flirt.

Joel raises a blond eyebrow. "But you think I can be trusted?"

"Let's find out." I lean closer and position my lips next to his ear. "Maybe I should tell you a secret." And then Captain Morgan revokes his magical powers, and I say the least-smooth thing I could possibly come up with: "Ben knows where we're hiding the homecoming float."

"Oh?" If Joel thinks it's a stupid thing to say, I'm glad he doesn't act like it. Especially since Cap chooses that moment to make me walk the plank, and my mouth starts to run independently of my brain in an effort to fight off a sudden wave of dizziness. By the time the wave passes, all I know is that Joel and I are laughing again, and I'm trying to pull him up onto the car with me, but we're both too drunk and too silly and he might as well be scaling a block of ice for all the progress we're making.

Finally he lands next to me on his back, smiling up at the night sky. It's a rare, unguarded moment, and it's so beautiful that I grab my camera and aim it at him. Joel mock shields his face and says, "No pictures, please!" Then he takes the camera from my hands and pulls me down next to him, holding it crookedly in front of us. "Not unless you're in it too." The camera clicks away, and when we finally prop ourselves up to a sitting position, he slings an arm around my shoulders and holds me close before snapping one more.

We turn toward each other as the final click sounds. There's hardly any space between us. We're breathing the same air, and I feel the rise and fall of his chest. His lips are right there, so perfect and kissable, and I don't have an ounce of self-control to speak of.

So I lean in and close my eyes.

And that's when Joel's foot slips off the bumper, and he lands with a graceless crunch of dead grass beneath his sneakers.

"Whoa," Ben says, appearing out of nowhere. He claps a hand on Joel's shoulder and nods toward the trail that winds through the woods. "Why don't we take a walk so you can sober up a little?"

Joel rubs his forehead like he's just realized it's killing him. "Yeah. Sounds like a plan." He takes a few uneven steps onto the path.

Ben places a bottled water in my hands. It's cold, and coated in tiny beads of condensation. "You coming too?"

"I'm gonna rest right here." I take a sip of the water, grateful for the coolness washing through my insides. "You're a good friend, Ben." I lean in to kiss his cheek. At least, that's what I meant to do. But he takes a step at the same time I move toward him, and our faces meet like a pair of bumper cars. "Sorry," I say through a fit of giggles. "You have so many heads, and I couldn't tell which one was real."

Ben gently pushes my shoulders until I'm propped against the windshield. "Go home, Macy. You're drunk."

"I can't go home. You brought me here!"

"No, it's a sayin—never mind. Lie down until Joel and I get back, okay?"

"Okay." I raise my pointer finger toward what I think is the general direction of his face. "Be warned, imposter Ben heads. I'll get you later." Ben shakes his head and starts to follow Joel, but stops when I pull his sleeve. "Hey, Ben? Do you think Joel will kiss me tonight?"

He detaches my fingers from the material of his shirt. "I don't know, Mace. I guess that's up to you."

As he walks away, I think I ask him why all his heads are such frowny faces. But I'm still being pulled under by the currents of booze in my system, and the moment short-circuits into a fragmented blur of chattering voices and music from car stereos and a starry sky spinning above me.

I think I must fall asleep, because the next thing I know, I'm blinking at the moon, wondering where the past few minutes have gone and thinking hard about where I am. I sit up and look around. The parking lot has cleared out considerably, and I have a moment of terror when I think my ride has left without me. Until I remember that I'm lying on it.

A rustle near the tree line makes my head snap in the direction of the woods, and I'm met with the sight of Joel and Ben returning from their walk.

Joel is slumped over, hands jammed into his pockets,

zigzagging unevenly over the path. When Ben tries to steady him, Joel swats him away. Twice. I can't tell if they've had a fight, or if Joel morphed from silly drunk to belligerent drunk.

Joel plunks down on the hood of the car like a sack of rocks, and Ben shoots an anxious glance at me. "I'm gonna go see if anyone else needs a ride." He steps closer, like he doesn't want Joel to hear what he says next. "And, uh, to see if I can find a bag or something. I'm pretty sure he's gonna blow."

Joel does look a little green, and the corners of his mouth have turned so far down that they're practically touching his jaw. I offer him my bottle of water as Ben walks away, and Joel shakes his head without taking it.

"Are you okay?" I ask.

He sinks against the windshield and covers his head with his hands. "Headache," he mumbles.

Before I can say anything else, Joel's cell phone chimes in the pocket of his zip-up. He pulls it out and stares at the screen for what feels like a full minute of silence, his jaw tense and his breath coming in harsh, shallow puffs.

"Joel?" I place a hesitant hand on his arm. "Are you sure you're all right?"

He slips the phone back into his pocket without looking at me. "Happy birthday email from Afghanistan."

"Oh." I squeeze his forearm. "I'm sorry your dad can't be here."

Joel snorts. "He said he hopes all my birthday wishes come true." He rolls away from me onto his side, like he's

182

forgotten that he's on the hood of a car and not getting comfortable in bed. "He's full of shit."

"Don't say that. You know he'd be here if he could."

"I'm glad he's not. I bet he is too." On the last word, his voice breaks. And then his whole body shudders, and sobs spill out of him like demons being exorcised. "I hate him," he chokes. "I fucking hate him."

It's the last thing he says before leaning over the side of the car and retching a flood of melted ice. I barely remember his words as my own nausea overtakes me, and our fun night at the slushie stand suddenly isn't so fun anymore.

Twenty

SENIOR YEAR

It's a picture-perfect day for the pennant hunt. Not too hot, a clear blue sky, and a hint of leaves shedding their green for cloaks of gold and red—everything I love about autumn in Georgia. It's so perfect that I decide to go for a run before diving into my homework and then heading over to Old Mill later in the afternoon.

When I get downstairs, it's chaos. Michael is wearing half of his breakfast, and my mother yanks his shirt over his head, snapping, "Get a new shirt and your brother and let's go. I have a lot to do today."

"Where are you going?" I ask.

"Zoo," Michael responds, at the same time my mother

says, "The boys have a playdate with Ethan. And we're going to be late."

I turn to Mom. "Ben's brother?" It takes only a heartbeat for the plan to form. "I can drop them off," I say, ruffling Michael's hair.

Mom eyes my running clothes—a hot-pink Dri-Tech tank top and tight navy-blue shorts—as if I'm about to walk out of the house in pasties and a thong. "Are you looking for a reason to run into Ben?"

Yep. I want explanations. For why he keeps telling me he wants to talk, but then clams up and storms off instead. For why I feel like I'm missing something every time I have a conversation with anyone lately.

Mostly it's because I'm not sure we can be friends again, but I still want to try. And I want to know why he doesn't anymore.

Mrs. Collins answers the door with a dishrag in her hand. Ethan runs up behind her, a red-haired blur.

"Ahoy, Captain Edgar!" Michael says with a salute. Of course, Aaron has to be a pain in the ass, loudly pointing out, "His name is *Ethan*," as they run like a pack of wolves toward the basement door.

"Macy," Mrs. Collins says, sounding pleasantly surprised. "We haven't seen you in a while. How have you been?" She nods to my brace before I can answer. "Cheerleading casualty?"

"Sort of. I'm not on the squad anymore, but my last injury never got the memo." I step inside at her prompting and immediately feel my boldness waver. Ben's mom has never been anything but polite to me, but more than once, the way I've caught her looking at me makes me wonder if she knows about the night Ben stowed me away as a drunken refugee in her basement. "How is everything with you?" I say.

"Fine, fine, though I have to wonder what I was thinking, volunteering to take four boys to the zoo. They're learning about mammals in school, and sometimes my good intentions get ahead of my common sense. We're waiting on one more." She waves toward the tall, wrought-iron stools at the kitchen island. "Sit down. I see your mother now and then at soccer games. We were just saying that we should get everyone together one day."

I'm willing to bet that it was my mother who did the saying. "Um, I was actually wondering—is Ben home?"

Surprise registers in her blue eyes before she dons her best motherly poker face. "He's in his room doing homework. I'll bring you up."

I've been inside Ben's house before, but never in his room. It's strange that I'm going there now, with things the way they are. It feels intimate to walk into his personal space. Like I'm about to plop down into the lap of a stranger or something.

Mrs. Collins knocks on the door and cracks it open,

sticking her head inside. "Ben? Macy is here to see you if you'd like to talk."

I realize what she's doing. The way she's blocking me from seeing him, guarding the minimal slice of entrance she's created, like she's ready to deny access and stand guard if Ben says the word.

She's protecting him from me. She doesn't think I belong here either.

But Ben must give the okay, because she pushes the door open wide before stepping past me to head back downstairs.

All I can think when I enter is that Ben's room is exactly like his personality: full of color and activity and things to discover. There are basketball posters on the walls, a book-case in the far corner overflowing with books and trophies and keepsakes, including a shelf of Superman figurines. A big, unmade bed with a navy-blue comforter and more pil-lows than one person could ever need is at the center of the room, with Ben's work clothes laid out at the edge. Ben is seated in front of his computer at a desk to my left. A pic-ture of Ethan is taped to the side of the monitor, and the face he's making reminds me of my brothers' silly expres-sions in the photo I used to wear around my neck.

"What are you doing here?" he says.

"Hello to you too." I walk over to his bed and straighten out the blankets before perching next to his familiar work shirt with the BEN name patch sewn beneath the left shoul-der. From the looks of his computer screen, he's writing a paper. There's a playlist docked in the upper right corner, and a guitar-heavy classic rock song rings though the speakers. "You've been avoiding me."

He lowers the volume on his music. "Haven't had much to say."

"That's funny, because you came to that conclusion while you were right in the middle of telling me we should talk—again. And then you saw the necklace from Joel, and suddenly it's like I'm a walking infectious disease. I thought we were over this."

"And I thought you were smarter than that."

I grip the edge of the bed. "Smarter than what? To let Joel give me a necklace? At least when Joel says he wants to work things out, he makes good on it. You used to be all about giving people a chance, or did that slip your mind when you gave me that judgy look for talking to Noah the other day?"

Ben's hand closes around a pencil lying next to his keyboard. "I have nothing against giving chances . . . to the right people."

I stand up. "And now you're the authority on 'the right people'? Is that why you asked Meredith to homecoming again this year? Because you're giving things another chance? Or are you not done stringing her along?"

The moment I finish, I know I've gone too far. This conversation is not going the way I intended, and I want to walk out the door, walk back in, and start over.

Ben's jaw tightens. "Was there a point to you coming here?"

I take a deep breath and rub my temples. "I'm sorry." I walk over to his bookshelf, trying to gather my thoughts. "I've been doing a lot of thinking lately. About last year, about everything." I pause at his shelf of trophies and realize they're all awards for basketball with his name engraved into the tiny placards on the front. "Why aren't you on the basketball team?"

Ben snorts. "Those are your deep conclusions about everything that happened last year? That I should be on the basketball team?"

"No," I say with a roll of my eyes. "But you obviously love it." I motion to the posters on the walls. "And I know you're good at it."

Ben's face softens, and he shifts in his chair. "I guess I always felt like competition takes the fun out of it. I like playing for rec teams and stuff, but joining the school team always felt like too much pressure. To win, to stand out, to be the best." He shrugs. "I'm happier without that. Plus I needed to work so I can help my parents out with college expenses next year."

I nod and pick up a figurine, one with Superman's fist extended in mid-flight. "I can respect that." I smile, hoping to change the previous tone of the conversation. "But I would've been your biggest cheerleader." I flush red when I hear the words in my own ears, and clumsily replace the statuette. "Your second-biggest, anyway. I think we both know Meredith is your first."

He looks down at his feet and I look down at the carpet, and we're right back to square one of awkward.

"There was a point to me coming here," I add in a hasty effort to change the subject. I sit back down on his bed as the sound of the front door opening registers in the background, signaling the arrival of the last member of the boy brigade. I know that once they leave, my excuse for being here goes with them. "I've been thinking a lot about that night at the slushie stand. And the more I do, the more I feel like that's the night when everything started changing. Don't you?"

Ben looks at his computer screen, down at the floor, and back again. "Changing how?"

"I was hoping you could tell me. Did something happen that night? Something that I either didn't see or don't remember?"

The pencil in Ben's hand taps a steady beat against the desk. He doesn't look at me when he answers. "It was like any other weekend. A bunch of drunk kids doing stupid crap that they end up regretting later."

"You weren't drunk, Ben."

His eyes finally meet mine. "I wasn't talking about me."

An exasperated sigh huffs from my throat before I can stop it. "If I did something stupid that night, please stop talking in circles and tell me what it was so I can apologize and we can move on with our lives."

Ben stands and puts his hands behind his head, stretching like he's been cramped in his chair for too long. Or like he's already tired of this conversation. To my surprise, he comes over and sits down next to me.

"It wasn't you. Okay?" he says quietly. "But if you're planning on making another go with Hargrove, I'll be honest with you: It's a bad idea." My mouth opens, but Ben plows ahead. "I'm not saying Joel's a bad person. He's not. But he's got a lot of shit on his plate, and he doesn't deal with it in the"—he stops, looking like he's struggling for the right word—"healthiest of ways, I guess you can say. He makes some pretty crappy decisions without thinking about how they affect other people."

It's almost exactly what Noah said, and it makes the hair on my arms stand up.

"I know firsthand that Joel does crappy things. But right now I feel like I'm the only one who doesn't know *why*. What I do know is that I ended up at homecoming alone, and I've spent the past year wondering if the fire at Meredith's was my fault. So what am I missing? Does it have something to do with why Joel hates his father?"

Ben's eyebrows pull together. "Joel doesn't hate his father."

"He hated him that night. He told me so. It was the last thing he said before he got sick."

Ben looks dubious. "Are you sure about that? You were pretty trashed."

"He was crying."

"Oh." The word comes out soft, almost guilty-sounding. "He was pretty trashed too." He says it like it's supposed to explain away Joel's tears. But in the pause that follows, it's obvious that we've realized we're both missing pieces of the puzzle.

And then, as if some greater power is determined to make this afternoon as uncomfortable as possible, the music from Ben's computer changes. It's a slower, gentler beat, one that we both recognize from the first note. One that never fails to send me back to the night of the homecoming dance, under the spotlight of a parking-lot streetlamp, swaying in Ben's arms.

One that made me forget for a minute that it was supposed to be the worst night ever.

"Remember this song?" Ben says.

"Of course I do." My next thought slips out before I can stop it. "I can't hear it without thinking of you."

Something about the way Ben looks at me tells me he's pleased with that answer. That maybe it was exactly what he wanted to hear.

The sound of the twins' raucous laughter rings through the house, and Ben clears his throat. "So I might not have joined the basketball team, but there might still be hope for a band."

"Oh?"

"I signed up for some refresher guitar classes right after . . . a while ago." His foot bounces against the carpet. He hesitates, then crosses the room to his closet and returns holding the same acoustic guitar he used to give Aaron lessons last year. A wave of nostalgia washes over me as he positions it across his lap.

I'm keenly aware of the empty space left by the moments lost between now and the last time I saw him with that guitar.

The feeling intensifies when Ben starts to play along with the music drifting from his computer. My throat tightens, and chills creep up my arms. It's like those guitar strings are tied directly to my heart, tugging with each note. Oh, crap. I am not going to cry right now.

Ben glances up, and our eyes meet for a split second before we both look away. He stops playing abruptly, and we shift a little farther from the other, like an unspoken agreement.

"You play really well," I croak. I draw a sharp breath and release it with the question that, until this moment, I didn't realize I badly wanted to ask. "So tell me, Ben. What didn't happen that night?"

His hand moves a fraction of an inch toward me, and his mouth opens. But then a stampede of footsteps sounds on the stairs, and in the next second the room is full of prepubescent boys. Ben greets them all with high fives or noogies, saving Aaron for last.

"Hey, dude. How are the lessons going?"

Aaron smacks Ben's outstretched hand as hard as he can, then runs his fingers over the strings of the guitar still sitting in Ben's lap. "I'm getting really good. You were a way cooler teacher, though."

Mrs. Collins appears in the doorframe, slinging her purse over her shoulder.

"We're heading out now," she says. "The boys wanted to say good-bye first." She checks her wristwatch. "And you need to leave for work soon, don't you?"

I stand up, taking the hint. "I'll walk out with you," I say to her.

I ruffle my brothers' hair and remind them to behave themselves. The minute they're out of sight, I lean against my car and heave a deep sigh. I'm a little relieved that I don't see Meredith's car in her driveway.

Between the things Ben and I talked about and the things we didn't, I'm leaving Ben's house with even more questions than I had when I walked in.

Twenty-One

JUNIOR YEAR

My head feels like it's going to explode. As my eyes work their way open, I try to remember what the hell I did to make me feel this way.

A vague memory of shaved ice drowned in booze floats through my mind, followed immediately by a wave of nausea.

I am never touching a snow cone again, virgin or otherwise.

I moan a little as I sit up, rubbing the sleep out of my eyes. And almost jump out of my skin when a guy's voice says, "Hey. How're you feeling?"

It takes me a minute to focus. If I'd had a few seconds longer to let my senses adjust, I would've realized that I wasn't home. Or at Jadie's house. Or even in a bed.

"Ben?" I croak. "Where are we?"

A few more blinks, and the three heads floating on Ben's shoulders converge into one, and I see that he's half lying on a black leather couch identical to the one I'm currently draped across.

"We're in my basement. You were pretty wasted last night, and Jadie was afraid her mom would call your parents. So she lied and said you met up with Meredith after the wedding and slept there instead."

Pieces of last night start rushing at me like my brain is in a batting cage gone haywire, and I cover my face with my hands, muffling another groan. "I told Meredith to text me after the wedding, and I don't even remember if she did. She probably thinks I'm dead."

Ben swivels into a sitting position, and if every artery in my head weren't contracting like a heartbeat and my mouth didn't taste like the floor of a sewer, I'd be giggling at the way his hair is flattened on one side and sticking up on the other like he stuck his finger in a socket.

"It's okay. Jadie filled her in on what was going on."

"Where's Joel?"

He points to the ceiling. "Upstairs in my room. At least that's where I left him. He might've decided to bite the bullet and take some blankets into the bathroom."

It's only then that I notice how puffy Ben's eyes are, and I realize he's been babysitting Joel and me all night.

"Ben. I am *so* sorry."

He assures me it's okay, but I feel even worse when he

tells me that he brought Joel upstairs so that Mr. and Mrs. Collins wouldn't know I was here. "They have a pretty strict 'no coed sleepovers' rule," he explains. "I told them I gave Joel my bed and I'd sleep down here. They're at church now, but"—he shifts uncomfortably over the leather—"I think they knew something was up."

"Parents always know." I can only imagine what mine are going to say after one look at me, and I haven't even seen myself in the mirror yet.

Ben rubs his eyes, and I'm almost certain it's to hide a grimace. Knowing that he's going to take heat because of me makes me feel ten times worse, and I didn't even think that was possible.

"Which is why, no offense, you guys should probably get out of here before they get back." He tosses his blanket aside. "Do you want to take a shower? The bathroom's over there." He points to my right. "Except you already know that, because you got pretty well acquainted with it last night."

I cover my eyes and shake my head. I'd rather eat one of the couch cushions than have to move from them, but I know I can't go home looking like death warmed over, wearing my clothes from last night.

Except, when I look down, I notice that I'm not wearing my clothes from last night. I'm not wearing *my* clothes, period.

I pull at the unfamiliar gray T-shirt. "Whose shirt is this?" I throw the blanket off my legs to find I'm wearing

Superman pajama pants. "What happened to my clothes?"

Ben scratches behind a bright red ear. "You sort of got puke on them." He points behind him to an open door in the far corner of the room, where a slice of a washing machine is visible. "I washed them for you, but I had to give you something to wear in the meantime."

"You *undressed* me?" I'm horrified. Utterly and completely mortified.

"No! I mean yeah. I mean—" Ben claps his hands over his face. "I mean, you mostly undressed yourself, but I had to help you. I didn't see anything, though," he rushes to add. "It was dark, and I swear I didn't look if I didn't have to."

I whimper and curl into the arm of the couch, throwing the blanket over my head. I am never, ever drinking again.

"Nice pants, by the way," I mumble from the safety of my cotton shell.

Ben laughs. "Sorry about that. I thought they'd fit you because they're old and too small for me." The blanket peels away from my face, and Ben peers down at me.

"You know," I say, "I'm starting to think you *are* Superman for all the times you've saved my ass."

He pauses like he's going to say something, then offers his hand instead. "Need help getting to the bathroom? I left an extra toothbrush in there for you last night. In case you forgot?"

The way Ben looks at me makes me feel like he's testing me. On what, I don't know. But I decide that's silly—I'm probably hallucinating. I sit up and take his hand, but I don't get to my feet. "You're such a good friend, Ben."

"You said the same thing last night." He gives me that look again, like there's a correct response to that statement, and it's starting to make me a little self-conscious that I have no idea what it is. So I go with:

"I owe you so big." I squeeze his hand to show him I mean it. "Whatever I can do, just let me know."

"Really?" From the way he brightens, I have to wonder if he's already thought of something. And then, as if he read my mind, he says, "Because there is something, but I'm not sure how you'd feel about it."

I snort, which makes every muscle in my torso smart. "Unless you're going to ask me to rob a bank, I'm pretty sure I can handle it."

"Okay. Um." A nervous-sounding chuckle escapes his throat, and he runs his free hand through his hair. The other is still holding mine, and as the seconds tick by, his touch starts to feel different. Less helpful. More . . . hopeful? "So I was—" he starts to say, but the creaking of the basement door interrupts.

"Collins," Joel's voice, raspy with sleep, or maybe lack thereof, calls down the stairs. "Where the hell do you keep toothpaste in this place? And, um, do you have a bottle of Fantastik or something? I need to clean your bathroom floor."

Ben drops my hand and claps his against his head. "Dude. I left a garbage can right next to you."

"I know. I missed."

I can tell Ben feels bad leaving me, but I say I'll be fine, even though I'm not sure it's the truth. I do manage to find my clothes and my purse in Ben's laundry room. When I pull out my cell phone, there are three missed calls from my mother and three texts from Meredith.

One text says BRIDESMAID DUTY = DONE, YOU GUYS STILL OUT?? The second came through about an hour later and reads IF YOU'RE GOING TO FAKE SLEEP AT MY PLACE, WHY NOT JUST SLEEP HERE FOR REAL?? And the third: GUESS YOU HAD A GOOD TIME.

Great. She's mad. But I don't have the time or energy to grovel right now, so I fire off a quick BE HOME SOON to my mother and drag myself into the bathroom. I get through a shower without incident, even if I do most of my washing seated on the tile floor of the stall. There's a connected workout room, and I get dressed in there. No one thought to sneak my overnight bag out of Jadie's house last night, so I try not to blanch as I turn yesterday's underwear inside out beneath the clothes that Ben washed for me. By the time I'm ready, Ben and Joel are each sitting on one of the leather couches.

Joel is pale, with dark circles under his eyes, and blond stubble glistens on his chin. I don't recognize what he's wearing, so I assume Ben lent him the gray sweatpants and blue T-shirt he has on. Even though he looks like he should be hooked up to an IV, he stands up and says, "We have to go. Ben's parents are on their way home."

"Are you okay to drive?"

He gives me a limp smile. "I can make the car go in a straight line, but I can't guarantee that I won't have to pull over between here and your house."

I'm praying for an uneventful drive as Ben walks us out to the car. Even through sunglasses, the morning light is so offensive that I can barely think of anything except making a beeline for my bed the minute I walk in the door. Ben gave me a sweatshirt to hide my walk-of-shame outfit, but it's early enough that my brothers might still be sleeping, and my parents will probably be reading the paper over coffee at the kitchen table, out of sight from the front door. That way I can make my escape without being spotted.

It doesn't occur to me until we're pulling out of the driveway that Ben never got the chance to ask for his favor. I make a mental note to text him later, when I can look at my phone's screen without feeling like I'm going to hurl.

It's a quiet ride home. We make it to my house without having to stop, and I tell Joel to text me so I'll know he got home in one piece. As I open the car door, he grabs my hand.

"Thanks, Mace."

"For what?"

He lets go of my fingers. "I don't know. I just felt like I should say it." He puts the car in gear. "Good luck."

"Same to you."

As he drives away, I unlock the front door and slip inside, noting the kitchen lights spilling onto the hardwood of the dining room floor. My parents are definitely in there. And just as I'm about to call, *I'm home*, and make a run for it, the sound of a gong reverberates in my skull, breaking my brain into a hundred pieces.

That's when my mother, father, and both of my brothers march into the dining room. Everyone is holding wooden spoons except for Aaron, who's wearing his noise-canceling headphones as Michael gleefully smacks away at the lid to one of the pots that are tucked under my parents' arms. A cacophony of clashes and pings and clangs rings through the foyer until I feel like the sounds are tunneling inside my head like tree roots and I might implode at any second.

"WELCOME HOME, MACY!" my family shouts in unison, and it's clear that this is an ambush.

They know.

"What are you guys *doing*?" I say, sinking onto the bottom stair, clutching my temples.

"Giving you the welcome you deserve," my dad replies. He punctuates it with a loud smack of the wooden spoon against the bottom of his pot.

"I got a text from Jadie's mother saying that you spent last night at Meredith's." My mom shifts her pot to her hip, her lips taut with anger and disappointment. "But when I asked Mrs. Kopala if I should pick you up while I was out this morning, she said you weren't there." Her eyes flash. "I called you three times, Macy Jean."

"I know, Mom. But by the time I saw it—"

"You were what?" Her question slashes off the end of my statement. "You could've been tied up in someone's basement, for all I know."

"Well, I *was* in someone's basement, but I wasn't tied to a post or anything."

My parents' expressions don't change, and my brothers give each other confused looks.

My dad holds out his pot, a beat-up hunk of stainless steel that my mother uses to make soup. "Hand over your phone and go to your room. We'll discuss this later."

There's a defeated *clunk* as my cell hits the discolored bottom. I slink off to my room knowing that I'll be paying for last night for a very long time.

It's a couple of hours later when my mother comes into the dark, quiet solitude of my bedroom and sits down on the edge of my bed with my cell phone in hand.

"Your friend Joel must be very worried about you," she says. "He keeps sending you text messages."

I roll over to face her, noticing that I feel a little hungry for the first time all day. "Am I allowed to answer him?"

"First tell me *why* he's checking on you so many times, and then we'll talk about it."

I tell her. All of it, or at least what I remember. And I don't leave anything out, because I feel like somehow she'd know.

Once I finish, she's quiet for a bit. "Macy." She pauses again, like she's deciding how hard it's necessary to ride me. "I don't consider myself an unreasonable parent. Nor am I ignorant. I'm well aware that kids your age are experimenting with a lot of things, especially alcohol. And I've never expressly forbidden you to drink, but that doesn't mean that I don't expect you to behave responsibly. That includes being honest with me. Telling me what you're doing, who you're with, and checking in with me when your plans change. I don't think that's asking too much. Do you?"

"No." In all honesty, this is probably the least dramatic reaction I've ever seen her have to anything. It's pretty humbling.

Mom must know she's twisted the knife enough, because she switches to interrogating me about Joel. She wants to know how close we are. Which, of course, is code for *Do I need to rehash the birds-and-bees lecture while I'm here?*

"We're friends," I say.

Mom raises an eyebrow. "But?"

"No 'but.'" Her stare is unrelenting, and she ticks my phone from side to side in front of her chest like a pendulum. So I tack on, "Yet?"

"Well." She turns the phone toward her, and the screen illuminates her face. "He wants to meet for coffee at Mugsy's, but since you're grounded—"

"No! I'm supposed to go to Meredith's and help finish the homecoming float today." Not to mention I still haven't responded to her text messages. She's going to kill me.

"I already made Meredith aware of your situation. The float will have to get finished without you." She hands me the phone. "I'm relinquishing this long enough for you to call and tell Joel he can bring your coffee here. I couldn't get a good read from the two minutes at the door when he came to pick you up." I have to laugh. "After that, your phone is mine until next weekend, unless you're in school or at practice. Which are the only places you'll be going."

Less than half an hour later, Joel pulls up to the curb in front of our mailbox and emerges from his car with a red Styrofoam Mugsy's cup in each hand. I'm praying my family will be gentle with their inquisition as I watch him from our dining room window. If the way I feel is any indication, Joel doesn't have the luxury of all his pistons firing right now.

My parents are already behind me as I open the door, so I can only hope Joel hears my telepathic apology for whatever discomfort they inflict on him. Even though they know that I made my own moronic decisions last night, having their first real conversation with him while he's shaking off a hangover and after I tried to lie about spending the night under the same roof as him . . . he hasn't made the best impression.

We get through the initial overly polite introductions, and Joel hands me my coffee so he can shake my father's hand.

"Good call on the coffee," Dad says. "Looks like you could both use it."

Joel gives a nervous chuckle, looking like he wishes he could jump into his cup and submerge himself. "Yeah. This—" He looks at me, floundering. "It's not a habit. Not even close. But yesterday was my birthday, and I guess I threw good judgment out the window." He ducks into his shoulders like a turtle missing its shell. "Sorry."

GINA CIOCCA

He's so embarrassed, and this is torture to witness. It doesn't help that my brothers have crammed themselves into the doorframe between the dining room and kitchen, eavesdropping with unabashed conspicuousness.

"Oh, well, happy birthday," Mom says coolly. "Older and wiser, eh?"

"And dehydrated," Joel adds.

Luckily, the stiffness in my parents' postures eases up after that, and the conversation becomes less interrogational. Mom even offers Joel a piece of homemade pound cake, and when he politely refuses, Aaron and Michael take it as their cue to drag him into the living room and test his video game knowledge.

"Are we allowed to walk down to the lake?" I ask as Michael insists on showing Joel the "cool trick" he learned to take down some evil ogre in a game that I'm always amazed doesn't give them nightmares.

"Don't be gone long," my mother replies.

Joel and I both breathe a sigh of relief when the front door closes behind us.

"Wow," he says. "They don't hate me or anything."

"They really don't." I hope I sound reassuring. "They're mad at me, and all they know about you is that you were with me last night. Makes you an easy target to play the bad influence. Then they don't have to put all the blame on me, because that's kind of the same as blaming themselves. At least I think that's their logic."

Joel shrugs deeper into his sweatshirt, even though it's

not cold out. "Makes sense. I got the 'man of the house' speech from my mom, plus the 'you're only doing this because your father isn't here to deal with you' guilt trip, which means I'll be getting a long-distance lecture from my dad later on. Not that it matters, when she already grounded me."

I throw him a quizzical look. "If you're grounded, how are you here?"

"I told her I was going to the car wash to get the puke off the exterior. She's running around with my brothers this afternoon anyway. As long as I'm back before she has to go to work, it's no big deal. My parents are great at ignoring things if it's more convenient to overlook them."

"So you babysit your brothers while your mom works?"

Joel nods through a slurp of his coffee. "Between Peyton's medications and his moods, he can be kind of tough for other people to deal with. Sometimes the neighbors will take them, or people from church. But most of the time, it's me."

"Wow. Can your mom really blame you for wanting to cut loose a little?"

He snorts. "From what I remember, I'm not sure it was worth it."

I wrap my hands around my cup as we round the corner at the end of my street, trying to come up with something to contradict him. I thought the haze shrouding my memories of last night would clear along with my headache, but it's like my brain has the same fragmented highlight reel playing on repeat.

"Were your friends from Mortonville giving you a hard time? I feel like you were upset about something." I also feel like an ass admitting that I can't really remember.

"They were mostly fine. There was this one kid I didn't expect to be there, and it kind of threw me when he was."

We trot down the planks that serve as steps to the path between the lakes and settle down on one of the benches. I lift my knees to my chest.

"Which one was that?"

Joel's face twists. "The jerk in the blue car."

I rack my brain, but come up blank. "Did he say something to you?"

"Something about a threesome when you and Ben wished me happy birthday." Now that, I vaguely recall. "I kept waiting for more. My parents almost took out a restraining order against him this summer. Kid's fucking crazy."

My eyes widen. No wonder Joel seemed on edge last night. He was watching his back the whole time. "Is that part of the reason you left?" I suddenly feel stupid. I always assumed Joel had a good life in Mortonville, and that transferring to Ridgedale was a downgrade. I never bothered to ask if maybe it was just the lesser of two evils.

Joel shrugs, staring over the lid of his cup at the murky water, and the faraway look in his eyes tells me his mind has gone elsewhere. "I guess you could say that." In the next blink, he's there with me again and pulling his phone out of his pocket. "I got some pretty funny pictures, at least. Actually, I have no idea who took half of these. Check them out."

He hands over his cell, and I scroll through the photos with my thumb. There are pictures of the football players and cheerleaders going shot for shot from the white paper sample cups, pics of Joel pretending to gag as Ben laps up his Pickle Juice slushie.

I snort. "You're lucky you were only pretending to puke in this one."

"Tell me about it."

"So who lost it first? Me or you?"

"I think I did," Joel says, a trace of guilt creeping into the words. "I started feeling woozy when Ben and I were in the—" He cuts himself off and pales so suddenly that I'm afraid he's about to be sick yet again.

"Joel? Are you all right?"

He licks his lips like his mouth has gone dry and eyes his cup. "Yeah. I think the coffee hit me the wrong way. Is there a garbage can around here?"

I nod to my left. "There's one at the playground. We can loop past it and take a different route back to my house if you want."

"Do you mind if we go now? I don't think I can stand smelling this anymore."

We get up and walk to the rec area, where the pool, tennis court, playground, and clubhouse are clustered at the center of the subdivision. Once Joel's coffee is in the trash, he doesn't seem as anxious to leave. We sit down on the swings and rock back and forth with quiet, absent glides.

I try to go a little higher, then realize almost immediately that it's a bad idea. I assume Joel has done the same when he suddenly stops, trenches forming in the wood chips where he plants his feet. As I'm scrambling to slow myself, he blurts, "Do you want to go to homecoming with me?"

I gawk at him as I drag my feet along the ground, forcing myself to a complete stop. I half expected puke to come out of his mouth. I did not expect *that*.

"Really?" I finally say.

Joel smiles. "Are you that shocked?" Then his expression changes abruptly. "Or do you not want to be seen on the arm of a former Pirate? Are you afraid I'll embarrass you?"

"No. God—you know I don't give a rat's ass about all that Pirate crap. I just—" I clap my hand over my mouth, but a giggle escapes anyway. *"Really?"*

Joel's grin returns. "Is that a yes?"

I nod, suddenly grasping that I got asked to homecoming by Joel Hargrove. While sitting on a swing set, hungover, in sweats, and not wearing a drop of makeup. I don't even have my camera to capture the moment.

And it could not be more perfect.

Twenty-Two

SENIOR YEAR

YOU'LL NEVER BELIEVE WHO I JUST PICKED UP OFF THE STREET.

Jadie's text reaches my phone a few minutes before her car pulls into my driveway. We're shooting the pennant hunt for the yearbook, and she volunteered to give me a ride.

And apparently she's giving one to Noah, too. Because he's sitting in the passenger seat of her car. When I reach the driveway, he steps out and motions for me to take his place while he folds himself into the cramped backseat.

"Wow, talk about an odd couple," I say as I shut myself into the car.

Jadie's head ticks toward Noah. Her black hair is in two French braids, and she's wearing cat-eye sunglasses. "Pirate Booty was having car troubles."

"My own fault," Noah adds. "I've been procrastinating taking it in for a recall. It picked today to bite me in the ass."

"He was standing in his driveway with his car and a puddle." Jadie shakes her head as she backs out of my driveway. "That poor car looked as guilty as my dog after he pees on the carpet. I couldn't leave his ass there."

Noah reaches up and squeezes Jadie's shoulder. Not that he has far to go. The car is so small that he's practically sitting between us. "Appreciate it."

Jadie's eyebrows lift and she casts a sidelong glance at Noah's fingers. "He's a handsy one, isn't he?"

A laugh that's half snort bursts from my throat, and I smile at Noah. "Yeah, he is."

"Sorry." Noah coughs and shifts back a little, or as much as he can when he's taking up half the car and sharing his seat with the Yearbook Club camera and Jadie's purse. He nods toward the lens staring up at him. "So how'd you both end up on photographer duty? Didn't feel like flipping a coin?"

"It's too hard for one person to cover the whole park after everyone scatters like cockroaches. Two people makes it easier," Jadie says.

"Plus Jadie is lost without me."

"Damn right. Oh!" Jadie holds up her pointer finger. "That reminds me—I recruited Renata Higgins and Criselle Woodley to help us with the homecoming bulletin board. It's gonna be awesome."

"Are they going to homecoming together?"

Jadie nods. "Renata posted a picture on the RF page this morning. You didn't see it?"

"These two girls?" Noah asks. To my surprise, he has the Ridgedale's Finest page up on his phone. He turns it toward me, and I smile at the picture of Criselle holding an armful of sunflowers while Renata beams next to her, dreadlocks wound atop her head.

"That's them," I confirm.

"Huh. Two girls going to homecoming together." There's definite appreciation in Noah's voice, but the way he looks at me when he says it makes me squirm. Like he's reminding me that he also did some asking, and never got an answer.

Jadie looks at him in the rearview mirror. "They do have lady parts, yes. Would you also like me to verify that they're black?" They both laugh, and I can tell that she's warming up to him. Even if she does call him "Pirate Booty."

"No, I think that's great," Noah says. "And even greater that no one's giving them shit for it."

"Give it five minutes," Jadie scoffs.

I nod, recalling the time someone wrote the word "dyke" on Renata's locker after she came out freshman year.

Noah settles into the seat and folds his hands behind his head. "Still. Some schools won't even allow same-sex couples at dances and stuff like that. Ridgedale's at least got the right idea."

"Too bad a school's policies can't change all the ignorant

people who go there," Jadie grumbles, and I know she's not just talking about Renata anymore.

Noah leans forward so that his face is right between ours. "Well, I'd be the last person to have a problem with it. Especially since they both have a date for homecoming"— he turns and fixes an expectant stare on me—"and that puts them one step ahead of me."

Jadie's jaw drops. "Not exactly the king of subtlety there, are you, Pirate Booty?"

Both of their eyes are on me now, and I practically jump out of the car when I realize we've reached the Old Mill parking lot. "We're here!" I announce a little too loudly.

We all climb out, and Noah hands Jadie her camera. She snaps a picture as he scoops me off the ground and throws me over his shoulder like a sack of flour.

"Forget I said that," he whispers.

"Put me down first."

He does, and holds out his hand. When I hesitate to take it, he adds, "No pressure, I swear."

The camera clicks again as my hand slides into his. "I'll deny saying this later," Jadie says as she adjusts the lens. "But you two make a cute couple."

As if by mutual agreement, Noah and I drop our hands. There are a lot of words I'd use to describe the relationship between him and me. But I'm not sure "couple" is one of them. And I think we both realize we need to make that call before anyone else gets used to the idea.

* * *

Meredith is in her element as leader of the hunt. We're all gathered at the large, semicircular observation deck that overlooks the creek, where she and Tyrell are standing with their hands behind their backs, scanning the group like camp counselors taking stock of their charges. Jadie and I have drifted to opposite sides of the group, circling with our cameras.

"Listen up, everybody!" Meredith calls, clapping her hands. As well as she can, anyway, considering she's holding an air horn. A few of the football players hoot and holler, and Tyrell holds his arms out toward her like he's giving her the floor. The look on his face says, *Shut up and pay attention.* Except for when he winks at Jadie. "Thanks for coming to the new and improved pennant hunt!" Meredith lets out a whoop, and Tyrell claps his hands, prompting the rest of the group to do the same.

I have to wonder what's so new and improved about it.

"So y'all know the rules," Tyrell says. "Six flags per team are hidden somewhere on the grounds, and your job is to recover as many as you can of your team's assigned color. You have one hour to report back here with your pennants."

"And," Meredith adds, stepping forward to quiet the predispersal rumblings. "Thanks to Noah Granger, number forty-two"—she points to the back of the crowd, where Noah is standing with his arms folded across his chest—"we have a little added incentive this year. The winning team gets Friday Night Eats on the losers. *And.*" She pauses for dramatic effect. "In addition to the blue and white flags you know to look for, there is also a purple flag hidden somewhere in the park. The person who finds it and brings it to Tyrell or me will get an automatic nomination for homecoming court." She waits, a look of satisfaction on her face at the excited claps and gasps ringing out around us.

If Noah was looking for a way to charm the pants off Meredith Kopala, getting people excited about the pennant hunt is definitely it. I catch his eye, silently asking when this happened and why I didn't know about it. He responds with a satisfied quirk of his lips.

"There's more," Meredith adds. "The person who finds the purple flag will also get to choose one more name to add to the ballot."

More enthusiastic buzz hums through the group, and a few of the football players give Noah looks of approval.

"Okay, guys," Tyrell shouts before he can lose us to the increasing frequency of chatter. "Try to stay in groups of two or more. When you find a flag, deliver it here to Meredith or me at this observation deck. When all the flags have been recovered, or at the end of one hour, whichever comes first, we'll sound the air horn." He points to Meredith, who holds it over her head. "That's your cue to stop what you're doing and report back. Everybody ready?"

There's a chorus of shouting and clapping, and then Meredith yells, "And . . . GO!" sending the first shrill blare into the sky.

Everyone takes off running, and Jadie seizes the opportunity to leap into Tyrell's arms and smack a giant kiss on his lips. "You start at the bridge," she calls out to me. "I'll go down to the creek. Meet me back here ten minutes before time's up."

It's not as surreal as I thought it would be, being on the flip side of the pennant hunt. I'm still at the center of the action, even if I'm not scaling trees and bridge posts in order to oust felt triangles from their hiding spots. It's a different kind of reward to chase the players with my camera, to capture their determination and their flails of victory. And I kind of like seeing it from this angle.

Still, it's hard not to feel a little nostalgic when I pass by the piece of abandoned machinery where I snatched the final pennant of the sophomore-year hunt. I almost broke my ankle in the process, but I limped to the finish line waving that flag over my head like it was one of Willy Wonka's golden tickets.

I pause when there's a rustle of movement on the opposite side of the wood barricade that surrounds the potbellied hunk of black metal. And raise my camera to my face when I spy a familiar muscular frame on tiptoe, reaching toward a ribbon of blue concealed in the same overgrowth as my flag two years ago.

Noah's footing falters at the sound of my camera's click, and the grin he flashes when he spots me makes me laugh— like he's embarrassed that he got caught taking this seriously.

"Found one," he says, brandishing the blue felt.

"Look at that. You don't even need to use it to cover your junk," I tease, recalling our first conversation about the hunt. I snap a picture of the face he makes at me. "Or is that your real plan for the purple one?"

"Were you surprised by that little tidbit?"

"You've been surprising me since the minute we met, Noah Granger."

He looks beyond pleased with himself. "There's no point in sweating our asses off out here for bragging rights and a picture. There needed to be more to it. So I brought up the idea to Tyrell, he ran it by Meredith, and they got it approved. It's no extra work to put another name on the ballot, and this way, maybe someone gets a shot who might not have had one." He fakes like he's going to throw the pennant at my face, then snatches it back at the last second. "I'm all about helping the underdog."

"I don't know if I'd call a crew of cheerleaders and football players 'underdogs,' but I admit"—I give him an approving once-over—"I'm impressed with the thought you put into it."

"Who knows? Maybe we'll end up on the homecoming court together. You and me, at the same time."

"That is generally the definition of 'together,'" I counter. "Though there's a better chance that unicorns will fly out of my ass."

Noah raises an eyebrow. "Are you talking about the odds of making the court, or the odds of the word 'together' describing you and me at homecoming?"

I twist the lens of my camera, knowing I can't put this off much longer. "It's not that I don't want to go to homecoming with you, Noah. It's that I . . . I have conditions."

He tucks the flags into his pocket and folds his arms across his chest. "And they are?"

"First, we go as friends." Noah's expression doesn't change, so I can only assume he expected me to say as much. Which is more than I can say for myself. I take a deep breath. "And second, you said you had not-so-honorable intentions when you asked me the first time. I want to know what they were."

At this he sighs like he would've preferred I ask him to shave my name into his hair. "It's not that big a deal—"

"Good." I make the word clipped, with no room for argument. "Then you won't have a problem telling me. Because last year I ended up dateless and on the outs with two of my best friends, and I'd rather not do that again."

Noah's eyebrows slant. "Wait, really?"

I nod. "Joel ditched me at the last minute. And then our homecoming float burned down that same night. He, um, takes full responsibility for one. But not the other."

Noah rubs at his chin, and from the pensive expression on his face, I can tell that at least some of this is news to him. And that he's not happy about it.

"Wow." He runs his palm along the underside of his jaw. "I heard about the fire. I saw it in the paper, or something. But I didn't know that you thought Joel had anything to do with it. Or that he bailed on taking you to the dance." He laughs, but there's an uncharacteristic skittishness to it. "I guess I should feel a little less like a prick in comparison."

"Because?"

He exhales another quick huff like he wants to get this over with. "Because you were right. I know you think that my asking you was part of the shit between Hargrove and me, and I'd be lying if I said it wasn't at least a small one." He squeezes my arm like he's afraid I might make a run for it. "I don't want you to think for a second that I don't really like you, Mace. I do."

There's a but. I know there's a but, because suddenly he's looking at me the same way that Joel does. Like there's something he can't say, and he's begging me to read his mind and say it for him.

"But you lied about kissing me on the football field," I say softly.

"Hey, what are you two doing back there?"

My and Noah's heads snap in the direction of the intruding voice. The ivy rustles as Ken Davenport lumbers into our hiding spot, the look on his face as smarmy as if he'd caught us with our pants down.

"Wow, Macy, you've really got a thing for Pirate dick, don't you?"

My face contorts with disgust, but I don't get the chance to respond before Noah steps in front of me and gets right in Ken's face.

"I don't see any Pirates, but I sure as hell see a dick." He spits the words with pure venom and then knocks Ken to the ground with an effortless, one-handed shove. Noah pulls me out of the brush while Ken's friend, a kid whose name I always forget but I know that his number is eighty-eight, scrambles to help him up. "Let's go, Mace."

I don't get a chance to say anything else, even though I'm dying for him to answer the question that Ken interrupted. But Jadie is waving me over in the distance, and Meredith and Tyrell are yelling the ten-minute warning from the observation deck above. So I tell Noah we'll pick this up later, and we part ways.

"No one's found the purple flag yet," Jadie says. "We might have to go into overtime. That's our moneymaker."

"'Moneymaker'? How did you go from joining Yearbook Club out of boredom to talking like paparazzi?"

She sticks her tongue out, her camera beeping as she flips through her shots. "Tyrell told me to stay near the waterfall, but I don't know how we're supposed to hang out there without giving it away."

"I think whoever finds it should nominate *you*," I say. "Right in front of Ken. It'll be the perfect revenge. I could highlight you on the blog and every—"

"Don't want it," Jadie cuts in. "I already told Tyrell. If anyone nominates me, I'm declining."

"*Why?*"

She looks up from her camera. "I love him. So I can't blame everybody else for loving him too. It basically goes without saying that he'll make the court, but that doesn't mean I want in. I'd rather shave my head as bald as Tyrell's before I accept pity votes from the same people who treated me like a joke at the diner last year."

"You really don't want to be on the homecoming court? I think you deserve it more than anyone else."

"That's just it, Macy. I don't need to earn my place with Tyrell, no matter what anyone thinks. Whichever girl stands next to him wearing a sash and a fake crown, he's still leaving with me. It's all a popularity contest, and I don't care enough about what other people think to put on a show for them."

I close my hand over my locket. Maybe, while she's being brutally honest, there's something else I should get her opinion on.

"Jadie, do you think I'm making a huge mistake by try-ing to be friends with Joel again?"

An expression that resembles nausea crosses her face. "Does this mean you said yes to homecoming?"

"He actually took back the invitation. He told me to go with Noah."

Jadie's jaw drops. "He did not."

"He did so."

She stops again and pulls me aside. "Honestly? Know what that sounds like to me? A giant. Red." She holds up the review pane of her camera, tapping the white pennant being waved by Anna Chen on the screen. "Flag." She lowers the camera and touches my wrist, guiding me up the rocky path toward the waterfall. "Look, I'm not saying this because I think Joel is, like, inherently a douche-us maximus, or even totally unredeemable. But you know how my parents bought me that book of Chinese fables as part of the whole keeping-in-touch-with-my-heritage thing? This situation with Joel reminds me of one of them.

"So in it, an officer is interrogating a bunch of suspects about a crime that no one is fessing up to. He tells them he has a magical clock that will chime when the perp touches it— or, you know, whatever you call an ancient Chinese criminal. So anyway, they all go into a room one by one to touch the clock, and as they come out, the officer examines their hands. Even though the clock didn't chime, he grabs one of the men and screams that he's the guilty one, and the guy faints in terror. Because, obvs, he committed the crime. And the way the officer figured it out was because he'd painted a layer of ink on top of the clock, knowing that the culprit's guilt would probably make him too afraid to touch it."

"Okay," I say, not sure where she's going with this. "Interesting."

"So what I'm saying is, Joel did an über-crappy thing by bailing on you last year. And the float burning down right after is beyond suspicious, and I think he knows both of those things. *But.* No matter how bad he feels, or how much he wants to take you to the dance this year, something is stopping him. So I have to wonder if homecoming is Joel's version of the clock. Or maybe it's *you.* The thing he feels too guilty to get close to, you know? It just seems like if he's inviting you and then taking it back, then maybe it's not such a good idea to trust him. Because it sounds like he doesn't even trust himself."

Her words settle deeper into my brain as we continue walking. I'm not sure I want to admit how much sense they actually make. Not only does it explain why Joel seems to be withdrawing—again—but it also explains why he hasn't come forward if he's the one who kissed me at the football game. I've been wavering over whether or not I'm willing to go down this road with him, but it looks more and more like Joel has already made the decision for me.

Twenty-Three

My first stop on Monday morning is Meredith's locker.

"Hey," I say as I come up beside her. "I'm sorry I've been MIA all weekend. My parents confiscated my phone as soon as I got home."

"The float came out awesome, in case you were wondering. And I saw the pictures you probably don't remember texting me. Looks like the crime was worth the punishment."

It's a jab, not an observation. Meredith needs to be in the center of the action at all times, and she hates when she's not. Especially when it means that I spent the night at Ben's house and she didn't. But I hope that when I tell her my news, it'll buff out some of the soreness.

"Definitely worth it. Joel asked me to homecoming."

Sure enough, her eyes get huge and bright and she gasps for ten straight seconds. "Shut up!"

I clasp her hands and try to control the involuntary bouncing that happens every time I think about it. "I know!" I lower my voice, but the words still come in an excited rush. "And I'm almost positive that your invitation is coming next. Ben told me he needs a favor from me."

"What kind of favor?"

"I don't know yet. Phonegate happened before I could find out. But I was going to his locker next, so—"

"Then why are you still standing here?" she cuts in, all evidence of her previous attitude gone. "Go!"

So I do. I run, actually. Until I get close enough to sneak up on Ben at his locker, poking both sides of his waist.

"You didn't warn me," I say. He jumps, almost dropping the book he's loading into his bag, and I giggle. "Ticklish?"

"Maybe." He slams the locker door. "And anyway, you didn't warn me either."

"About what?"

He pulls his phone out of his pocket and holds it up. "That your mom would be answering your texts for the rest of the weekend. Though I kind of figured something was up when you didn't check in."

I tell him the story of my post-slushie welcoming and consequent grounding as we head down the hall. When I get to the part about Joel surviving my parents' interrogation, I say, "So did you know he was planning to ask me to homecoming or what? Because if you did, you're not a very good informant."

I'm 100 percent teasing him. But Ben stops and stares at me like I sucker punched him.

"He did?"

There are so many possible ways to read those two simple words. I can't tell if Ben is upset that Joel didn't tell him first, upset that he still hasn't found the courage to ask Meredith, or just upset, period.

"I guess he didn't tell you?"

"That's putting it lightly." He shakes his head. "He told me he wasn't going at all." His voice rises on the last word, like he's working very hard to subdue a tidal wave of anger.

"Well, I guess he changed his mind? It seemed pretty spur-of-the-moment, if that makes you feel any better. I'm sure he would've told you if he'd thought about it."

Even as my mouth is running, I'm racking my brain for reasons why it matters so much. And it occurs to me that maybe Ben was stalling on asking Meredith until he could convince Joel to go with me. It makes sense that he feels a little slighted in that case, and if it's true, then I can add it to the list of things I owe him for—

"Oh!" I say. "I never got the chance to ask about the favor you wanted. I meant to, and then my cell phone got taken away. So what did you need?"

Ben lifts the straps of his bag off his shoulders and shrugs. It's a gesture so small and sad that it makes my heart sink. "Forget it," he says. "I'm an idiot."

I reach for his arm when he tries to turn away. "Ben? What's wrong?"

"Nothing. It's pointless."

"You didn't think it was pointless yesterday."

He detaches me from his sleeve, and something shifts between us, the kind of shift that makes my stomach feel both too full and too small.

"Yesterday's not today."

The rest of the week is a blur. Ben finally asked Meredith to homecoming by holding up a sign in his bedroom window as she stood in front of hers, and everything after that has been a whirlwind of preparation and pep rallies and appointments.

Speaking of which, I can't keep the grin off my face as my hairdresser turns me loose from her chair, my hair a masterpiece of flowy tendrils. I've already had my nails painted with a sheen of iridescent sparkle, and I can't wait to see how it looks against the sparkly lavender fabric of my dress.

I also can't wait to see Joel's face when he sees me. I can't wait to see *him* in a suit. I can't wait to see him, period. My excitement levels are a little ridiculous, and I could not care less.

My mother *ooh*s and *aah*s as I turn to face her, as does pretty much everyone in the salon. The girl who takes my place in the chair says, "Do mine like that." And I don't blame her one bit.

"Not to be the heavy," Mom says as we shut our respective car doors in the parking lot. "But I want your word that you're going to be safe tonight. No repeat performances of the last time you went out with this Joel character."

"He's not a *character*, Mom. He's a boy. And we'll be fine. I promise."

"And you'll check in with me if you're running late, or if your plans change?"

"Cross my heart."

"Good." She smiles lovingly and brushes a tendril away from my face. "You look beautiful."

I settle into my seat and reach for my purse to see if I have any new messages as Mom puts the car in gear. When I pull out my cell, there's a text from Joel. My heart pumps a little harder. I wonder if he's as excited as I am.

When I open the message, I have to read it three times before it registers. My hands go cold and clammy around the phone.

I'm sorry but I can't make it tonight. Mom got called into work and I have to watch my brothers.

My mother must hear the air rushing from my lungs, because her head snaps toward me and she asks what's wrong.

I have to stare at the screen for a few more seconds before I can turn the croak in my throat into an answer. "Joel canceled. He says he has to watch his brothers tonight so his mom can work."

"*What?*" It's a miracle that we don't swerve into oncoming traffic with the intensity of her reaction. "Can't she switch with someone? Can't someone else watch them? It's three hours before the dance!"

"I guess not." I've graduated from shocked to numb. "It's not his fault, Mom."

But that doesn't stop my throat from constricting with the threat of tears. I can't believe this is happening.

"I'd babysit them myself if we didn't have the boys' banquet tonight. I just don't understand how this could—" Mom holds up her hand, takes a deep breath, and composes herself. "I'm not letting this night be ruined for either one of you. We'll figure something out." She keeps one hand on the wheel and digs in her purse on top of the center console with the other. "You said Joel lives in Willowbrook, right? The Miltons live there too. Remember Agnes? She watched Michael when Aaron had his accident. Her son doesn't play soccer anymore, so she won't be at the banquet. I'm sure she wouldn't have a problem taking Joel's brothers for a few hours."

I'm filled with hope so quickly that I'm surprised it doesn't emanate from my body like beams of light. "You think so?"

"I'm certainly going to ask. If she can't do it, maybe she can recommend someone else in their neighborhood."

Mom is already on the phone with Mrs. Milton as we pull into our driveway. She orders me to go upstairs and do my makeup, as if a change in plans isn't even a possibility. And because everything in me wants to believe it, I go. But first I send a message back to Joel.

Sɪᴛ ᴛɪɢʜᴛ. Wᴇ ʜᴀᴠᴇ ᴀ ᴘʟᴀɴ.

I try to stay calm while I put on my face, but it's not easy. Especially when outside the bathroom, my house is chaos. Michael and Aaron are fighting over the guitar that Ben left for Aaron to practice with. I jump every time my mom's cell phone rings, which feels like every five minutes.

Meanwhile, mine remains eerily silent.

The mirror betrays the shake in my hands when I'm finishing off with a coat of mascara. And that's when Mom appears in the doorframe. One look at her face tells me everything I need to know.

"So Mrs. Milton was more than willing to take Joel's brothers tonight," she says softly. "But we kept getting voice mail when we called the number you gave us. She thought maybe there was a problem with the phone, so she took it upon herself to go over to the Hargroves' house." Anger flashes in her eyes when she pauses, and all I can do is wait for the bomb to drop. "Joel's mother isn't at work, honey. She answered the door. Joel, on the other hand, was nowhere to be found."

I sit down hard on the edge of the tub, cold prickles of nausea climbing up my throat. Why would he lie to me?

Mom sets her cell phone on the sink and kneels in front of me. "I'm so sorry, Macy. Mrs. Hargrove had no idea that Joel had used her as a cover. He actually told her that *you* canceled on *him*. She tried calling him as soon as Agnes explained what was going on, but apparently he's turned off his phone." Her teeth clench. "He must know he's going to have a lot of people to answer to for this. Including me."

She looks ready to kill him with her bare hands. But all I can feel are waves of devastation crashing over me. The excitement that was building all day—since Joel asked me to the dance, really—bursts all around me, as fragile and fleeting as soap bubbles.

And when my mother pulls me to her and hugs me tight, I can't hold back. Rivers of painstakingly applied mascara flow down my cheeks and into her shoulder, while chords of "Smoke on the Water" drown out the sound of my sobs.

Twenty-Four

SENIOR YEAR

There's a ruckus near the waterfall, and Jadie gasps. "Shit! We missed it!"

We both take off toward the noise, negotiating the rocky incline of the creek bed as fast as we can. The word "Rigged" is shouted seconds before I see Noah sauntering toward us, one arm raised above his head and a shit-eating grin on his face.

He's holding the purple pennant.

"Rigged!" number eighty-eight shouts again. "Riiiiiigged!"

"Whatever helps you sleep tonight, you sore-ass loser," Noah claps back, never breaking his stride. He tosses the flag into the air and snatches it in a victorious fist.

Meredith's head pokes over the guardrail at the observation deck, and she yelps, "The purple flag has been found!"

The air horn wails, followed by groans and shouts and the sound of feet rushing to reconvene from all over the park. Luckily, Jadie's snapping away with her camera, because I forget mine even exists.

"You know what they're thinking, right?" I say in a hushed voice when Noah reaches my side.

"Of course. That because it was my idea, I somehow cheated. The real question is, do I give a shit?" He clears the steps to the observation deck two at a time, clutching the pennant high over his head. In other words: *not a single one.*

When we reach the deck, Meredith positions Noah between herself and Tyrell and waits a moment for the stragglers. The more people gather, the louder the protests become when they see Noah holding the purple flag.

"Look at them," Jadie whispers. "Five seconds into not getting their way, and they've all reverted to two-years-old."

And Ken, of course, is the loudest of them all. "What the fuck, Tyrell?" he barks. "Why'd we even bother coming if the whole thing was a fix? Granger should be disqualified."

"*Hey,*" Tyrell booms, raising both arms above his head to quiet the protests. "Y'all need to take a seat. The purple flag was Noah's idea, but the only people in this park who knew where it was hidden are Meredith and *me.* Nothing was rigged. Nobody cheated. *Are we clear?*"

"He's so hot when he's authoritative," Jadie says, and I swear her eyes actually turn to hearts.

"So if we're done being sore sports," Tyrell continues,

"I suggest we give it up for the cheerleaders and Noah Granger, winners of this year's pennant hunt." He slams his hands together in three loud claps. The rest of the group follows his lead, though only half of them applaud with any kind of enthusiasm.

"All right, Noah," Meredith says. "You know what this means. Your name will officially appear on the ballot for the homecoming court, and you'll get to choose one other partner in crime." I wince. If people think Noah cheated, that wasn't the best choice of words. "You'll have until Monday to decide on your nomination—"

"I don't need until Monday," Noah cuts in, rocking on his heels. His gaze fixes on me. "I nominate Macy Atwood."

My jaw drops. There's a rustle of gasps before Jadie gleefully shoves me off-balance, and then I'm trying my hardest to pretend that every eye in a ten-foot radius isn't on me. I've stood in front of crowds fifty times this size and never felt as scrutinized.

"Macy!" Meredith trills. "Noah Granger has nominated you for the homecoming court. Do you accept?"

Joel told me I'd be doing myself a favor if I went to homecoming with Noah. And Ben warned me against going with Joel. What do I have to lose?

"Of course she does," Ken says before I can respond. "Macy can't get enough of Pirate—"

"I ACCEPT," I say, drowning out the predictable rest of his comment. Under my breath I grumble, "Come up with some new material, Ken."

I make my way to the center of the deck amid lackluster applause, at least from the cheerleaders. And I guess I get it, because I'm no longer part of their camp. I voluntarily hung up my pom-poms when I feared they all saw me as a traitor after the fire last year. But that doesn't take away the sting of knowing my fears weren't unfounded.

"Pretty sure I just saw a unicorn fly out of your ass," Noah murmurs with a wink.

"Congratulations, Macy," Meredith says quietly. She turns to the crowd. "Cheer girls! Assemble for a winners' picture!"

While she's distracted organizing the squad, Noah leans in to me. "Mace," he whispers. "If I tell you that I wish it *had* been me who kissed you on the field . . . can I still be your date for homecoming?"

I look up at him. I shouldn't feel like a block of granite dropped into my stomach—I suspected it all along.

In my head, I always knew the kiss might've been a fluke. A tasteless joke. Someone taking advantage of being in the right place at the right time.

In my heart, I wanted to believe it was so, so much more than that.

And until two seconds ago, there was at least someone who wanted to take credit for being part of it. Now all I have is a memory that obviously meant nothing to the person I shared it with.

"Did you know Joel works at the Mill Club?" I demand.

"Was that why you brought me here to ask me to homecoming?"

Guilt floods Noah's eyes. "It—might have had something to do with it."

I turn away with a disgusted sound and put a step of distance between us. *Less than honorable. Pff.* What a jerk.

Noah hangs his head. "So I guess that's a no?"

The disappointment in his voice is the first blow to my resistance. The second is the fact that I asked him to be straight with me, and now I feel like I'm punishing him for it. But the third, as much as I hate myself for it, is the realization that I might have to go to homecoming alone again this year.

Been there, done that.

"I get it, Mace," Noah says solemnly. "I hope you find whoever kissed you."

I sigh. If we're really going to wipe the slate clean, then I need to check my wounded ego at the door. "Do you really want to go with me to homecoming? Because whoever he was, he doesn't. So—"

The side of Noah's hand brushes against mine. "It's a date. As friends?"

I hook my fingers around his and give them a quick squeeze. "Friends."

Jadie's camera clicks as Noah hugs me to his side. I wonder if my guilt will show in the pictures. Because I'm thinking of Joel, and the haunted look in his eyes the last time we talked. And even though he's sent me signals more mixed than a salad and I have every reason to believe that he's chosen to walk away from me yet again, I feel like I might've made this decision a little hastily.

But as I scoot closer to Noah and stare into Jadie's lens, I have to believe that a hasty decision isn't necessarily the wrong one.

The hunt lasted only an hour, and the post-hunt swim about another. But I feel like I pulled an all-nighter. My head is pressed against the glass of Jadie's passenger side window, and I'm only half listening as she and Noah joke about their homecoming outfits. He's teasing that he's going to make me wear a tux while he wears a dress as a show of support for Renata and Criselle.

"Watch what you say, Pirate Booty," Jadie says, her finger pointing backward at Noah's face. "She'll totally hold you to it." When I don't answer right away, she pokes my side. "Back me up here, Macy."

I sit up straight. "Noah can wear a dress if he wants, but I only got to wear mine for all of five minutes last year. I have lost time to make up for."

I hope he doesn't call me on the half-assed smile I flash. Drama aside, going to the dance with Noah will be a great time, and that's all that should matter. Whatever my problem is, it's not his fault.

We pull into the Arbor Creek entrance, and I'm kind

of wishing I'd had Jadie bring me straight home instead of agreeing to stop at her house and powwow about the next RF spotlight and the homecoming bulletin board after we drop off Noah. It shouldn't take long, but it seemed like a better idea when we came up with it yesterday.

Especially when we pull up to Noah's house, and I see his car still sitting in the driveway.

"What the hell?" he says under his breath. "My dad was supposed to call the tow truck."

If I'd never fallen down the rabbit hole of looking at my photos from last year, the University of Georgia Bulldogs decal that I'd never noticed on Noah's rear window wouldn't mean a thing to me. Except that it had also appeared in the background of at least four of those pictures. On a car the same shade of electric blue.

The jerk in the blue car.

All I can hear is Joel's voice in my head.

My parents almost took out a restraining order against him.

Noah's father appears at the front door, waving his son into the house. I have to get out of the car to free him from the back, and while he's fiddling with the lever to release the seat, I swipe through my phone to take another look at the pictures I sent myself. A quick zoom of one of my and Joel's drunken selfies confirms it. Not only is the car the same, but that's definitely Noah, a year younger and with much shorter hair, leaning against the rear fender.

Glaring at us.

I click out of the screen as Noah emerges from the car and hide the phone behind my back. He tells me he'll call me later and leans in to hug me.

His eyebrows knit together at my stiff response. "You sure you're all right?"

I nod. I'm also sure that Noah is the jerk in the blue car.

And that there's way more to his rivalry with Joel than either of them is telling me.

Twenty-Five

JUNIOR YEAR

Meredith steps away from me to assess her work, grinning as she closes the tube of lip gloss with a triumphant snap. "You look *amazing*, Macy Jean."

I don't know how I let myself be convinced to go to the dance. Walking into homecoming alone is right up there with "lick a tarantula" on my list of things I have zero desire to ever do. But my friends rallied so fast and so fiercely that I didn't have much choice. Meredith practically flew over to my house, her hair still in rollers, her makeup half-done, and fuzzy blue slippers on her feet. She'd barely set foot in the front door when my phone started blowing up with calls and texts from other girls on the squad, begging me not to let Joel ruin the night.

It's a little late for that. But I don't want to seem weak. I don't want Joel to think he got the better of me, even if he did. And I don't want to turn my back on the people who actually want to be around me on account of the one person who doesn't. So I found myself sitting on the toilet cover, letting Meredith fix my wrecked makeup while she and my mother buoyed me with compliments and one-upping each other thinking up appropriate punishments for Joel.

"Forget running him up the school's flagpole by his boxers," Mom says, leaning against the bathroom doorframe. "When he sees what he missed out on, he'll be kicking himself until his butt is bruised."

When I step in front of the mirror, I can't help but agree. Meredith did a fantastic job of hiding the blotchy, puffy evidence of my disappointment. And when I put my dress on, the reflection staring back at me is as pretty as a picture.

I just wish she didn't look so sad.

It's not so bad at first, being at homecoming without a date. My friends take extra care to stick by me, bringing me punch and dragging me out to the dance floor every five minutes. It's not that I'm not still disappointed and hurt and confused. But for a while, the feeling of being loved is like a bandage, holding together the pieces of me that are threatening to fall apart.

A short while. Because soon enough the fun, upbeat music gives way to a sweet, slow guitar melody. Everyone starts heading to the dance floor in pairs, and I'm staring at my hands and feet, hoping no one makes a big deal if I sit out. Hoping even harder that no one tries to force me into a slow dance three-way, the most uncomfortable act of third-wheeldom I could imagine.

Jadie says, "Be back in a minute, Macy," as Tyrell leads her to the center of the gym. I gather the skirt of my dress and take a seat a few bleachers up. It's the first time since Meredith showed up at my door in fuzzy blue slippers that I've been alone with my thoughts, and they waste no time wandering into dangerous territory.

I don't get it. It's not like I coerced the invitation out of Joel; he seemed so happy when he asked. And yet at some point he'd told Ben that he wasn't going to the dance at all. Whatever happened to change his mind, it obviously didn't stick. Because I'm here. And he's not.

As I watch all the couples sway, I can't help it: I'm uncomfortable. And worse, I'm jealous. Each beat of the music is like a chisel, chipping mercilessly at my mask of indifference. I'm supposed to be out there with them, with Joel. Laughing, dancing, having a good time. Not sitting by myself, wondering why he decided that the last place he wanted to be tonight was with me. What the hell did I do wrong? And how many more times will I have to retreat to this spot tonight, asking myself the same damn question?

I don't want to stick around to find out. I thought I could do this. And maybe I can, but the truth is, I don't want to.

So I grab my stuff and hurry down the bleachers, then

make my way along the wall to the closest exit. I'm supposed to spend the night at Meredith's after the dance; all the cheerleaders are. The homecoming parade is tomorrow afternoon, and we thought it made sense to have everyone crash in one place, especially since it's the place where the float is located. But I just want to curl up in my own bed. I have my house keys, and it's not far to walk home. I'm sure Meredith will forgive me for meeting them there tomorrow.

For walking out on the dance . . . that might be a different story.

The tightness in my throat releases a little as soon as I step out into the cool night air. I fill my lungs with it, telling myself that if I can wait until I'm home to crumble, then maybe I won't have to fall apart at all. I don't want to waste one more tear on someone who handles a football with more care than he handled my feelings.

I make it a few steps down the sidewalk that lines the parking lot before the door I just exited crashes open behind me.

To my surprise, Ben comes flying out. The sleeves of his dress shirt are rolled up to his elbows, and the black-and-blue tie he chose to match Meredith's dress flaps against his torso. "Macy? Where are you going?"

"Home."

"No, no, no." He clears the steps in what looks like one leap, and then he's at my side, gently taking my arm. "What are you gonna do, walk? I'm not letting that happen. Please come back inside."

"I'll be fine walking. I brought flip-flops." I hold up the small Godiva shopping bag housing my spare footwear, like that makes everything okay. I try to pull my arm away, but he doesn't relinquish it. "Please let me go. I just want to get out of here."

"Mace, I'm really sorry about Joel. If I'd had any idea that he was going to pull something like this, I would've—I don't know, done something. Warned you. Somehow." He exhales, and it's such a remorseful sound that I feel like I should be comforting him instead of the other way around. "I should've warned you," he says again.

"How could you warn me about something you didn't know was going to happen?" Unless— "Did he say something to you? About any of this? Because the way you reacted when you found out he'd asked me was . . . a little strange."

Ben looks at the ground and releases my arm, putting his hands into the pockets of his pants. "I was mad at him for something else, and I guess I kind of took it out on you. I didn't mean to."

"Why were you mad at him?"

He starts to say something, then stops. "It's complicated. And what he did tonight is way worse. But still." He takes a step closer. "Please don't leave."

"Look, Ben." I squeeze his hand. "I really appreciate everyone trying so hard to make this better. But I don't feel better at all. I feel . . ." The knot in my throat springs back to life, strangling my last words. "So stupid." And now I feel even dumber for being on the verge of tears, so I gather the skirt of my dress and say, "I'll see you at the parade tomorrow."

But he holds my arm again when I try to leave. "Wait. You didn't even get to dance."

"Yes, I did."

Mischief lights his eyes. "Going to a dance doesn't count unless you've slow danced at least once." And then he's holding his hand out, offering it to me.

"Ben. I'm not going back inside."

"No need." He takes my shopping bag and places it on the ground, right before leading me over to the streetlight a few paces away. "How about right here? Look, we've even got our own spotlight." He motions at the halo of illumination that falls around us, pooling in a semicircle at our feet. I'm shaking my head. But I'm also smiling, because it's sweet. "Come on, Mace," Ben says, soft but insistent. "One dance, and then I'll take you home myself." He holds out his hand. "Okay?"

My responding "okay" is barely audible. I lay my hand on top of his, and he guides it up to his shoulder, and then we're holding each other the same way we were that day on the homecoming float. Except I'm not Meredith, and this isn't practice.

Which reminds me: "Isn't Meredith going to be looking for you?"

"She had to help with a decoration emergency. I'm sure she won't miss me for a few minutes."

"I bet she will." And maybe it's because my day has been

so tumultuous, or because my emotional energy is all but sapped. But something about being this close to Ben, feeling the warmth of his body, breathing the summer-air scent of his cologne mixed with the smoky smell of lit fireplaces on a crisp autumn night, is the nicest sensation I've experienced in a long time. I want nothing more than to relax into him and stop thinking so much.

So I do. I rest my head beneath his shoulder. For a few quiet seconds, there's only us, and the far-off, dreamlike sound of music escaping the gym.

"Meredith is lucky," I say, more to myself than to anyone else. "You're a keeper, Ben."

One of his hands moves to the center of my back. "So are you, Mace."

Not everybody thinks so. But I let the thought die as a silent frown on my lips, because bringing up Joel doesn't feel worth it anymore.

Twenty-Six

SENIOR YEAR

"Do I just *ask* him about it?" I know it's not the first time I've posed this question to Jadie, but I'm having a hard time focusing right now. "I don't get it. Noah's always made it sound like Joel is the troublemaker. Like he's the reason things are shitty between them. But if that's the case, then why would *Joel* need a restraining order?"

Jadie presses the barrel of a pen against her lips and leans against the wall her bed is pushed up next to. She's sitting cross-legged on top of her kaleidoscope-patterned comforter, looking thoughtful.

"Joel said his *parents* almost took out the restraining order, right? So they might not know the whole story. They could've seen something that made them think Noah was the instiga-

248

tor." She shrugs. "It could've been something. It could've been nothing. Your guess is as good as mine. But I don't see the harm in getting the real story straight from the horse's mouth."

"Which horse?"

"Whichever one will give you an answer."

I should know by now that getting a satisfying answer from Joel about anything is not a likely event. We left things unfinished the last time we talked, and so many times before that. It's like there's some kind of invisible blockade that springs up between us anytime we get within an inch of being 100 percent honest with each other, and I want it gone once and for all. Even if it means I have to ask him point-blank about the kiss in the dark, and face the fact that it meant something to only one of us.

I spot him slipping into the library before first period on Monday, and I hasten in after him. He drops his bag onto an empty table in the back, and in seconds my hand is on the chair next to his.

"Can we talk?"

Joel looks up, and nothing in his expression says that he's glad to see me. "I forgot to study for a quiz and I have ten minutes to cram. No offense."

"None taken." I pull out the chair and sit down anyway. Much to Joel's dismay, if his frown is any indication. "I'll be fast. I promise."

Joel pushes his notebook aside with a grimace, like he's waiting for a punishment.

"Remember when you told me you almost took out a restraining order against someone from Mortonville?" He doesn't react at first, just keeps staring down at the table. I wonder if maybe he *doesn't* remember telling me. But then he nods once, and I continue. "That was Noah, wasn't it?"

Joel turns to me. "Why is this coming up now? I told you about that more than a year ago."

"Because it doesn't make sense to me that one minute you're pushing me off on him for homecoming, telling me I'm better off going with him than with you, and the next minute I realize that you almost had to make it illegal for him to go near you. Seriously, Joel. What's going on here?"

"Look, the restraining order thing, it got blown out of proportion. Noah showed up at my house one night, and my parents caught us fighting and blamed him for the whole thing. We'd already gotten in trouble at school once, and it was like what you said about me with your parents that day. . . . They thought he was corrupting me, or something. Even though we were kind of both being idiots. I still think he's the bigger idiot, but that doesn't mean he's not the better choice. If that makes any sense at all."

"None."

I sit there, hugging my book bag to my chest, staring him down so he knows I'm not going anywhere unless he does better than that.

"Look," he says again, and this time it prickles with condescension. "What it comes down to is that I don't have a chance in hell of giving you what you want. He at least has a shot."

"What exactly is it that you think I want from you, Joel? You asked *me* to homecoming, remember? Both times. All I've ever tried to do is be your friend. And yeah, maybe last year I would've liked more than that, but this year I would've been fine never speaking to you again. So if you went through all this trouble to make up with me just to prove to yourself that you don't feel that way about me, then I'd say that's a pretty shitty thing to do." I stand up and fling my bag over one shoulder. "Almost as shitty as what you did the night of the blackout."

I'm rooted to the spot, watching his reaction. Waiting for the moment of truth. He swallows hard, staring at his thumb as it runs along the edge of the table.

"I guess," he finally says, "that might not have been the best decision." He looks up at me, and guilt and sadness shine in his eyes with a thousand other emotions I can't read. And one that I can.

Relief.

It's plain to see when he forces half of his mouth into a smile and adds, "But at least now you know."

I'm not prepared for how disgusted I feel. Or the lump that forms in my throat.

I push in my chair with such force that the legs stay planted in the carpet and the backrest bounces off the table's edge with a smack. "Yep. I know that you used me and then left me in the dark when you decided I wasn't good enough for you. Although, at this point, I'm starting to think no one is."

It's as much as I can manage without giving in to the shake in my voice. I turn and stalk out of the library as the first bell rings, my body aflame with hurt and rage. I can't believe I let Joel Hargrove ruin even one more minute of my life. I was stupid enough to let my guard down, even with Ben and Noah and an entire parade of warning signs telling me not to.

I'm as angry with myself as I am with him.

Of course, part of me knows I shouldn't be this disappointed. I tried to prepare myself to let go of what I now know for sure was a fantasy that vanished under the glare of stadium lights. I told myself that if the kiss on the football field was more than just a kiss, then the person who initiated it wouldn't stay hidden in the shadows like some kind of reverse Cinderella.

That kiss was my glass slipper. Except, instead of leading me to the prince, it led me to the same brick wall I slammed my head into last year.

Fool me once, shame on you. Fool me twice, shame on me. The first time Joel crushed a piece of my heart, I'd given it to him willingly. The second time, he stole it while I wasn't looking. And then stomped all over it when the lights came up.

Shame on me indeed. I've been blind to so many things. And there's not a blackout in the world that I can blame for it.

Twenty-Seven

JUNIOR YEAR

The thump of Ben's heart beneath my cheek matches the rhythm of the song pulsing from the school. As it reaches its crescendo, Ben pulls his cell phone out of his pocket. "So what do you think about capturing this moment?" he asks, almost like he's afraid I'll turn him down. "I know there're a lot of things about tonight that you probably want to forget. But I'm kind of hoping that right now isn't one of them."

I smile, and it's small but real. "This is probably one of the few things about tonight that I'll actually *want* to remember."

Ben crouches a bit as he extends one arm and drapes the other around my shoulders. I wrap mine around his waist and press my face against his, savoring the last seconds that

I'll get to hug him like this. It's kind of weird to think that I'm going to miss it, but I think it nonetheless. He taps his phone, and the moment we see our faces with the horrendous fish-eye effect of the screen, we burst out laughing, the same way we did the day we danced in Meredith's garage.

"Be cool, be cool," Ben says, forcing his face into a more composed smile. Except that I'm watching him on the screen, and it makes me crack up even harder. And I'm so grateful for the rush of release, for ending this night on a high note—and for him—that I do something even I'm not expecting. I lift up on my toes and kiss his cheek.

The camera clicks, and Ben turns to me, rubbing at the pink imprint of my lips with an embarrassed grin. "Now, that's a keeper," he says, holding up the photo. I agree, and he returns the phone to his pocket.

The song from inside is down to its final notes, and I wrap my arms around him again while I still can. "Thanks, Ben," I whisper into his shoulder.

"Are you sure you won't stay?"

I pull back with a sigh. And even though I mean to say no, when I look up at his face, I forget to actually form the word. He's watching me with those wide, inquisitive eyes, and all I can think is, *You really are beautiful.*

But more than that, I'm thinking about his question. And wondering why staying suddenly doesn't sound like such a bad idea.

The song is over. But something is different. Everything is alive—the air, my body, the space between Ben and me. This should be good-bye, the part where we go our separate ways. Except neither of us moves, and I wonder if he feels it too.

Goose bumps spring up on my skin as his hand travels up my arm. His lips part.

"Ben?" Meredith's voice says. "What's going on out here?"

We shoot away from each other like repelling forces. Meredith is standing in the doorway, holding one of the glass doors open. Any thoughts I had about staying are obliterated when I see the look on her face. I'd give anything to turn the clock back and run off like Cinderella at midnight if it would mean not having to face the wounded, betrayed look in her eyes. Or the fact that I'm the cause of it.

Ben takes a few steps toward her. "Macy's having a tough time, and I saw her trying to sneak out. I followed her so I could convince her not to leave."

Meredith lets the door slam behind her. When her arms wrap around her torso, I can't tell if it's to protect herself from the chill in the air, or from what she saw.

"Looks like you were making quite the effort," she says.

"I wanted to go home instead of sitting out every time a slow song came on," I pipe in. "So Ben gave me a pity dance."

I wince inwardly as the words leave my mouth, because it feels gross and wrong to write it off like that. But I can't let this night be ruined for one more person. Especially not my best friend.

"I was just coming to get you," Ben rushes to add. "I promised I'd take Macy home if she danced with me, and she kept up her end of the bargain. I couldn't convince her to stay."

Meredith snorts. "Since that's obviously what you really want."

"Mer—" Ben starts to say, but cuts off when Meredith's hand shoots up to silence him.

"You know what?" she says. "Why don't I do you both a favor, and *I'll* be the one who leaves?" Her glare cuts over to me. "It's pretty clear who's actually the third wheel here." She laughs, sharp and without humor. "A pity dance. That's a good one, Macy."

My mouth drops open, but my protests are swallowed by the wail of an approaching siren. All three of us turn toward the main road, where a fire truck and an ambulance are hot on each other's trails, turning into the entrance of Scarborough Farms—Ben's and Meredith's neighborhood.

We all notice them at the same time. The wisps of smoke and intermittent flashes of light in the distance. Not someone's fireplace, like I initially thought. An actual fire.

"Oh my God," Meredith says, removing her shoes in one swift motion and rushing down the steps. "That's near my house."

Meredith takes off running, with Ben right on her heels. I follow suit, throwing on my flip-flops and catching up to them as they cross the street. We're only a few paces onto the sidewalk, but it's clear the fire engine is stopping right in front of Meredith's house.

"Oh my God!" she shrieks again. I've never seen her run so fast in my life. I'm panting by the time I reach the edge of her lawn, where Meredith stands with her hands over her mouth, eyes wide and flashing with fear. Ben rubs her arm and babbles words of reassurance, even as smoke pours from all three garage doors and flickers of orange flash behind the glass panes.

The firefighters yell at us to stay back, and an EMT comes over to ask if anyone is in the house. Meredith shakes her head, explaining that her parents went to a play tonight. Her neighbors have started to gather, and one brings a blanket to drape over her shoulders.

"Ben!" someone calls, and I turn to see Mrs. Collins running over from across the street. "My God, what happened?" It's a good thing she doesn't wait for an answer before ushering us to her front porch, because none of us has a clue. "Wait here," she says, indicating their porch swing. "It's safer. Meredith, honey, I'm going to put on some tea, and I'll try calling your parents. Nobody move until I get back."

We sit in a row, looking anywhere but at one another. The exchange from a few moments ago still hangs in the air as heavily as the gray billows of smoke. No one says a word.

After a few tense minutes, or maybe it's only seconds, I follow Meredith's tear-filled eyes across the street. One of her neighbors is pointing a fireman in our direction. He's holding a trash can in one hand. When he starts to jog over, Meredith shoots to her feet.

"Fire's out," he says, wiping his face with the sleeve of his coat. "Luckily, it was pretty well contained, but there is some damage to your kitchen. All things considered, it's minimal. Can't say the same for your float, though." Meredith nods woodenly as he holds up the garbage can. "This appears to be where it started. Cigarette butt that wasn't properly put out."

"No one in our house smokes," Meredith says.

He jiggles the can. "We found this in the middle of your float. I'm assuming the fire wasn't started by anyone who lives in your house."

She looks at him like he slapped her. That's when Mrs. Collins opens the door, her cell pressed to her ear. "Meredith, I've got your dad on the line. Oh wait, Brad," she says to the phone. "One of the firemen is right here. I'll let you talk to him."

She hands her cell to the firefighter, and I watch, not really hearing or seeing anything in front of me.

Pranks to a homecoming float are nothing new. But this is way too extreme to be a prank. I have a terrible feeling that someone meant for this to happen.

Someone who should've been at homecoming but wasn't. And who spent a lot of time right across the street from the float without even knowing it.

Unless he did.

Were there signs that I totally missed? I remember the way Joel said that he didn't care about having to give away the ring his father used to wear around his neck. At the time, I didn't think anything of it. Now it seems like a pretty callous, unfeeling thing to say.

And then there was the question he asked the day he invited me to homecoming: *Are you afraid I'll embarrass you?*

Did he mean that literally?

No matter what, it didn't make sense that Joel would have some secret agenda to earn our trust and then turn on us. For what? To trash our float and then ? I come up blank. There's no glory in this. He can't even take credit, unless he wants to pay a serious price. Several of them.

Nope. It doesn't make sense at all. But it also doesn't make sense that he's supposed to be here right now and he's not.

I stand up and pace the lawn as Mrs. Collins offers their guest room to Meredith's family.

"My parents are going to take you up on that," Meredith says, wrapping up the call. "But I was supposed to have half the squad sleeping at our house tonight. I need to see if we can move it to someone else's place."

"Not a problem," Mrs. Collins replies. "We have plenty of extra blankets if you decide you want to stay. Speaking of which, let me go put fresh sheets out for your parents." She starts to head back inside, but stops when she catches sight of me, almost like it's the first time she notices I'm there. "Do you have a way home, dear?"

"I'll take her, Mom," Ben says.

"*I'll* drive her," she counters. "You stay with Meredith until her parents get here. Be back in five minutes."

She hurries into the house, and I stare at Meredith, who's texting away, most likely sending an FYI to the other girls about the sleepover. It's like she forgot I'm here. "Everyone can stay at my house," I offer. "I'll call my parents right—"

"I am not staying with you." The ice in her voice could've put out the fire on its own. "And neither is anyone else."

"Mer," Ben says, getting to his feet. "Don't be mad at Macy for the dance thing. It wasn't her fault." He tries to touch her arm, but she swats his hand away.

"It's not just the dance thing, Ben! How am I supposed to trust either one of you? Because, newsflash, *I don't*." Meredith wraps her arms around her torso again. "And I want to know right now which one of you told," she snaps. An invisible fist squeezes my stomach. "Because it's pretty obvious who did this, and you two traitors have been so busy bending over backward to be his friend that you've seriously sucked at being mine." Ben opens his mouth to say something, but Meredith's venomous glare cuts over to me. "Was it worth it, Macy? Getting stood up?" She points across the street. "Having my house almost fucking burn down? All because you wanted poor, misunderstood Joel to feel accepted? Is that why you told him? So he'd feel like part of the crowd? Or were you just hoping to throw me off your trail while you went after Ben?"

"Meredith, I'd never—"

"That's not what happened," Ben cuts in sharply.

"Then what did?" Her glower is unrelenting and fixed

on me. "Maybe you talked in your sleep the night you all holed up together at Ben's house?"

She has no idea how close she actually is. And even though I can't remember for the life of me if the words actually left my mouth at the slushie stand that night, the confession is ready to pour out of me.

"I told him," Ben says before I have a chance to form one word. He looks from my shell-shocked face to Meredith's and back again. "Quit trying to find a way to blame Macy for everything, Mer." His shoulders sag. "I'm not saying that I think Hargrove did this. But if he did, it's my fault."

"Ben." His name is an aghast shriek on Meredith's lips, which lapses into a stunned croak. She looks from her house to him, like she's trying to grasp the connection between the two. "How *could* you?" She points toward her scorched garage. "Look at my *house*. How are you even still defending him right now?"

Ben holds up his hands like he's shielding himself from her wrath. "I can't tell you for sure that Hargrove was never here. But." He looks at me, and the guilt in the curve of his mouth sends instant prickles of dread over my skin. "It doesn't seem likely . . . if he is where he says he is."

My mouth drops open, filling with the taste of smoky air.

"I know what you're thinking, Mace," Ben continues. "But I had no clue he was going to bail until after he did."

I swallow over the dry, singed taste in my throat. "You said you should've warned me."

"That's not what I meant. I was trying to say that I wished I *could've* warned you."

I don't believe him. It's one more thing that doesn't add up, and I'm tired of feeling left in the dark. "Where is he?" I ask through gritted teeth.

Ben hangs his head, scuffing one of his leather shoes against the grass. "At his grandmother's in Buford." Meredith makes a sound that's a cross between disgust and disbelief. "I have my own reasons for being pissed off at him," Ben continues, his posture wilting. "But he . . . he asked me to tell you he's sorry."

I don't feel a flicker of sympathy at Joel's secondhand apology. He lied to me, he let my mother scramble around trying to solve a problem that didn't exist, and he stood me up. Now he wants to use a middleman to make it right?

"You can tell Joel that I'm done with him. No. On second thought, I'll tell him myself. I'm not going to sink to his level and use someone else as a mouthpiece because I don't have the guts to do it myself." I take out my phone, ready to unleash my rage into my fingertips. I stare hard at Ben. "I don't need *anyone* in my life who can't be honest with me."

The moment the words leave my mouth, I wish I could reel them back and swallow them up. But when Meredith says, "Funny, I was thinking the same thing," I see my chance. The chance to reverse some of the damage I've done. The chance to step back from the line I crossed when Ben became more than just Meredith's neighbor and started being my friend.

Mrs. Collins returns then and beckons me over with her car keys. She insists that Ben stay with Meredith while she drives me home, unaware that Meredith wants nothing to do with either of us. Or that if I'm going to get back in my best friend's good graces, I have to find a way to stay as angry with her son as I am right now. But it's a price I'm willing to pay.

Tomorrow, when the smoke clears, it'll all be better. I'll call Meredith, and I'll apologize again. I'll offer to help repaint her garage. We'll agree on how silly it all was, and we'll figure everything out.

Maybe I'll even get some sleep tonight, as long as I can keep believing my delusions.

Twenty-Eight

SENIOR YEAR

"It was Joel," I say to Noah as I land hard in my seat at our bio table. I take out my notebook and start to flip through without looking at him. "He's the one who kissed me."

Noah looks dubious. "Are you sure?"

"As sure as he is that it was a 'bad decision.'" I emphasize the last words so he'll know they were Joel's and not mine.

"He said that?" Noah's eyebrows pull together, and he runs a finger back and forth over his bottom lip, like the statement isn't perfectly self-explanatory.

"In plain English."

"Where did you say you found that picture the next day? The one of the tattoo?"

What? I'm in crisis mode, and he decides to ask the most random, least relevant thing ever?

"Uh, on the field, where the platform had been. Why does that matter?"

Noah shrugs, flipping through his textbook. "Just curious."

I'm annoyed, and I'm having a hard time hiding it. Of all people, I thought I could count on him to commiserate and have my back. After all, Joel's let him down in the past. But he seems oblivious to the fact that I could use a friend right now.

Until I demand, "But *why*?"

He turns to me, and the pensive demeanor vanishes. "No reason, okay? Sorry if I made you more upset by asking a dumb question." He gives my fingers a brief squeeze, then takes his hand back to prop his face against it, hunching into his textbook.

Closing me off.

But not before I catch sight of what I could swear is a triumphant smirk that he's making every effort to keep me from seeing.

The gym is decorated and thrumming with energy. Last year's pep rally was fun, but this one feels different. It's my last, and the first where I'm nominated for the homecoming court. I've tried to tell myself that I don't care if I'm voted in or not, but truthfully, hearing *my* name announced on the same field where I spent three years cheering my heart out on the sidelines would feel like confirmation that no one blames me for what happened last year. Or an apology, if they did.

I don't have to wait much longer to find out. Principal Fielding smiles beneath the scoreboard, microphone in hand, waiting for the applause and chanting to quiet. As soon as he says, "I know you're all excited for homecoming weekend," it starts right back up again. Once he has our attention, he makes us sit through another variation of the speech he's given for the past three years: the homecoming tradition of bringing current students and alumni together, the importance of school pride and spirit, and a list of some of the more distinguished alumni that we can expect to see on campus this weekend. Including the former king and queen from more than a decade ago, who will officially crown this year's royalty at the game tonight.

And then, finally, he holds up the piece of paper in his hand. "So without further ado, here are your homecoming princes and princesses for this year!" He calls off the names of a boy and a girl from the freshman, sophomore, and junior classes, who all make their way to the center of the basketball court.

"As for our upperclassmen," he says, "give a big Ravens round of applause for your senior princess . . . Macy Atwood!" A cheer explodes through the gym, and a rush of heat flashes through me. This is nothing like the reception I got at Old Mill. People are screaming and clapping and patting me on the back. As I jog out to take my place in line, I hear: "And your senior prince . . . Noah Granger!"

I gasp, and while the clapping continues, it's noticeably less enthusiastic. About half of the football team cheers Noah on with big, manly claps, while the other half passes looks of *Are you fucking kidding me?* back and forth between them. It's more of the same in the stands. People are either ecstatic or indignant.

Noah side-bumps me as he joins the line. When I do it back, he winks. I reach for his hand. Maybe I imagined the odd vibe between us earlier, and if that's the case, I'm happy to forget about it.

Except that his fingers slip through my grasp before he clasps them behind his back. His stance widens, and just like that, I'm closed off again.

"And now," Principal Fielding continues. "The moment you've all been waiting for. As you know, the homecoming king and queen are traditionally seniors who are also exemplary students. They're conscientious, dedicated, and involved. And this year, I think you've done a particularly great job of recognizing those qualities in your king and queen. They are . . . Tyrell Davis and Meredith Kopala!"

I'm screaming and clapping and ricocheting off the bodies on either side of me like a Ping-Pong ball before he can even finish pronouncing Meredith's name. I'm so excited for her. Honestly, I'm excited for me, too. Maybe being on the homecoming court together will be the thing that finally helps Meredith and me put last year in the past, where it belongs.

I look up at Noah, and he gives me a cocky half smile. "Guess we're doing this together at the same time after all," he says.

I grin back at him. If this moment is any indication, senior year homecoming is already showing serious promise over last year's nightmare.

Twenty-Nine

SENIOR YEAR

Renata Higgins makes a sweeping bow as I approach the main doors to the gym, my book bag slapping against my back and a plastic shopping bag full of pictures dangling from one hand.

"I was starting to think you'd skipped out on us, *Your Majesty*," she says.

"Sorry." The word comes out breathless, thanks to my rushing. "My pictures fell out of my locker and I had to improvise a storage system." I hold up the plastic bag. "Good thing my mom is a bag hoarder and makes me carry one of these at all times."

Jadie and I spent lunch in the yearbook room, printing up the photos from the Ridgedale's Finest page, as well as some of our favorites from our cameras. We stashed our pics in our lockers until after school, when we'd start piecing together our vision of the ultimate showcase of student life: a collage of four-by-four photos, interspersed with print-ups of favorite quotes submitted by the students and captions from the Ridgedale's Finest page.

"Congratulations on making the homecoming court," Criselle says. A paper cutout is draped over her arm, a quote that reads, *We try and keep our eye on the big picture, but the picture keeps getting bigger.*

"Thanks." I can't help it. I beam.

Renata motions to the empty gym. "I know the bulletin board is supposed to be a surprise and all, but how did you guys convince Queen Meredith to move the perky-saurus squad elsewhere for practice?"

"Friday is usually weight training day," Jadie pipes up, dropping a stack of photos onto the hall monitor's desk. "They're upstairs in the auxiliary gym. Should we get started?"

We spend a few minutes going back and forth about how to best lay out the pictures, toying with the idea of arranging them oldest to newest, or trying to cluster similar themes. But in the end we decide to let them fall where they may, so there's a surprise to discover, no matter where you look.

I have to laugh when I see everyone else's neat, uniform piles of photographs compared to my haphazardly stuffed bag. I must've opened my locker too quickly, because all the pics I'd stacked in my cubby toppled like a house of cards, landing in a heap of faceup and facedown messiness. I'm about to dump the bag and give them some semblance of orderliness, when my cell phone starts to ring.

"What's up, Mom?"

"Can you be home in ten minutes?"

"Why? What's wrong?"

"Nothing. The doctor's office called to say they had a cancelation. If you can get out of what you're doing, we can finally get that wrist looked at."

I'm torn between wanting to be angry at her for calling the doctor without my permission, and wanting to jump for joy at the thought of finally getting some relief. I didn't plan to wear my ugly brace at homecoming, but my swollen arm won't score much higher on the attractiveness scale.

I rush over to Jadie, who has already swooped in on the picture pile, and explain the situation.

"Will you be mad if I go?"

She assures me that she and her minions have the bulletin board covered, and tells me to leave.

"See you at the game tonight, *Your Majesty*," she calls after me as I practically skip out of the building.

An X-ray, a tendonitis diagnosis, and a cortisone shot later, I'm already feeling better. My arm looks neglected and abused, like it's been stranded on a deserted island for a few years. But I'm so happy to have full access to all my limbs again that I don't care.

Mom takes me home after the appointment so I can change into something nice. All the members of the home-coming court will be driven down to the football field in fancy convertible cars loaned by parents or teachers, and then we'll have to walk out onto the turf and be introduced before the game starts. It's usually a quick ceremony, but the attendance tonight will easily be in the thousands, and I'd be lying if I said I didn't have butterflies.

My brothers beg to eat at Chick-fil-A beforehand, which isn't the most royal of dinners. But I get through it without my meal becoming part of my blue maxi dress, so it's good enough for me. As far as not being asked, "What if you trip?" at least three times by two eight-year-olds, that's where I don't fare as well. They then take turns cracking themselves up by inventing enough disastrous scenarios that it actually starts to mess with my head—until we pull up to the school.

There are four sleek, shiny convertibles lined up in front of the pillared brick of the main entrance. Each has a sign on the door with the names and ranks of the court members who'll be riding in it: a red Cadillac that I know belongs to Principal Fielding's wife for Meredith and Tyrell, a black BMW for Noah and me, a yellow Corvette for the junior prince and princess, and then a blue Volkswagen for the sophomores and freshmen to share. My heart jumps into my throat with excitement, and since I don't have my camera, I pull out my phone to capture how perfect everything looks.

My parents drop me off before heading back down the driveway. They always park at Meredith's house and then walk back, to avoid the nightmare that the school parking lot can become on game night. As I approach the lineup of cars, Tyrell is circling the Cadillac, shooting the breeze with Principal Fielding about the gas mileage and the paint job. He nods when he sees me and comes over to give me a hug.

"Look at you, working with two arms again," he says, twirling me around. "Congratulations."

"Thanks. Are Meredith and Noah here?"

"I haven't seen Granger yet, but I think Meredith went inside to pick up her flowers." He glances back at the front entrance, and right on cue, Meredith emerges from the doors in a white dress and matching heels. There's a silver sash across her torso, and in her arms is a big bouquet of roses that are the same deep red as her lip gloss. I excuse myself and run up the stairs to greet her.

"Hey! You look so pretty." I'm all smiles and sunshine, but one look from Meredith tells me that something has already rained on her parade. My face falls. "What's wrong?"

She sets the roses down at the base of a column and folds her arms across her chest. "I went to see your bulletin board after practice." She says it like that in itself is an explanation. But I have no idea why a collection of pictures would bring such a harsh, defeated note to her voice and so much sadness to her eyes.

"Is there something wrong with it?"

She makes a disgusted sound. "Come on, Macy. What

were you getting at by putting that picture of you and Ben up there?"

"What picture? I didn't—" I try to tell her that I didn't get to work on the board and that I haven't even seen it myself, but she cuts me off.

"The one from the dance last year. The one you apparently took when you and Ben snuck off together. Ring a bell?"

Of course it does. But there's no possible way that the picture she's talking about could've made it onto the board. I've never, ever seen it on the RF page, and I was just scrolling through on the ride over. I don't even have a physical copy of it. And neither does Jadie.

"I swear to you—"

Her hand shoots up to silence me. "Look, Mace. We both know that Ben would rather go to this dance with you than with me. And maybe I'm an idiot for saying yes again, and I'm definitely an idiot because I keep hoping things will change, but you didn't need to go rubbing it in my face."

"Meredith, I would *never*." I take her wrist, hoping to make her feel the desperation she's ignoring in my voice. "I didn't put that picture on the bulletin board. I had to leave for a doctor appointment. I didn't put *any* pictures on it."

Her red lips purse. Both of her hands go up in a *Never mind* motion, and she scoops up her flowers before taking a step down. "You know what? It doesn't matter. The real question is, were you lying to me when you said nothing happened between you and Ben? Because we both know

Joel is a dead end. So if there's something going on, I think it's about time you admitted it to yourself. And to me."

Her heels click furiously against the stairs, and I rush down after her. I manage to catch up before she can reach the Cadillac, and pull her aside.

"You're wrong, Meredith. Ben didn't ask me to the dance. He asked *you*. And even if I did like him, I'd never do that to you."

She puffs an amused snort, though she looks crushed. Beaten. Let down. But there's an undeniable edge of vindication in her voice when she says, "Then why is history repeating itself?"

Thirty

SENIOR YEAR

Horns blare, and the cheer of the crowd grows louder as Noah and I wave from the backseat of our homecoming car, which creeps toward the football field at about two miles per hour.

"So you and Collins, huh?" Noah says. Great. He caught the tail end of my fight with Meredith. "And here I thought you had a thing for Hargrove."

"I did. I do. *Did.*" It's hard to keep up the Miss America facade when I'm this rattled. "I guess someone put a picture of Ben and me up on the bulletin board, and Meredith thinks I did it to spite her."

"And why would she think that?"

"When I left homecoming last year, I was upset about

being ditched. And Ben came outside to dance with me. He asked if we could take a picture, and in it, I'm kissing his cheek. That was when Meredith found us. And that's the picture that somehow wound up on the board."

"Oof. That sucks."

"Tell me about it. And then the fire happened, and she didn't speak to me for almost a year. Even though it wasn't like that between Ben and me."

"I don't know. A romantic dance under the stars, outside the gym while the rest of the school, including his date, is inside? I can see how she'd think that's something, Mace."

"It *was* something." I shake my head, wondering how the wrong words escape my mouth so damn often. "I mean, it wasn't, but sometimes—in the back of my mind—*ugh*," I bite at my cuticle, realizing I'm about to tell Noah something that I've never admitted to anyone. That I haven't even completely admitted to myself. "Sometimes I think it could've been. If she hadn't come out right at that second, sometimes I wonder if . . . maybe it might've been."

Noah arches an eyebrow. "Oh?"

I respond with a feeble shrug. "But most of the time, I'm pretty sure I imagined it."

It starts out as a singular jolt, and then Noah's muscular torso is full-on shaking with chuckles. "I don't mean to laugh, Mace." Funny, he could've fooled me. "But after one look at Meredith's face today, and knowing absolutely nothing else about the situation, I can tell you with total certainty: You didn't imagine it."

GINA CIOCCA

And just like that, it's real. I don't know why I believe
Noah, who wasn't even there, when he confirms something
I've spent the past year second-guessing. But hearing him
say it makes it a living, breathing reality, and suddenly the
thing that didn't happen is the thing that almost did.

But what difference does it make now?

It doesn't. Whatever that moment under the streetlight
might've had the potential to be, it passed us by. And it's
probably better that way, because I meant it when I said I
wouldn't do that to Meredith.

Not again.

By the time I'm able to sneak off the field after halftime, the
school is locked. I'm dying to see the homecoming bulletin board for myself, but it's not going to happen tonight. I
even try to flag down Jadie after she snaps some group shots
of the homecoming court, hoping she'll have photos handy
of the finished product. But Principal Fielding intercepts
me, requesting pictures with the alumni and Meredith and
Tyrell.

As I stand there, taking in the lights and the noise, I
find myself wishing that Ben were here. There are so many
things I want to ask him and a hundred things I feel like I
should apologize for. A hundred others that make infinitely
more sense if what Noah said is true.

But what I really want is for Ben to tell me that Noah
is wrong. Because much like the night I stood on this field
in total darkness, in the arms of a boy I thought I knew

278

but didn't, I'm going to keep going back to that moment under the lamppost. It's going to replay in my mind until I've examined it from every possible angle.

And then I'm going to drive myself mad wondering what could've been instead of accepting what isn't meant to be.

Thirty-One

SENIOR YEAR

We win the game, and the energy in the stadium is palpable. I know the guys are going to be extra amped at the diner tonight, but for once I don't feel a pang of longing at having to miss it. I run over to Noah as soon as he and the other players are done high-fiving the members of the opposing team.

"Hey," I say, tugging the sleeve of his jersey. "Any chance you want to skip Friday Night Eats and hang out with me tonight?"

Noah gives me a suspicious look. "Are you skipping because you're hiding from Meredith?"

"No. I always skip." He looks like he's going to lecture me, so I don't give him the chance. "Please? We can eat somewhere else if you're hungry. I need to give her and Ben some space tonight."

"Mace. You can give them all the space in the world, but it's not going to make Ben want her if he doesn't. Has Meredith considered that?" I shrink, at a loss for how to answer. His face softens, and he touches my shoulder. "Look, I wish I could hang out, but I'm meeting up with an old friend. Any other night, I'd be there in a heartbeat."

"Oh. An old friend from Mortonville?"

"Yeah."

"A touchy-feely friend?"

He grins. "According to you, I have no other kind."

I'm disappointed, but I smile anyway. "Don't do anything I wouldn't do."

"Same goes for you. And that includes hiding out in your house to keep someone else happy in their delusions." I give him a look that says *Touché*, even though I have no intention of changing my mind about the diner. I wave and start to walk off, but he calls after me. "I'll shoot you a text if I'm done early. My friend and I are just hanging out at my place, but"—he runs a hand through his hair, and there's an air of nerves in the gesture—"I'm not sure how much we have left to say to each other. Either way, I'll see you tomorrow."

I tease him that he'd better not show up wearing the same dress as me, and then we part ways. As I'm turning to go, I nearly collide with Jadie.

"Oh my God, I've been dying to talk to you," I say.

"What's the problem?" She detaches my hand from its

clawlike grip on her arm. "Glad to see there was no permanent damage from brace-zilla."

"Meredith is all bent out of shape about one of the pictures that went up on the bulletin board. Do you have any idea how a shot of Ben and me from last year's dance would've made it up there?"

"Yikes. All I know is that if it was in the pile, it went on the board."

"But it wasn't on the RF page. And I sure as hell didn't print it up, so how did it get into the pile?"

"No idea. I'm guessing Criselle or Renata put it up, because I'm not even sure which one you're talking about. All I know is that the board came out way too amazing for drama."

Principal Fielding beckons her over again, and I say good-bye before she can ask about going to the diner. Still, I feel like I need to warn Ben about the situation, so I take out my cell phone.

FYI, THERE'S A PIC OF YOU AND ME ON THE HOMECOMING BULLETIN BOARD. DON'T KNOW HOW IT GOT THERE, BUT M IS UPSET.

When I'm watching a movie half an hour later, neck-deep in my bedsheets, I still haven't heard a peep—from Ben or from Noah.

And even though I told myself I was going to take tonight to relax before the homecoming dance, the silence only makes me restless. I get up and throw on some yoga pants, then head downstairs.

Soon I'm back in my car, heading out into the night.

*   *   *

I make a few aimless left turns before ultimately pointing the car in the direction of Noah's neighborhood. I know he's busy, and it's not my intention to insert myself into his plans. But I guess I'm hoping to catch a glimpse of whoever he's hanging out with tonight, because he so rarely goes into detail about his life in Mortonville.

One of the few traits he and Joel share.

The houses in Arbor Creek are almost identical—midsize brick ranches with matching bay windows and peaked roofs. In the dark, it's hard to remember which one is Noah's, until I spot the house with the Bulldogs lawn sign by the front walkway.

The one with Joel's car in the driveway.

I pull over to the curb and press my brake, idling in the street. This can't be right. Noah said he had plans with an old friend tonight, and unless he was using a very creative version of the word "friend," he couldn't have meant Joel. Then again, they *were* friends at one point. . . .

My curiosity is piqued. The shade drawn over the bay window is open a crack, but Mr. Granger's profile in an armchair is the only thing I see inside. So unless I develop X-ray vision in the next ten seconds, I'm pretty sure I've hit a dead end as far as sleuthing this out. Still, despite the voice in my head that's telling me to turn around and go home already, I turn off the car. And that's when I hear a rhythmic *thump, thump, thump* coming from outside.

I squint into the distance, and sure enough, two boys

are heading away from me toward the tennis and basketball courts in the center of the subdivision, one bouncing a basketball off the asphalt as they walk.

And maybe it's a really stupid, nosy thing to do, but I wait until Noah and Joel turn the corner. Then I get out of my car, and I follow them.

I stay several paces behind, sneaking around the tall chain-link fence that surrounds the tennis court, doing my best to avoid the crunchy carpet of pine straw between the fence and the surrounding trees. I stop when I reach the corner, where I can watch the basketball courts without being seen. I'm very confused, but mostly I'm intrigued.

They spend a few minutes running the court, dribbling and stealing and shooting, with grunts and the scrape of their sneakers against the clay as the only sounds.

Then Noah stops and passes the ball to Joel. "Remember the last time we were on the courts over at your place?"

Joel's body language changes instantly. His shoulders tense, and he keeps his eyes on the ground, watching the ball smack against the pavement. "Yeah. So?"

"So that's kind of where it all started."

Joel shoots the ball at one of the four hoops stationed on each side of the court. It rolls off the rim and bounces into the grass. "Not sure why it matters." He retrieves the ball and lines himself up for another shot, his back turned to Noah.

Noah snorts. "It matters because it's the whole reason we're here."

"No." Joel grips the ball between his hands. "We're here because you said we should try to be friends." He sends the ball flying into Noah's abdomen. "Same as you and your homecoming date."

Whoa. I'm not sure what I did to deserve the bitter, derisive way Joel mentioned me, but the sneer in his voice makes the hair on my arms stand on end.

"I already apologized for that. And Macy and I *are* just friends; we both knew it wasn't going to work as anything else."

Joel throws his arms open in indignation. "How do you think an apology is going to undo all the shit you put me through this past year? Everyone hates me, and you get to walk around like nothing happened. But it's great to know that you're *sorry*." He spits the last word like it stabbed his tongue.

Noah takes a few steps forward, pointing at Joel's face. "I've done some shitty things, and I'd take them back if I could. But don't you dare try to act like this didn't all start with *you*. I was willing to put it all out there, lay everything on the line, and instead you fucking ran." He moves closer as he speaks, his eyes flashing. "You ran and hid, like you always do, and you blackmailed me on top of it." His finger jabs the center of Joel's chest, and Joel falters. "So is it worth it? To get to keep fucking lying to yourself?" This time Noah gives Joel a full-out shove, sending him stumbling backward. But Noah still doesn't back down, matching each move Joel makes, close enough to steal the air from his lungs. Joel's back collides with the post of one of the basket-ball hoops, and Noah glowers at him. His chest shakes with a sarcastic laugh. "Have you even said it out loud yet?"

Their eyes are locked, their chests heaving. Joel's jaw is set tightly enough to crack his teeth.

And then I see it. A split second before Joel grabs a handful of Noah's shirt, I recognize it. Something has been simmering between them, and it's on the verge of boiling over. Something I thought was hate but isn't even close.

No, that's not hate at all. That's *heat*.

"Why do I have to say it at all?" Joel says.

And then he pulls Noah to him, and their mouths meet with the fierceness of two people whose resolve just crumbled under the weight of holding back their feelings for too long. Joel's fingers thread through Noah's hair, and there's not a breath of space between their bodies. They're kissing like no one is watching. Because they don't think anyone is.

Except that I'm so stunned by the sight of them that a gasp escapes my mouth a millisecond before I manage to clamp my hand over it. And the boys are so consumed with each other that they probably wouldn't have noticed, but when I take a step backward to make my escape, my foot hits the pine straw in the exact right way to render a loud snap beneath my sneaker.

Joel and Noah jump apart, as their heads whip toward the direction of the sound. I know there's no point in running—they'll only cut me off on the other side of the tennis court. So I take a tentative step from behind the fence and come forward, watching the horror on Joel's face melt into confusion.

"I—I'm sorry," I say when no one else speaks.

"Macy," Noah says. It's both an admonition and a question. "What are you doing here?"

"I don't really know. I got restless sitting at home, and—kind of curious, too, I guess. This is where I ended up." I twist my fingers. "So you two . . . your 'history' . . . You're gay?"

Joel shifts on his feet. "He's bi," he says, nodding toward Noah. His voice drops and he stares at his shoes when he adds, "I'm gay." When he glances up at Noah, his lips are set in a sad line. "Happy now? I said it out loud."

I'm surprised, even though I shouldn't be, when Noah responds by hooking an arm around Joel's neck and kissing the side of his face. Noah being affectionate is nothing new. But having been on the receiving end of his affection for a while now, it's taking me a second to adjust to watching him touch someone else. Especially when that someone is Joel Hargrove.

"Are *you* happy?" Noah counters. "Because that's all that matters."

Joel responds by pressing his face into Noah's shoulder. He certainly doesn't *look* happy. He looks scared to death.

Noah holds out his free hand to me. "Come on, Mace. We have a few things to talk about."

Thirty-Two

SENIOR YEAR

Noah leads me to one of the benches alongside the basketball court. Joel and I both sit, while Noah stands.

"So you guys are—were?—a thing?" I hedge.

"Were," Noah says softly.

Joel draws his knees up and wraps his arms around them. "I wanted to tell you about a thousand different times. I really did."

I reach out and squeeze his arm. "Then why didn't you?"

He pauses, swallowing hard. "Because saying it means there's no taking it back. And I don't want to be gay."

"One of the reasons we're no longer a thing," Noah mutters. But then he sits down on Joel's other side, bumping him to the center of the bench. And takes his hand.

Which Joel promptly takes back and slips between his knees.

There are so many things making sense to me now. All the times Joel seemed on the brink of telling me something important, only to back down at the last second. The way he'd look at me, silently begging me to figure it out for myself. His conviction that he was going to let down his father by being human.

He's happy because I let him keep his delusions.

I hate him.

"Your parents don't know, do they?" I ask.

Joel snorts. "They know. They're just happier pretending they don't."

"Except you don't know that, because you've never actually sat down and talked to them," Noah says.

Joel tenses, and I shoot a look past him at Noah, shaking my head.

Noah clears his throat and sits back a little. "Sorry."

"It's not . . . it's not something I've always known," Joel begins. "I mean, maybe part of me did, but I was pretty slow to catch on. I dated a lot of girls—and most of the time there was no reason why it shouldn't have worked. Except that it never did, and I couldn't figure out why." He traces his eyebrow, the way he always does when he's nervous.

"I thought I was defective. It wasn't until freshman year that I realized I had a crush on a guy. And it freaked me the hell out. I told myself it was some fluke thing, and I tried to fix it by dating more girls, sleeping with more girls. I completely ignored the question of why they were never enough."

Joel's foot starts a nervous thumping against the ground, and he looks at Noah, silently asking him to take over.

"I had a girlfriend at the time," Noah continues. "For me, being bi wasn't something that confused me, but the thought of openly being with a guy was one of the few things that ever scared the shit out of me. I'd never taken it past hookups on the down low, and I always figured I'd keep it at that. But then sophomore year, I hurt my knee." He nudges Joel, and there's so much tenderness in that small gesture that I have no idea how I never saw what really exists between the two of them. "And this kid got the job of bringing me my assignments while I was out of school.

"We'd never talked much before, but the more time we spent together, the more we clicked. Our dads were both in the service. Our moms are both basket cases. Plus he helped me with my homework, carried my books for me when I was on crutches. And then one day I told him I was sick of being cooped up and on my ass, and he brought me over to the basketball courts at his place so I could walk around for five minutes without my mom having a heart attack. And that night ended pretty much the same way as what you saw a few minutes ago."

Joel picks up again. "We hooked up a lot after that. And I *know* my parents suspected, or at least my father did. I'll never forget the way he looked at Noah the first time he stayed for dinner."

"Like he wanted to perform an exorcism and then board up the house to keep me from ever getting back inside," Noah mutters.

Joel turns to me. "You have to understand, Mace. My parents say that people being gay doesn't 'bother' them, but what they mean is that it doesn't bother them as long as it stays the hell out of their house. They don't get that tolerating something at arm's length isn't acceptance. The same way my dad doesn't get that I'm not some math problem he can solve for the 'right' answer." He taps his temple. "The logic doesn't add up."

"So is that why you broke up? Because you didn't want to come out to your parents?"

Joel grimaces and glances at Noah, who looks at me. "In the super-oversimplified version, I guess you could say that," Noah says.

"I didn't even want to come out to *myself*," Joel adds. "But then, toward the end of sophomore year, we knew my dad was going to be deployed again, and my parents decided to sell the house and move here." He sucks in a deep breath. "And Noah started saying things I wasn't ready to hear. Talking about coming out, not having to sneak around anymore."

"I'd broken up with my girlfriend," Noah interjects. "I came out to my parents. I even brought up moving in with my dad so I could transfer to Ridgedale too. Start over together, you know? I was ready to do whatever." He turns dark eyes on Joel. "But he wasn't."

Joel slumps against the bench. "I waited until summer vacation and then stopped taking his calls. Told him I'd met a girl, said I'd made a mistake. I swore I'd deny every word and use my dad's connections to get him expelled if he ever told anyone what happened." He shrugs a heavy shoulder. "I wanted a fresh start too, but not the one he had in mind."

"Wow," I breathe. "So I'm guessing this is where the whole restraining order thing comes in?"

Noah scoffs. "I showed up at his house to try to get him to talk to me. Pops didn't appreciate that. Especially when things got heated and I broke a picture of dear old Granddad." I must look a little horrified, because he tacks on, "By accident. Geez."

To my surprise, Joel chuckles wryly. "It was a pretty symbolic thing to break, considering it's my dad's favorite weapon in the psychological warfare arsenal."

"*If* that's what he's doing," Noah counters.

Joel shoots up from the bench and rounds on us. "It *is* what he's doing." He looks at me. "You wanna know how Noah's father reacted when he came out to him? Handed him a condom and said, 'I don't care who you're banging as long as you're safe about it.' And because it was that easy for him, he thinks it's that easy for everybody. But my dad knows exactly how to get under my skin, how to make me feel like a failure without ever saying the words."

He gestures at me. "Like that story he told you about why they named me after my grandfather. He does it to mess with me. That same bullshit line that he says all the time—'you can do anything you put your mind to'—that's his way of telling me he knows. He knows he makes me fucking hate what I am, and what he's really saying is, 'Fight it, Joel. You don't have to be something we're both ashamed of.' Because he doesn't want to deal with it, and he doesn't want to have to face what *he* is either. He preaches all about love and acceptance and courage. But at the end of the day, he's still a homophobe with a gay son."

He falls onto the bench and buries his face in his hands. I hate that he's been carrying all this on his shoulders and never said a word. Everything could've been so different if he'd opened up to me like he wanted to.

"He pulled the same shit in his welcome-back speech at the football game," Joel continues before I can say anything. "That night, I was going to tell everyone, including him. I couldn't stand it anymore, and I just wanted to get it over with and make everything right. With you, with Ben, with Noah. I was sick of hiding. So I posted that picture of you and me and Ben to the school's page, as kind of a placeholder for the conversation I planned to have with you later. I had another picture with me that I've never shown to anyone. Except my dad. Only, I didn't show it to him; he found it while he was snooping through my phone."

"The picture of my tattoo," Noah murmurs.

His tattoo?

Joel sits up straighter. "How did you know?"

"Macy found it on the field the next day."

"You didn't tell me it was of *you*," I say.

Noah turns away from me, using his hand to push his hair up off his neck. Beneath the curtain of his dark locks are the familiar black lines of a fern-shaped snake that, until now, I only saw in a colorless photograph. He lets his hair fall into place, and when he repositions himself, there's something sad and somber in the lines of his profile.

"Defiance," he says. "That's what it stands for. And the shape of the snake is an Adinkra fern that means 'I am not afraid of you.' I got it when I made the decision to come out."

"He wanted me to get the same one," Joel says quietly. "And I was going to. I printed the picture, but then I thought, maybe I should wait to get the tattoo until I tell everyone. I should've known I was giving myself an out."

Noah looks at me. "I had a feeling that it meant something, you finding that picture. I just didn't think it was anything good. But then you and Joel had that fight, and I started to wonder if it was a sign that he was coming around. 'Hoping' is a better word, I guess."

Joel's arm twitches and stretches slightly, and for a second I think he's going to put it around Noah. But then it falls back at his side, and he continues to fiddle with his hands like he's not sure what to do with them.

"I had it with me while my dad was making his speech," Joel says. "I guess I was being superstitious, holding on to it so I wouldn't chicken out. And I swear to you, it was like he sensed it, and he had to go and shake me up by telling that story about me learning to ride my bike." He looks up at me, desperation shining in his eyes. "He refuses to see who I really am. And now you know why I hate him for leaving and dread him being home."

I sigh. "God, Joel. I wish you'd told me."

"Me too, Mace. When I met you, I knew I liked you. I either wanted you to be the first person I told the truth to, or the person who made it not true anymore." He snorts a soft laugh. "You can guess which one I went for." When I'm quiet, he asks, "Do you hate me?"

"I'll be honest. It's a shitty feeling, knowing I was used. But hate you because you're gay? Never." I motion toward Noah. "I mean, we have the same taste in guys." They both laugh, and even though I'm glad to lighten the moment, there are more questions lingering. "I have to wonder, Joel. What else have you been keeping from me?"

He looks at me out of the corner of his eye. "Ben and Meredith both know about me. But I'll let them tell you how." He looks exhausted all of a sudden, like he can't take another step now that he's finally stopped running.

Noah stands abruptly and starts to pace in front of us. "Speaking of Meredith." He drags a hand through his hair. "I guess this is where I should make a confession of my own." Joel looks at me, my confusion reflected in his face.

"So I thought Joel was full of it when he told me he'd met a girl," Noah says. "Or I figured if he had, he was using her and it wouldn't last. But then I saw the two of you at Snow in Georgia that night, and he actually seemed happy. And even though everything in me knew he wasn't into girls—" He stops and shakes his head. "Holy shit, Mace, was I jealous of you." He starts to pace again. "I hated both of you. And I hated myself for being such a goddamn coward. Backing down from anything isn't my style, but there I was, surrounded by girls myself, covering up that I'd had my heart ripped out by a guy. So I did some things that I'm not proud of."

"Like?" Joel asks, an urgent edge to his voice.

Noah stops, hooking his thumbs into the waistband of his shorts. "I decided I was transferring to Ridgedale whether you wanted me there or not. But that part you know. As for the other part . . . I guess I should just freaking say it." His eyes dart from Joel to me. "I set the fire in Meredith's garage."

"You?" I say at the same time that Joel says, *"What?"*

Noah kneels in front of me and takes my hands. "It was mostly an accident, and I'm so sorry, Mace. My dad and I ran into Joel that day at the grocery store. While he was picking up your flower for the homecoming dance."

Joel's posture stiffens. "Yeah," he says. "That was the day you totally fucking threw me and told me you were moving in with him and coming to Ridgedale for senior year. *You* were the reason I couldn't bring myself to show up that night."

Noah looks incredulous. "Dude, if I threw you for a loop, you sure as hell didn't let on. Because believe me, I wanted to ruin your night. I wanted you to be pissing your pants at the thought of having to see me every day.

And instead all you did was say you had to pay for your girlfriend's flower and walk the hell away." Noah releases my hands and sits on the ground. "I got stupid drunk that night." He hazards a glance at me. "I overheard you, at the slushie place. Telling Joel that Ben knew where the float was hidden. But you didn't say where, so I followed you back to Ben's place in true stalker fashion. Meredith's parents came home as I was leaving, and I saw it in the garage."

Oh my God.

After all this time, I finally know for sure. I *didn't* open my mouth. And Joel might not have started the fire, but I gave enough away that I still feel like it's all my fault. I have no idea how I'm going to bring myself to tell Meredith. She forgave Ben when he falsely confessed, but for Meredith, Ben is the exception to everything.

And he knows it. There's a violent lurch in my stomach as I realize that Ben covered for me.

I can only imagine what my face looks like, because Noah quickly adds, "Don't think I'm saying you're to blame in any way, Mace. You didn't force me to go over there the night of the homecoming dance. You didn't know Meredith's dad was going to leave the garage door cracked open because he'd been touching up the paint, and you sure as hell didn't make me sit on that float feeling sorry for myself or put the bottle of vodka in my hand. I did all that. The same way I spilled half of it into the trash before I threw in the cigarette. It's the dumbest thing I've ever done in my life."

"You know everyone assumed I did it, right?" Joel spits out.

"I do now. It was one of the things I wanted to tell you tonight. I had no idea you'd skipped out on the dance until Macy told me. Trust me, I feel even shittier knowing you took the blame."

Joel stands, his hands clenched at his sides. "That's exactly what you wanted. You came here to make my life hell, and now you expect me to believe that you feel bad about it? Seems to me like everything played out exactly the way you planned, right down to the way you used Macy to get back at me." Joel turns to me. "He hasn't gotten to that part yet. But in case you thought he really cared about you, he doesn't." He turns back to Noah. "I don't think he cares about anyone but himself."

He's halfway across the lawn in three strides, and Noah and I both jump to our feet.

"You know that's not true," Noah calls after him. "No matter what I told myself about moving here to get back at you"—his voice rises in volume and urgency as Joel continues to retreat—"*I just wanted to be with you.*"

Joel stops, then looks up at the sky. When he turns around, every wall he let down in the past half hour is firmly back in place. "I can't, okay? I'm sorry."

Noah makes a move like he's going to take off after Joel, but I put my hand on his arm. "Give him some space," I say.

Noah releases a frustrated, primal grunt into the air before collapsing onto the bench. I sit down next to him, waiting for him to get his bearings. After a long, quiet moment, he says, "I really fucked up, Mace."

"I think we've all made our share of mistakes."

"I'll talk to Meredith if you want. I won't say anything about how I knew the float was in her garage. I'll lie if I have to. It's the least I can do." He reaches over to take my hand, and I let him. "Joel's right, you know. I mean, not totally right. But he wasn't wrong when he said I wormed my way into your life to get a rise out of him." His thumb runs along the inside of my wrist, the same way he touched me at Old Mill Park when he kissed me. Only, this time it's different—not a come-on but an apology. "I came to Ridgedale thinking the two of you were together. But then when I saw that you weren't even speaking, I thought I could screw with him by getting close to you. Make him jealous, because he knew I at least had a chance at falling for you."

I nod, but I'm finding it hard to look at him. "In other words, you used me."

He sandwiches my hand between both of his. "At first, yes. And you have no idea how sorry I am. Because I really am your friend, Mace. It's why I backtracked after I asked you to homecoming, and why I stopped lying about that kiss—I knew I was being a sadistic little prick, and I couldn't do that to you." He stops short and says something that he's said to me before. "I like you. I do."

I lay my other hand on top of his. "You like me," I say with a shrug. "But you love him."

Noah laughs, one quiet, incredulous note. "Yeah," he says. "Probably could've saved myself a lot of trouble if I'd just opened with that."

And then, because it wouldn't be Noah if he wasn't taking me completely by surprise, he lays his head in my lap and starts to cry.

Thirty-Three

SENIOR YEAR

Noah insisted on still taking me to the homecoming dance. I told him he didn't have to, that I understood if his heart wasn't in it. But he interpreted that as *I'm disgusted by you and never want to see to you again*, and the only way I could convince him otherwise was to say we were still on.

In all honesty, disgust is the last thing I feel. For him, or for Joel. Our friendships might've started under less-than-truthful circumstances, but it doesn't mean they're not real. I'd be lying if I said Joel's confession didn't bring up more questions, but at the very least, I understand his motivation.

Which is why I pick up the phone and call him the minute the digital alarm clock on my nightstand reads 5:50— exactly fifteen minutes from the time I last texted him.

It rings long enough that I'm mentally preparing a voice mail message, but then there's a click. "Mace? What's up?"

"I texted you and you didn't answer. I got nervous."

Joel chuckles. "I saw your text, and I'm fine. No running off to Buford tonight, I promise. But I'm not coming to the dance."

"Please, Joel? I hate knowing that you're going to be home by yourself."

"I won't be by myself. I'll be with my parents and my brothers."

I sigh. "You know, I never got to dance with you last year. I was hoping to make up for it tonight."

The line goes quiet. Then he says: "Is it okay if I come over for a minute? There's something I want to tell you anyway."

I can only imagine what he's referring to, and Noah will be here to pick me up in half an hour, but I tell Joel of course he can stop by.

When the doorbell rings ten minutes later, I'm one step away from being ready. My dress is still hanging in its plastic bag on my closet door, but my hair, makeup, and nails are all dialed up to homecoming level. So I'm not all that embarrassed to answer the door in my bathrobe and slippers.

I open it to find Joel standing outside, holding two yellow roses. Before I can do anything more than smile, my mother walks into the foyer, saying, "Macy? Who's at the—" She stops short when she sees Joel. I haven't told her anything about what happened on the basketball court, and my instincts to usher Joel to safety before she can start in on him kick into high gear.

"Joel," she says, the pitch of her voice surprised but casual as she eyes the flowers. "You know Macy already has a date for homecoming, right? You were supposed to take her *last* year."

Too late. I open my mouth, but Joel steps into the foyer, wiping his feet on the welcome mat. "I know, Mrs. Atwood. She's going with my ex-boyfriend." He sucks in a breath. "I'm gay." My mother's eyes bulge, and I'm pretty sure my expression is almost the same as hers, but for different reasons. Joel exhales, sheepishly holding out one of the roses to my mom. "Sorry," he says. "I haven't told my parents yet, and that was practice."

She reaches for the flower, her mouth opening and closing without a sound. Finally she says, "You're gay?" Her gaze switches to me. "And so is Noah?" I nod, deciding I'll correct her terminology later. The stunned look on her face turns to confusion. Guess her personality radar didn't pick up on that little nugget. "How did you end up with gay dates two years in a row?"

"Luck?" I say, and she turns to Joel, twisting the flower between her fingers. My mother is almost never at a loss for words, and I have to hold back a snicker as a high, nervous laugh skitters from her throat.

"Well. Congratulations." Her eyes dart from Joel to me and back. "Is that the right thing to say? I've never had anyone come out to me before."

Joel considers it. "That works. And I really am sorry for what I put Macy through last year."

She nods, pressing the flower to her nose. "If Macy forgives you, then so do I." She steps back toward the kitchen. "Good luck telling your parents. And thank you for telling me."

I nod toward the stairs. "Come up to my room." We jog up the stairs, and I close the door behind us, giving Joel a push on the arm. "Definitely didn't see that coming. You were amazing."

"Glad you thought so. My heart feels like it's gonna beat right out of my chest and take off down the road."

I sit on the edge of my bed. "Are you really planning to tell your parents?"

Joel stares at the remaining flower in his hand. "I have to, Mace. Maybe not tonight, but soon. Denying it won't make it go away. And . . . the more I say it out loud, the more I think I'm learning to be okay with that."

"Noah would be really proud of you." I tap the comforter, not wanting to be too pushy with what I say next. "I'm not the only one who'd like to dance with you tonight, you know."

"About that." Joel steps forward, holding out the flower. "This is for you. I bought you a yellow rose corsage last year, but . . . obviously I never gave it to you. So I brought two flowers to make up for this year and last, only . . ." He swings around to look at the door. "I ended up giving the other one to your mom. Sorry. It felt like a good move."

"It was." I laugh, brushing the silky petals over my lips.

Joel pulls his cell phone from the back pocket of his jeans and sets it on top of my dresser. He presses the screen a few times, and then a familiar song starts to play.

The song.

My spine straightens, and the flower drops to my lap. "How did you know about this song?"

Joel freezes, looking almost frightened by my reaction. "What about it?"

"Last year, when I walked out of homecoming. Ben followed me outside and asked me to dance with him. This was the song that was playing."

"Oh." Joel fumbles with the phone, and a different melody starts up. "Weird coincidence, I swear. Is this better?"

"Better for what?"

He holds out his hand. "May I have this dance?"

I study him to see if he's pulling my leg, but his eyes are so earnest and the set of his mouth betrays the tiniest bit of nerves. It's so sweet that I can't say no. So I take his hand, and we start the first dance of the night, right there in my bedroom.

"You don't have to wear that," Joel says, nodding toward my dresser, where the locket he gave me is laid out next to my earrings and bracelet for tonight.

"But I like it."

"I know." He shakes his head. "Only, it was never mine to give. That's one of the things I wanted to tell you before the dance tonight."

"What do you mean?"

"So, remember how I said Meredith knows about me? It's because I told her. The night that they gave my dad the welcome-home celebration, that was the night I planned to come out. I pulled her aside before the game because I was sick of everyone thinking I had something to do with the fire. I promised her that I hadn't been anywhere near her house that night. And then I blurted it out."

"How did she react?"

"She hugged me. Which I didn't expect, but it gave me the boost I needed to feel like I could tell everyone else. I made her promise not to say anything until I gave the okay. But then my dad got onstage at halftime, and we all know what happened after that." He grimaces. "I thought she'd kept her word, until you came into the library that day and mentioned the 'shitty thing' I'd done the night of the blackout."

I pull back and look up at him, a cold sensation brewing in my veins. "Wait. When you said you'd made a bad decision—you meant coming out to Meredith?"

"Yeah. I thought she'd blabbed and it was blowing up in my face. But what you said right after made me realize that you must've been referring to some other shitty thing." He jerks his head in the direction of the necklace. "That was the only other thing I could think of. Because I didn't buy it for you. I didn't even pick it out. I found it near the football field that morning when I was waiting to meet with you and you never showed." He hangs his head. "The rest was all bullshit I made up on the spot."

I stop dancing, retracting my arms from around his neck. "So you didn't kiss me when the power went out?"

"Kiss you? Mace, I got within an inch of telling you I was gay. Why would I kiss you?"

"Because *someone* did. And then walked away without a word before the lights came up. *That* was the shitty thing I meant."

"Oh." He draws the word out, like he's giving himself an extra second to make sense of this. "So it was never about me finding some kid's necklace on the ground and passing it off as my gift to you, or the fact that it was only one of about a thousand lies I told you?"

"Joel, whatever lies you told me, yes, they hurt my feelings. But they're water under the bridge, okay? Clean slate. I've had enough experience with grudges to know that it's not the route I want to take." I pause. "There's not more, is there?"

He scratches his head. "No. That covers it. But I want you to know, Mace. The idea behind the necklace was real at least. I did want things to be good between us again, and I'm sorry I screwed it up a second time."

"You could make it up to me by coming to the dance," I say with a hopeful bat of my eyelashes. Joel immediately starts to squirm and stutter, so I don't drag out the torture. "Kidding, Joel. I'm kidding. It was worth a shot."

A knock sounds then, and my mother pokes her head into the room. "Hey. Door open when friends are in your bedroom, please. Gay or not." She winks. "And can you see if Noah is running on schedule? I want to make sure we have plenty of time for pictures."

Joel retrieves his cell phone as she makes her way downstairs. "I should get going. If I do end up talking to my parents tonight, I have to figure out how to do it."

I pull him into a hug and wish him luck. Before he can go, I tug at his hand, hoping he won't think I'm prying. "So," I say. "What about Noah?"

"Noah's made some pretty stupid decisions. But then again, so have I." He releases my hand and puts his in the pocket of his jeans. "I have to figure out where we go from here."

I so want to point out that he seemed to know exactly where he wanted things to go when he kissed Noah on the basketball court, but it's not my call. So I bite my tongue and we say good-bye.

Once he's gone, I take my heart locket from my dresser and sink into the armchair in the corner of my bedroom. I flick it open and stare at the empty center. In a way, Jadie was right when she compared Joel to the fable about the painted clock. Only, I was never the downfall that Joel was so afraid of; it was Noah.

As my palm closes around the heart, I feel like it has lost some of its meaning. I wanted to think of it as Joel's promise to start over, the same way I was hoping for that kiss in the dark to be the beginning of something special.

I close my eyes, letting myself relive that moment for the first time in a long time. Letting my insides flutter and the warmth spread from my head to my toes. When I open my eyes, I grab my phone and send a text to Joel. Something he said isn't sitting right, and I need him to clear it up.

As I wait for his answer, I lose myself in the memory again. And just for a minute, I let myself wonder if an abandoned locket on the football field might mean something totally different from what I originally thought.

Something that, up until now, I haven't allowed myself to hope for.

Thirty-Four

SENIOR YEAR

It's almost a shame that Noah and I mutually friend-zoned each other, because with his dark hair and smoldering eyes and his suit, the boy cleans up like he stepped right out of an Armani ad.

He's unusually quiet as a group gathers to take pictures in front of the fountains near the town hall green. The clouds are backlit and turning pink with the sun's descent, the perfect backdrop for what's supposed to be a perfect night. Every time a camera or cell phone clicks, I envision the next wave of Ridgedale's Finest photos. The smiling faces, the arching water, arms around shoulders and hands touching waists. And then I think about what no one else will notice. Like the concerted effort that Ben and Meredith arc making to keep as many people between us as possible. Ben never did respond to my text about the bulletin board, and I wonder if he's angry at me too. Again.

I watch Noah, hooking his finger into the collar of his shirt every five minutes like it's suffocating him. I wonder if everyone sees it, if they assume it's because it's too starched or too tight, or if they have any idea that he doesn't want to be here.

At least not with me.

I point my lens at the sky to capture one thing that actually is perfect tonight. As I lower my camera, ready to cap it and leave it in Noah's car in favor of my less cumbersome cell phone camera, I notice someone standing at the edge of the fountain, his own cell phone aimed at the pink plumes. My breath catches when Ben turns around as if he felt my stare. His mouth turns up into a smile, like he knew we'd be thinking the same thing. Like we're in on the same secret. And I bring my camera to my eye, freezing one more perfect image forever.

It isn't long before we're all filing into the gym entrance. I shoulder my way through the crowd to the bulletin board. Taking in the whole thing, it really is a work of art. Almost the entire school is represented: Athletics, arts, teachers, coaches, and lunch ladies all make appearances in the four-by-four squares. It's a colorful mosaic, spotlighting the high points of everyday life.

And I get that that's the point.

Still, I can't stop myself from zeroing in on that one photo, the memory of Ben and me that has existed only inside my head for the past year. It makes me feel like no time has passed at all, even though the entire board is evidence of the contrary.

"Oh, I see it," Jadie says, coming up behind me. She motions at the picture with a hand that's intertwined with Tyrell's. "No wonder Meredith's mad. That is ridiculously cute." She shoots a glance at Noah. "No offense, Pirate Booty."

Noah smirks. "I was actually thinking the same thing."

Jadie leans in and, more quietly, says, "Do you want me to take it down?"

I consider it. But in that same second, I spot Ben over Jadie's shoulder. He eyes the photo, and the Charlotte Brontë quote beneath it: *The human heart has hidden treasures, in secret kept, in silence sealed. The thoughts, the hopes, the dreams, the pleasures, whose charms were broken if revealed.*

His eyes find mine again, and I tell Jadie to leave the picture where it is. And then we let ourselves be carried off by the current of bodies making their way insto the gym.

Meredith and her crew did a fantastic job with the decorations. I take in the spectacular sight of metallic teal-and-silver streamers twisting and curling from every corner of the room, meeting at the giant disco ball in the center. White Christmas lights twinkle everywhere, and silver and teal balloons float around the room like ghosts.

Noah bats one away as we grab a seat in the bleachers. "Are you sure you're okay being here?" I ask. "You seem a little out of it."

"It's not that I don't want to be here." But the way he pulls at his collar again makes it hard to believe. "I can't stop thinking about last night. I wouldn't blame you for hating me, Mace."

"Well, I don't, okay? It's like I told Joel: Everybody makes mistakes. Let's deal with it and move on."

Still, my eyes dart into the crowd, scanning for Meredith. I hope the mention of Joel prevents him from noticing.

"You talked to Joel again?"

I nod. "I can't make any promises, but I think he's coming around. He cares a lot about you."

"He also cares way too much about what other people think. I mean, I get it. I do. I'm bi, and I feel like that's even harder for people to wrap their heads around. I hid for a while too, because I knew coming out meant facing people who have to make everything a shit show. But Joel is so convinced that his dad is one of them, and he hasn't even tried to talk to him yet. He spends so much time reading into every little thing his father says, of course he's going to psych himself out. I just— Would someone really waste all that effort to reverse-psychology their kid into staying in the closet?"

I twist the skirt of my dress around my finger, recalling the way Mr. Hargrove told me that my troubles with algebra were only a matter of "making the wires connect."

"Obviously I can't say for sure. But Joel's dad does have a tendency to make you feel like there's only one right way to do things."

No sooner have I finished the thought than Renata and Criselle walk by with their fingers intertwined, mercifully oblivious to the two boys snickering behind their hands in their wake. Realization comes over Noah's face like the dawn. He drags a hand across his forehead like he's angry at himself for even asking the question.

"He's right, isn't he? My parents didn't freak out, but that doesn't mean I know what his are thinking. And then on top of it, I came here and messed with his head even more." He drops his face into his hands. "Why am I such a dick, Mace?"

I curl my hand into the crook of his arm. "Hey. Quit talking about my friend that way." I pull gently. "Let's go take a walk."

Noah shifts in his seat, but before he can get up, his eyes fall on something near the main doors. I follow his stare right over to Meredith and Ben.

"I need to talk to her," he says. He stands, despite my best efforts to keep him on the bleacher.

"Don't. Please? What good will it do to confess now?"

"I'll leave you out of it. Don't worry."

I get to my feet, a good three inches taller than usual, thanks to my shoes. "It's not that. We both ruined homecoming for her last year. Can we at least pick a different night?"

"What is this 'we' crap, Macy? We've been over this, and it's my fault, not yours. Besides, what difference does it make if the damage is already done?" He hazards another glance over his shoulder. "I'm going. After the way Collins looked at you when he walked in, I think he'll be grateful if I keep her busy for a few minutes anyway."

He takes off in the direction of one set of doors, and I take the opportunity to slip out through another. The bulletin board has been pulling me like a magnet since I arrived, and I seize the chance to take another look, to really study the stories laid out by Jadie and Renata and Criselle.

But when my gaze falls on a picture of Joel and his dad standing behind a podium on a makeshift stage in the middle of the football field, I have to wonder: what about the stories these pictures have left untold?

"I got us in trouble again," a voice says behind me, making me jump. I turn to see Ben coming toward me, his hands in the pockets of his tan suit pants.

"Ben. What are you talking about?"

He nods to the bulletin board. "That picture. Why are you acting like you don't know how it got there?"

The question miffs me. "Because I don't. It wasn't part of the project, and that's the last picture I would put on display knowing that Meredith would see it."

Ben's eyes narrow in equal parts confusion and annoyance. "Macy, I slipped that picture into your locker the day of the homecoming game. To—answer your question. About what didn't happen that night." He looks from me to the board. "How could it get from there to here without you knowing?"

An image of a pile of photographs landing with a smack at my feet flashes through my mind, and suddenly at least one thing makes sense.

"I already had all the other pictures in my locker. Everything fell out when I opened the door, and I was in a rush, so I stuffed them into a bag without really looking. Then I had to leave before the board was finished. But"—I turn to the image of me kissing his smiling face—"how does that answer my question?"

So tell me, Ben. What didn't happen that night?

He shakes his head. "The answer's not in the picture. It's *on* it. I wrote something on the back." He gives a short laugh. "Something you managed not to see."

"I'm sorry, Ben. I didn't—" My head swivels from him to the photo. "What did it say?"

"It's stupid."

And suddenly I'm seeing his face, not the way it looks right now but a year ago when we had a conversation almost exactly like this one. Right after Joel asked me to homecoming.

Ben? What's wrong?

Nothing. It's pointless.

Only, this time I know better than to believe him.

I spot a hall monitor's desk beneath the trophy case on the opposite side of the entryway, and stride toward it.

"Macy, don't." Ben tries to block me, but I swerve

around him, dragging the metal legs across the linoleum and up against the cinder blocks beneath the bulletin board. When I throw my clutch down and try to step up onto the desk's attached seat, his arms circle my waist and he sets me back on the floor. "Look, the way this has all turned out, it's pretty much a sign that I should never open my mouth. So leave it alone, okay? Tonight's not the time or the place."

It's basically what I said to Noah a few minutes ago. Only, Noah didn't heed my wishes. But Ben's looking at me pleadingly, and when his eyes flick down to the locket around my neck, I can't bring myself to follow in Noah's defiant footsteps.

At least not in front of Ben.

"Wait until after the dance," he says. "Can you do that?"

"I think I can handle that."

"Thank you. Can we go back inside now?"

"Actually, I'm waiting for Noah. We're going for a walk. If you see him, tell him to meet me outside?" I scoop up my bag and half turn toward the door.

Ben's shoulders relax, and he nods. "Yeah. I should get back to Meredith anyway."

He tries to be subtle about checking over his shoulder as he walks away. I wait until the door to the gym slams shut behind him, and then I waste no time kicking off my shoes and scrambling back onto the desk. I chip my nail polish freeing the picture of its staples, but I don't care. As it comes loose, my clutch vibrates against the surface of the desk. I bend down and pull my phone out to see that Joel has finally responded to the question I texted after he left my bedroom.

I'd asked, WHAT MAKES YOU THINK THE LOCKET BELONGED TO A KID?

When I see what he's written, my heart stops.

BECAUSE IT HAD A PICTURE OF THE SUPERMAN SYMBOL INSIDE.

I steady myself against the wall, holding my phone against the same spot where Ben once drew an *S* inside the center of a heart. With my other hand, I pull free the photo of Ben and me and turn it over. There, in Ben's skinny handwriting, is one simple sentence:

I should have kissed you the first time I had the chance.

Thirty-Five

SENIOR YEAR

I slump onto the desk's surface, my feet on the attached chair. I must read the words thirty times. Deep down I knew that this was what he meant. But seeing it for myself makes something shatter inside me, some part of my heart that I didn't realize I was keeping under lock and key.

I bring the picture to my lips and close my eyes, letting myself imagine what it would've been like if Ben had kissed me the first time he had the chance. But when I edit out the moment when Meredith walked in and replace it with Ben's lips meeting mine, it happens again—I'm reliving *that* kiss. The one that's been haunting me since the night of the blackout.

And when I open my eyes, the reason why is staring me in the face.

Sitting on the desk, I'm at eye level with the photo that Meredith took of Jadie and me on the football field before the power went out. Our arms are around each other, our faces touching. And there in the background, in the far-left corner of the frame, someone stands leaning against the chain-link fence. Not on the outside of the track with the rest of the spectators, but within the confines of the field, like someone who has an in. Someone with a mop of dirty-blond hair and red Converse sneakers. Someone who should've been at work that night.

My eyes fall to the picture in my hand, and I read the words scrawled on the back one more time.

I should have kissed you the first time I had the chance.

The *first* time.

I'm pretty sure I know what happened the second time.

One of the gym doors bursts open, nearly startling me off the desk. To my surprise, Meredith is standing before me in her glorious one-shouldered red dress.

She spots the picture in my hand. "Don't take that down because of me. I'm sorry I flipped out on you." She lets the door close behind her. "Jadie told me you never got to work on the bulletin board."

I told her that too. If I could concentrate on anything other than the knowledge that Ben was on the field the night of the blackout, I'd be offended that she had to hear it elsewhere before she believed me.

"I understand why you were upset," I say. I understand it better than ever. But I don't have the heart to tell her that.

"It wasn't about the picture, Macy. I mean it was, but it's more about what the picture stood for. Which is me being an idiot." My mouth opens in protest, but Meredith cuts me off. "No, hear me out. I'm not saying that anything happened between you and Ben last year, but whether you acknowledged it or not, something changed between the two of you a long time ago. I saw it happening, and I tried to ignore it." She hugs herself, the same way she did when she found Ben and me dancing outside. "But ignoring things doesn't make them any less true. And . . . based on the conversation I just had with Noah, and the fact that you're not here with Joel, I'd say that's a lesson we both learned firsthand recently. Right?" My head moves up and down, but words are failing me. "So," she says quietly. "Just know that if you're ready to stop ignoring it, I'm not going to stand in your way."

The sound of paper crinkling makes me realize how hard I'm squeezing the picture. "Meredith, I don't want to lose you as a friend again. No matter what."

"I'm not much of a friend if people I care about are unhappy because they're trying to protect me from losing something that was never really mine."

"And I'm not much of a friend if I don't tell you that the float burning down was all my fault."

"Macy," she says with a sharpness that surprises me. "Did you set the fire?"

"No, but—"

She cuts me off, slicing the air with her hand. "Then it wasn't your fault. And yeah, maybe not so long ago I would've had a very different reaction to all of this. But I was also a lot dumber then."

I want to leap off the desk and hug her. But before I can do anything, the door next to her bursts open, bringing with it a blast of music and a bewildered-looking Jadie.

"There you are!" she says to Meredith. "Fielding is asking me all these random questions about the homecoming court's first dance like he thinks I share brain cells with you and Tyrell or something. So go talk to him, because all I know is that you'd better keep your hands where I can see them when you dance with my boyfriend." Her eyes dart over to me, and her face brightens. "Did you see that picture of us? Isn't it cute?"

Her heels click against the linoleum as she walks over to the bulletin board. Behind her, Meredith blows me a kiss and says, "We'll talk more later, okay?"

Jadie throws a confused look over her shoulder. "What just happened here?"

I point to the picture of her and me. "This cute picture of us? Look who else is in it."

She cranes her neck until her face is within half an inch of the wall. "Wait. Is that Ben?" She turns to me. "Ben was there that night?" I offer her the photo in my still-shaking hand and watch shock burst over her face as she flips it from one side to the other. "Oh my God." The pitch of her voice drops to demonic. *"Ben was there that night."*

"Mm-hm. And this"—I point to my necklace—"isn't really from Joel. He found it on the field after the blackout." Jadie's jaw is practically touching her chest as I motion to the spot where Meredith was standing. "And Meredith basically gave me her blessing to go after Ben, and all I want right now is to get in there and find him, but—" There are too many "buts" to even finish that sentence. I slump against the wall. "I'm a mess, Jadie."

"Scoot over." She bumps her body against me until I'm sitting in the chair, and she takes my place perched on the desk, wrapping an arm around me. "So this is kind of like the first birthday party I had when we moved to Ridgedale, and Meredith bought me a huge tin of gummy bears because she didn't know yet what a chocoholic I am. I acted like I was all excited when I opened them, because I didn't want to hurt her feelings. But then months later, she came to my house and saw that the tin was still full, so I had to admit that I'd rather set my hair on fire than eat a pound of rubbery, chemical-flavored bears. Only, you know, not that blunt."

I don't bother to hide the *WTF* expression on my face. "I don't see the connection."

"My point is that I didn't tell her the truth because I was afraid she'd be upset. But in the end, it bothered her more that she hadn't given me something that made me happy. So if she gave you the go-ahead with Ben, it probably means two things: One, your happiness really is important to her. And two, she's Meredith Kopala. She's hot, she's smart, and hell, she's the freaking homecoming queen. She's finally figured out that she doesn't want to be someone's gummy bear if she can be someone else's Twix bar."

I crack up laughing. "Wow," I say as I'm trying to catch my breath. "That was profound. I think you should write your own book of fables."

"Confucius has nothing on me."

We both dissolve into giggles, and then Jadie points at the picture I'm still holding. "What are you going to do with that?"

"Um, I didn't think that far ahead."

Jadie hops down from the desk. She gives me an assessing once-over, before her eyes fall into my cleavage. Not that there's much of it, because my dress's neckline is straight across, but before I can ask what she's thinking, she's plucked the picture from my fingers and slipped it— and her hand—beneath my dress, somewhere between my boob and my armpit.

"I was thinking more along the lines of my purse as a short-term solution," I say, adjusting myself when she finally steps away.

"Eh, what's a little groping between friends? Next time find an easier way to keep Ben close to your heart." She flashes a knowing smirk and taps the rounded surface of my locket. "Like maybe here." I wrap one hand around the pendant, and Jadie grabs the other. "Come on," she says. "Let's go find your prince."

"God, poor Noah probably thinks I bailed on him."

Jadie slaps her forehead. "Not *that* prince."

But he's the one I need to find first. And when I do, he says, "Go. Finish what you started." Like I'd be crazy to *not* finally face this thing that Ben and I have been dancing around for longer than either of us were even aware.

I pull Noah into a fierce hug, promising him that I'll be back. He kisses my cheek, and there's no doubt in my mind that he understands. He came here with me tonight knowing that his heart belonged to someone else.

And maybe he knew before I did that I'd done the same thing.

Thirty-Six

SENIOR YEAR

I weave through the crowd amid the sound of thumping bass, bobbing balloons, thrusting hips, and flailing hands. Meredith stands in one corner talking animatedly to Tyrell and Jadie. But I don't see Ben anywhere. It's like he vanished into thin air, and it feels too much like the disappearing act he pulled the night of the blackout.

But as I'm about to turn around and scan the floor again, a hand grabs my wrist. I turn to find myself looking into Meredith's eyes.

"He went out to the car," she says. "To get my backup balloons." She nods toward the door. "It's okay if you want to follow him." And even though verbal diarrhea is usually my MO in times of uncertainty, I can't seem to do anything except stare alternately at her face and the spot where she's touching me. She responds with the most affectionate eye roll I've ever seen. "Let me rephrase that. He's parked near the gate to the football field. Now get your ass outside."

I throw my arms around her neck and squeeze for a quick second. Then I turn and charge toward the door.

I see Ben before he sees me. He slams the car door, then props a box of decorations against his torso as he hits the remote lock. Slipping the keys into his pocket, he adjusts the box and starts toward the school. Until he spots me and stops in his tracks.

"You didn't wait, did you?" he says.

"No. But I think maybe we've waited long enough." I take a few steps toward him. He slides the box onto the roof of his car and leans against the door, jamming his hands into his pockets.

With the exception of the muted noise from inside, it's quiet as I stop with only a few feet remaining between us.

"It was you that night. On the field, during the blackout. Wasn't it?"

There's a terrifying heartbeat when he doesn't respond, and I'm afraid I'm wrong. But then his eyes meet mine, and all pretense falls away.

"It was me," he says. "I kissed you. I don't know what to say, except that my better judgment must've shorted out with the power. If you want to kick me in the nuts, you can." He watches his shoe scuff against the asphalt. "I'm surprised

327

you didn't figure it out sooner. It's not like it was the first time."

"What are you talking about? You said yourself"—I pull the photo of him and me out of my dress—"we missed the first chance."

Ben gawks, though I'm not sure if it's at my answer or because I produced a picture from my side boob.

"You really don't remember, do you?"

Something about the word "remember" makes goose bumps rise on my skin. There's only one night that's caused me to agonize over things I half recall. But the notion that there's more, that Ben knows something I've blanked on entirely, is terrifying.

I swallow over the dryness in my throat. "Is this . . . about that night at the slushie stand?"

"You were right when you said everything started changing then, Mace. Only, nothing changed. Not the way I thought it would. And definitely not the way I wanted it to." He taps a fist against the car door. "I'd been thinking about you way more than I should've for a while. And not thinking about Meredith the way I used to. But I didn't know how to tell either one of you that I was having second thoughts about asking her to homecoming, or how to clue you in on what was going through my head. But then, that night, I didn't think I had to. Because when I was helping you get changed out of your clothes, you kissed me."

"I—I did?"

"You told me I was a good friend, and you said you owed

my real head a kiss. Then you leaned up to kiss my cheek, I think, and you missed. Only, you didn't stop. And it was . . . not friendlike at all."

I cover my mouth with my hand. He might as well be telling me about someone else's life, because I can't recall a single second of this. All this time, I thought I'd gotten myself in trouble that night by saying or doing something I couldn't remember. And I had. Just not the thing I was afraid of.

"You were asleep five seconds later, but I thought you felt the same way I did. That it wasn't just about Meredith anymore," he continues. "I was going to ask you to homecoming and everything. Only, I never got the chance, because Hargrove pulled the ultimate dick move and did it first even though he—" His lips tighten as he cuts himself off and looks at me with last year's hurt still fresh in his eyes. "And you acted like nothing had even happened, anyway."

"Ben." His name comes out as a plea. "I'm so sorry. I had no idea."

"You never saw me when he was around. And even when he wasn't, you only saw what you wanted to see."

My heart plummets. I feel like I've had a blindfold ripped off my face, one I never even realized I was wearing.

"You knew back then, didn't you? That Joel is gay."

Ben kicks at a pebble on the asphalt. "He tried to kiss me while we were in the woods at Snow in Georgia."

"Oh." Well, that's definitely new information. "Is that why you were so angry with him?"

Ben's eyebrows pull together. "No. God, Mace, give me some credit. He was trashed, and he was so embarrassed when I pulled away that I felt awful. So I asked if I could tell him something about me that no one knew. That way we'd be even. And what I told him was how much I liked you. How I wanted to ask you to homecoming instead of Meredith, but I didn't know how to do it without both of you hating me. And then he turned around and stabbed me in the back so he could keep using you as a cover." The corners of his mouth turn down. "I was so mad. Mad that he'd use my secret against me even though I'd promised to keep his. Mad at you for being so oblivious. But then when he ducked out on you at homecoming, I felt guilty. Like I'd wished it on or something."

"That's why you said you should've warned me."

Ben nods. "And then when we danced, I thought that I hadn't been wrong. That maybe something was there after all. But it's like you said." He slides his hands into his pockets and hunches his shoulders. "I missed my chance."

Until he found another chance on a dark football field, and went for it. I want to ask him about that night. I want him to tell me what changed, why then. But there's something else I want to do more.

With our picture still in hand, I close the remaining distance between us. My arms wind around his neck and one hand brushes against the softness of his hair, guiding him down so I can press my lips against his.

And the moment his mouth meets mine, I know. *This*

A KISS IN THE DARK

was what I felt in the darkness. The same explosions of warmth zinging through my body like shooting stars. The familiar fit of our bodies. The taste of cinnamon and citrus that I tucked away somewhere in my subconscious, awakening into a craving.

I know you, I thought on the field that night.

And I was right. This is the kiss I've relived every time I've closed my eyes. Ben is the sunset I failed to notice for far too long.

When I pull away, we're both breathing hard. "It *was* you," I say. And then, because kissing him is so much better than not kissing him, I go in again. "But why?" I whisper against his lips. "What was different about that night?"

"I couldn't take it anymore," he says softly. "You and I were starting to get back on track, but I didn't want to be just friends again. I wanted to tell you how I really felt. So I picked this out"—one of his hands leaves my waist to trace the locket at my collarbone—"and carried it around with me for, like, a week, trying to get up the nerve to give it to you. I planned to put that picture inside." He indicates the one I'm holding. "But that felt, I don't know, presumptuous. Like I expected you to feel the same way, even though I had no reason to think you did. So I put the Superman picture instead and told myself that I'd switch it out later, as a surprise. You know, if things . . . went well."

"But?"

"But then I ended up not having to work, and I went to the game. I saw you looking at Jadie's phone, and you seemed

331

freaked out. So I checked out that picture page, and sure enough, there we were, staring back at me like everything was starting all over again. Like a bad omen, reminding me that I don't exist to you when Hargrove is around." He runs the tips of his fingers up and down my spine. "It took all of five seconds for me to back down. But then the lights went out, and somehow, there you were. And I had to do it. I had to know if part of you remembered."

I close my eyes and press my face into his neck, bracing myself for what's coming next.

"And the first thing you said afterward," he continues in that tone that's ripping my heart out, "was Joel's name."

"Ben." His name comes out as a desperate apology. I place a kiss on his neck, squeezing him tight. "I didn't know. I didn't even think you were there."

"Still. I was kind of hoping that part of you wanted it to be me. But when you said his name, I got flustered and took off. To make matters worse, I lost the necklace. And who finds it but freaking Joel, and then uses it to ask you to homecoming. Because why stop at one bad omen when you can have a whole collection?"

He snorts, and I cover his cheek with my hand. "Don't be angry at Joel for that. He didn't know the locket was yours when he gave it to me."

"I know. But it felt like one more sign pointing to 'Give up, Ben.'"

"Have you talked to him since?"

"Sort of. But I didn't think we could be friends as long

as he was going to keep using you. Or as long as you were willing to let him."

I tuck the picture back into my dress and drop my clutch so I can hold his face with both hands. "I've spent a lot of time not seeing what was right in front of me. But if you let me"—I brush my lips against his—"I promise I'll never miss another chance to kiss you again."

Ben's hand slides up the back of my neck and into my hair. Our lips meet, and then we're completely wrapped up in each other, making up for all the kisses we've lost and wasted.

And right as I'm wishing this moment would never end, I hear something that brings it crashing to a halt.

Thirty-Seven

SENIOR YEAR

"Macy. *Pssst*. Macy!"

Ben and I break apart, and I squint into the distance. "*Joel?*" A hesitant form creeps away from the outer wall of the school and steps into the light from the streetlamp. "Joel!" I say, taking in his khaki pants and button-down shirt. "You're here! Did you—"

"I told them. And it wasn't terrible, but it wasn't great, either." He rubs at the back of his neck. "At any rate, I don't think I'm ready to go inside or anything." He nods toward Ben. "I was kind of hoping I could take a cue from Collins, actually, and ask Noah to come dance with me out here."

"Noah?" Ben blurts. I squeeze his hand, hoping he'll get the hint. "Oh," he says, and then he's cool.

"He's not answering his texts, though," Joel continues. "So I'm sorry to interrupt, but do you think you can go get him for me?"

"Of course!" I tug Ben's hand, and he grabs the box of decorations off the car with his free one. We start toward the school, and I call over my shoulder that we'll be right back. A slow song starts up as we're entering the gym foyer, and I'm so consumed with getting to Noah that I almost forget that Ben didn't come here with me tonight and we're on borrowed time. Until I hear Principal Fielding say, "Please give a round of applause to your homecoming king and queen, Tyrell Davis and Meredith Kopala!"

"Shit," I say, coming to a stop. "This is the homecoming court dance." In the next instant, I've already dismissed it. "Whatever. They won't miss me." Ben sets the box of decorations on top of the desk I'd left beneath the bulletin board. I take his hands. "Listen. I know you have to get back to your real date at some point tonight. But since she's occupied for at least the next few minutes . . . can you save this dance for me?"

"A real dance? Inside the actual building?" An adorable grin lights his face. "I'll wait right here."

"Too bad we can't stay at Ridgedale another year," I tease. "Next time we might've made it inside the actual gym."

I give him a quick peck, but when I start to walk away, he pulls me back. "Just so you know, Mace, Meredith and I have talked about this. About us. Maybe not as soon as we should've, but it's not like you said. I didn't string her along."

I nod as his grasp drops. When I return a few minutes later leading Noah with one hand, Ben is exactly where he said he'd be.

"Collins," Noah says, slowing down despite my best efforts to haul him toward the door. "I'm really sorry for everyth—"

"No time for talking," I scold him, pulling his arm with all my might. "Your prince awaits."

Noah scans the darkness through the glass pane of the door, and the corners of his lips curl upward. "Wish me luck, Mace."

I do, landing a smack to his backside as he heads out the door. "Sorry," I say. "I guess I get handsy when I'm happy."

He's still laughing as the door shuts behind him.

"Hey," Ben teases, pulling me into the foyer in front of the bulletin board. "Just because he's gay doesn't mean I like watching you smack his ass."

I place my clutch on the desk chair and wrap my arms around his waist. "He's bi. And relax, it's not like I did this." I let both my hands wander down to Ben's rear end and give it a gentle squeeze. And all I can think is, *I just grabbed Ben's butt, and this is weird.*

Except it wasn't weird, and I liked it. A lot.

He must be thinking the same thing, because he says, "Wow. If someone had told me yesterday that Macy Atwood would be groping my derriere today, I would've laughed in their face."

I do laugh, because only Ben could use a word like "derriere" non-ironically, and be so damn cute while doing it.

Then I smile up at him, remembering the words he once said to me when things weren't quite this amazing. Only now they are.

"Yesterday's not today." I brush a gentle kiss across his lips. "Thank God."

"Wait. What happened to our picture?"

I tap my chest. "Right next to my heart, where it belongs."

He pulls my cell phone from my open clutch on the chair. "What do you think? Should we go two for two?"

"I think we can pull it off."

Ben holds the phone out, and we press our faces together. Only this time, it's him who turns and presses his lips to my cheek as the camera clicks. When I look at the photo, I'm beaming.

It's perfect. And I'd probably spend the rest of the night staring at it, if not for the text message that comes through at that exact moment.

When I click on it, a new picture pops up. It's Joel's face, grinning back at me as Noah plants a kiss on his cheek. A reenactment of Ben and me from last year. The caption reads: Taking a page from your book. Thanks.

I text back about fifty hearts before clicking over to the new picture of Ben and me.

"Should I post it?" Ben asks.

"No." I press my nose against his. "Let's keep this one for ourselves."

I smile again at the screen of my phone. Then I take out the old photo and hold them side by side.

Pictures don't always tell the whole story. Sometimes they are worth a thousand words, and other times they tell a thousand lies. But then there are the times when photographs capture perfectly the things we failed to see, things we didn't even know about ourselves.

And sometimes they're a perfect spotlight, like a halo of light from a streetlamp, on the moments that become memories all too quickly. And if we're lucky enough to capture those moments, we can hold them in our hands long after they're gone. We can share them with the world, or we can keep them like beautiful secrets, only for ourselves.

But in each one, there's a story to discover. And I couldn't be happier with the ending to mine.

ACKNOWLEDGMENTS

It took a village to get this novel written, and if I've forgotten to mention anyone who had a hand in making it possible, please know that I am grateful from the bottom of my still-seventeen heart.

As always, the first thank-you goes to my agent, John M. Cusick, for being the bee's knees. Thank you for having my back, and for always knowing exactly how to make a story better.

To my editor, Nicole Ellul, thank you for wading through several mucky drafts of this book, and helping me find and polish the salvageable pieces. The evolution of Macy's story wasn't easy, but almost nothing worthwhile ever is. I'm glad you stuck it out with me.

Big hugs to my readers, critiquers, and cheerleaders, whose insight, kind words, and gentle corrections were far too generous for the draft you read: Rebecca Phillips, Cam Montgomery, Dahlia Adler, Brianna Shrum, and Brett Jonas. You all rock.

To Sarah Blair, thank you for the playdates and text conversations that saved my sanity. Being a writer mom is hard, but having a friend who knows that firsthand makes it a little easier.

A huge thank-you to Stephanie and Meghan Copenhaver, for giving me the peace of mind to work while knowing my son was in good hands. Had you not answered my desperate SOS for a babysitter, there's a very good chance that this book still wouldn't be finished.

Thank you to all the other people who afforded me writing time by keeping my little guy occupied: the wonderful teachers at his preschool, my parents, in-laws, Aunt Gloria and Uncle Joe, and my husband. Every minute counts, and I appreciate every single one you gave me.

Dom, thank you for introducing me to Georgia, the place that not only became *our* home, but the setting for Macy's home, school, and her favorite spots. Being here isn't always easy, but that doesn't mean I'm not in love with the place itself. Thank you also for bringing me to a high school football game when I was afraid I'd forgotten what they were really like. (I hadn't, thank God.) But most of all, thank you for reminding me that I achieved my dream, and that's the only thing that should matter.

ABOUT THE AUTHOR

Gina Ciocca graduated from the University of Connecticut with a degree in English. She relocated from Connecticut to Georgia, where she lives with her husband and son. You can find Gina online at writersblog-gina.blogspot.com.